BRANDED

BRANDED

Linda Hearn

LUMINARE PRESS
WWW.LUMINAREPRESS.COM

Printed in the United States of America

Cover Illustration by Ruth Sanderson

Luminare Press
442 Charnelton St.
Eugene, OR 97401
www.luminarepress.com

LCCN: 2023908602
ISBN: 979-8-88679-198-3

To my best friend and biggest supporter—
dearest Jeffrey.

CHAPTER 1

uillermo Foxen shook the reins, urging his cow pony on. The bay gelding took a few stuttering steps, snorted, and resumed trotting through the oak grove, but it wasn't long before he drifted off the trail again.

"Ay, caramba, Benito!" Guillermo snapped at his pony. "I get it. You want to go home. So do I, but first we have to find those strays!"

A thunderstorm the night before had sent cattle scrambling for cover on his family's sprawling Rancho Tinaquaic. Separated from the herd, the cows were easy prey to the coyotes, puma, and grizzlies that roamed the oak-studded hills. In the wild backcountry of Alta California in 1846, there was safety in numbers.

Though it was early afternoon, little light filtered through the arched canopy. Guillermo scanned the shadows, searching for the black cows. As he rounded a bend in the trail, a gust of wind punched him in the face. He tucked his chin as leaves swirled around him and came to a halt. Standing in the stirrups he cocked his head this way and that. Guillermo noticed Benito's ears prick forward as he sniffed the air. "You heard it, too, huh, amigo? Sounded like voices. Maybe Angel met up with someone."

The wind howled as clouds scudded overhead. After several moments, he sat back down and patted Benito on

1

the neck. "I don't hear it now. Probably the wind. Vámanos." He tugged on the reins, determined to find the strays and escape the dreary woods.

A few minutes later, Angel, youngest son of the rancho's majordomo, came loping toward him down the trail.

Guillermo asked, "No luck finding them?"

Angel pushed back his hat and scratched his bandana-covered head. "Saw a heifer and her calf a while ago, but they hightailed it into the willows. No sign of 'em now. Must be following the creek toward the river."

"Shh-h! Hear that?" asked Guillermo.

"What?"

"Voices."

Benito whinnied and pawed the ground.

"It's just the wind. There's no one else out here," Angel said.

"I know I heard something." Guillermo raised his hand. "Listen!"

In a spooky voice, Angel said, "*Oo-oo-ooh!* Maybe it's one of Petra's ancestors." Petra was the Foxens' head house servant. The Foxen tract was located on the site of an old Chumash village, and there were many superstitions among the rancho's Indian servants about the spirit world.

"Go ahead, make fun of me if you want," said Guillermo. He and his sisters had hunted arrowheads, grinding stones, and bone tools along the creek for which his family's land grant was named. Their collection decorated his mother's rose garden. "Ever wonder what happened to the people? Why they abandoned their village?"

"Could have been Tulares or some other warring tribe. Could have been sickness, flood, drought…who knows?" Angel shrugged.

They continued through the grove until they approached

a clearing at the base of two hills and paused. Guillermo's eyes swept over the area and came to rest on a patch of ground under a gnarled oak. "Sometimes I wonder if my uncle's death was some kind of an omen."

"Omen? Ha! You've been listening to Old Fernando, haven't you? He's as superstitious as the Chumash."

"You have to admit, though, it was a freak accident. Ausencio was an expert rider. He'd ridden this way many times between his father's rancho and ours." A chill ran down Guillermo's spine, and he shivered. "I can't help but wonder."

"Ay, caramba! Wonder about what? That this place is... cursed? That your uncle was killed for settling on Chumash land?" Angel spat. "That's ridiculous!"

"No, it's not! For all we know, his death could have been an omen. Think about it. There's gotta be a burial ground nearby. We could be passing over it now."

Angel sighed heavily. "Accidents happen, Guillermo, even to the best riders. Don't listen to loco superstitions." He pointed to his head. "They're no good for you up here!"

Cr-aaa-ck!

Both boys flinched at the sound of rifle fire, and their horses whinnied. Angel shot Guillermo a look of puzzlement. "Who could that be?"

"Probably someone from Grandfather's crew. Chasing off a bear maybe." The sound of men's voices and the neighing of horses rose above the wind. "Hear that? Voices!" exclaimed Guillermo.

Cr-aaa-ck! Cr-aaa-ck! More shots rang out in quick succession.

Both horses reared and pawed the air. Guillermo leaned forward and patted Benito on his neck. "No wonder you've been skittish today!"

3

"Has to be two shooters," Angel said. "No one can reload that fast…unless…" His eyes widened. "*Ándale*! Let's climb the hill and see who it is!"

Guillermo hedged. "Uh…I don't know."

"What's wrong with you? This is your father's land. You have a right to know who's trespassing."

"I know…but whoever it is, they're not going listen to me." He glanced up and down the canyon, biting his lip.

"So, you're going to ride off like some scared rabbit?" Angel's dark eyes bored into Guillermo's. "Come on. Come with me, or I go by myself. Your choice."

Guillermo was trapped. He knew he'd never hear the end of it with the crew if he rode home without seeing who the shooters were. He was protective of the rancho's lands, they were his birthright. He would be owner of the rancho someday. The thought made him proud.

"So…you coming or not?" Angel pressed.

"Sí, but just a quick peek, and then we tell our fathers."

They rode twenty yards down the canyon before swinging off their mounts and looping their reins around an oak. Guillermo folded over the top part of his thigh-high boots and tied them below his knees so he could move more easily. Angel took off up the hill.

Benito nudged Guillermo's shoulder and neighed. Guillermo rubbed the cow pony's forehead before digging a dried fig out of his saddlebag. "I'll be back pronto." He ran to catch up with Angel.

He followed where Angel's spurs had cut a zigzag path into the carpet of leaves. With each soggy step, his feet sank into the muck. Soon his boots were soaked as he trudged up the slope. Angel waited for Guillermo near the top. They covered the final hundred feet on legs that burned from exertion. A caballero did not walk on two legs if he could ride on four.

A giant oak ruled the summit, and the boys hid behind its massive trunk. The acrid smell of gunpowder drifted up from below. Angel pushed back his hat, crouched, and pointed to a rocky outcropping ten yards away. The next thing Guillermo knew, Angel was gone. Now it was his turn.

He made the sign of the cross. "Dear God, please protect us."

CHAPTER 2

"¡Híjole!" Guillermo and Angel gasped as they peeked around the rock. They could hardly believe their eyes. Canvas tents had sprouted on the meadow where cattle grazed the day before. Pack animals were being unloaded by a motley collection of soldiers, mostly gringos. Haggard-looking men huddled around campfires, cleaning their rifles and smoking. At the bottom of the hill, two Indians were bent over a partially skinned cow. Steam rose from its body into the chilly afternoon air. Her calf lay motionless nearby. Angel had driven the strays directly into the sights of a rifle!

Guillermo caught a glimpse of a flag that snapped arrogantly in the breeze above one of the tents. It was a faded red, white, and blue American flag. The Americanos were intent on conquering the Mexican province, extending their nation from the Atlantic to the Pacific. The Americano army was setting up camp on his family's rancho and killing their cattle! Anger burned in his chest. He turned and whispered, "Vámonos! We must warn our fathers to hide the horses!"

They darted back up the slight incline and disappeared over the crest of the hill. The trip down proved to be a balancing act as they sloshed their way through the muddy ground. Guillermo's lanky frame proved harder to control than Angel's compact body, as his boots kept sliding out from beneath him, causing him to slip and slide down the hill. Angel was yanking on his horse's reins and galloping away by the time Guillermo reached Benito. He swung into the saddle and followed in pursuit.

On the trip out of the oak grove, Guillermo leaned far to the left and then to the right to avoid the whips of tree branches that whizzed overhead. He focused on covering as much ground as possible. The thundering hooves seemed deafening in the still woods. For several minutes, both riders charged through a tunnel of dappled light. Guillermo had narrowed the gap between Angel and himself as they approached an opening to the field. Angel burst out of the woods and slapped his horse's rump to accelerate, and Guillermo followed close on his heels. Benito's strides lengthened, and in no time, the cow pony was in a full gallop. Guillermo leaned low on the withers and fell into Benito's steady rhythm.

They were nearing the trail for home when the hairs stood up on the back of Guillermo's neck. Instinctively, he glanced up the hill to his left. A lone figure on horseback stared down at them. Tall and spectral, he looked like a statue against the pale sky. The only movement came from the fluttering of the feathers in his long braids. He made no effort to conceal himself, and there was a boldness about him, making Guillermo feel as if he were the trespasser. The thin outline of a rifle rested on the pommel of the saddle. A bow peeked from behind one shoulder.

"An-gel! AN-GEL!"

The other boy turned back, glowering. "What?"

"Up there!"

Confused, Angel let up on the reins, allowing Guillermo to catch up with him. His eyes widened at the sight of the Indian scout. He spurred his horse and shouted, "*Ándale!*"

They raced across the field in tandem, spraying clods of dirt behind them. From time to time, Guillermo stole a glance back to see if they were being chased. To his relief, no one followed. When the final bend in the trail came into view, he held his breath.

Thank heavens! Joaquin, his father's favorite mount, was tied to the broken ship's mast that served as the Foxen hitching post. Not having to search the open range for his father would save time.

Convinced there wasn't a moment to lose, Guillermo galloped into the hacienda's yard, calling, "Papá! Papá!" He yanked hard on the reins and waited for someone to come out of the adobe. He said to Angel, "We need to let the horses out of the corral and drive them…"

The door flew open, and Guillermo's ten-year-old sister, Ramona, stepped onto the veranda. "Hola, Guillermo! We just finished seeding the raisins for Papá's plum pudding! Want some?" For the past week, the Foxen household had been a beehive of activity preparing for La Nochebuena feast that was five days away.

"Not now, Ramona! I need to talk to Papá. Hurry, get him! It's important!"

"What is it?" she asked, wrinkling her pixie nose. Of the six Foxen children, she most resembled their English father with her fair complexion and golden hair.

"Ramona! Just get him! Now!"

Her head snapped back, and her eyes welled with tears.

"Oh, no," he groaned. "Don't cry, I didn't mean…"

Don Julian's bulk filled the doorway. Benjamin Foxen had been renamed Don Julian when he underwent baptism in order to marry Doña Eduarda in the Catholic faith. "What's going on?" he bellowed. "Did I hear you yell at your sister?"

"Yes, but Pa-Papá, I-I..."

"No excuses! Apologize now!" He crossed his arms and tapped an immense shoe on a plank of the veranda. "I'm waiting..."

"I'm sorry, Ramona. Thank you for sharing your raisins," Guillermo said, trying to sound more contrite than he felt. The Americanos could be coming at any moment, and here he was wasting time apologizing to his sister!

She sniffed. "I just wanted you to have some. Here." On tiptoes, she extended a handful of squished raisins.

"Thank you." The saddle creaked as he leaned down to accept her offering. "I'll eat these as soon as I tell Papá something. It's chilly out here. You'd better get back into the house, or you'll catch cold."

"I will, but first I want to give Angel some."

Angel thanked her promptly, but she was not to be hurried. With deliberate slowness, she made her way up the steps. She stopped to linger beside her father, but there her luck gave out.

"Get inside now, and make sure you close the door tight to keep out the draft," Don Julian said.

Ramona's shoulders slumped as she made her way into the house.

"What's all this about?" asked Don Julian as he stepped off the veranda and approached the boys on horseback. As he drew closer, he squinted. "What's wrong, mijo? You look like you've seen a ghost."

"That's what I've been trying to tell you! The Americano army is camped near the mouth of the canyon, and they're shooting our cattle!"

"Well, for criminy sakes, lad! Why didn't you say so?"

"I tried, but..."

9

"The Americanos? You're sure?"

"We saw them with our own eyes!" Guillermo turned to Angel for confirmation.

"Sí, jefe! An Indian scout saw us!"

With relief, Guillermo saw his father absorb the news. "Shouldn't we drive the horses deep into a canyon like Commandante Janssens ordered?"

Don Julian stared off into the distance, his bushy eyebrows knitted in concern. "By Jove, I didn't expect this. They must have camped at Rancho Nipomo, and Captain Dana directed them here. How else would they have found us?" He stroked his jaw with a meaty hand. "No, mijo. In time of war, invaders can take what they want. It would be better for us to cooperate."

"Papá! We can't afford to give them our remuda!" The remuda was the collection of horses from which the ranch hands selected their mounts. Each horse in the herd of specially trained cow ponies was valuable. Losing one of them was unthinkable.

Guillermo's mother stepped out of the adobe with his littlest sister, Juanita, tugging on her skirt, clutching a rag doll. Baby Alejandro rounded out the six Foxen children.

"Let's not frighten the girls," Don Julian whispered under his breath.

"What is it? Is something wrong?" asked Doña Eduarda.

"Now don't get alarmed, but the boys were telling me they discovered the Yankee army camped down the canyon a ways. They kilt some of our cattle."

"Yankees?" She gasped, and her hand flew to her breast in alarm. "How did they find us?" She pulled her shawl tightly around her shoulders to ward off the winter chill.

Guillermo's sisters Martina and Panchita had wandered

onto the veranda to see what the commotion was about with Ramona close on their heels. "Yankees? Did someone say the Yankees are coming?" asked seven-year-old Panchita.

"Don't worry, dear," Doña Eduarda said. "They have no interest in bringing harm to paisanos like us."

Guillermo's concern about hiding the horses was racing to panic, as each moment passed.

"What should we do, Julian?" Doña Eduarda asked.

Before Don Julian could answer, Angel pointed down the north trail and exclaimed, "Here they come now, jefe!"

All heads swiveled to see four riders galloping down the trail.

CHAPTER 3

"Papá, what about the horses?" Guillermo pressed.

"First things first, then we'll deal with the horses."

"Ay, yi, yi." Guillermo despaired. If they waited, it might be too late! He and Angel exchanged anxious glances as the visitors approached. The lead rider sat ramrod straight on a fine gray stallion. Two Indians in fringed buckskin rode slightly behind him, and a fourth rider brought up the rear.

Doña Eduarda tucked a loose strand of hair into the braid circling her head. Bracing herself to meet the visitors, she drew herself up and gathered Ramona and Juanita to her side. Don Julian strode to the hitching post to wait for them.

When the leader came riding up, he touched the brim of his black felt hat and called out in a clipped voice, "Good day, sir! Lieutenant Colonel John C. Fremont, leader of the California Battalion that's been charged with taking back the pueblos of Santa Barbara and Los Angeles from the Mexican rebels." Although he had the refined look of a gentleman, his sunken cheeks testified to having endured privation; they were only partially concealed by a neatly trimmed beard. The silver buttons on his blue jacket glittered with newness. His icy, blue eyes surveyed the welcoming party.

"Welcome to Rancho Tinaquaic, sir. I'm William Benjamin Foxen, but the locals call me by my Catholic name, Don Julian."

"Good afternoon. Captain Dana sends his greetings. We camped on his rancho last night, and he suggested I come see you. You're English, I understand." Looking around, he continued, "Idyllic spot for a homestead." Fremont's eyes swept over the adobe hacienda that lay nestled in a stand of stately oaks. Behind it, willows and sycamores lined the meandering creek that hugged the bottom of a steep hill. "Don't imagine you get many visitors out this way."

"No, we don't," Don Julian said. "When we do, it's a special occasion. Have to say, this tops them all. We all expected you to stay on the main trail."

"We would have, except we're in sore need of horses and food." Fremont dismounted and handed his reins to the nearest Indian scout.

Don Julian's horse, Joaquin, turned sideways from the hitching post and nickered a greeting to Fremont's horse. The gray had been recently groomed and looked regal with his white mane and flowing tail. He answered with an aloof whinny and a tail swish.

Don Julian escorted Fremont to where his family stood waiting. "Sir, I would like to present my wife, Eduarda Osuña Foxen."

Doña Eduarda motioned for Martina to take charge of the wide-eyed Juanita, moved to her husband's side and bowed her head. "Bienvenidos, señor."

Fremont removed his hat and bowed at the waist. "Gracias, señora." Addressing both husband and wife, he said, "I apologize that we had to kill some of your cattle. Our provisions have run low, and my soldiers are weak and in need of meat. My quartermaster will leave you with script entitling you to be reimbursed from the US government ten dollars for each animal."

"Thank you. That's mighty generous, sir," said Don Julian.

Guillermo and Angel exchanged glances. Híjole! That was five times what they received in trade for a cow's hide!

Doña Eduarda's hand flew to her mouth. "O Dios mio! José de Jesús! What are you doing here?"

All heads turned to the dapper man with the handlebar mustache who had been partially hidden by the Indians. "Eduarda, sí, it's me, José!" José de Jesús Pico removed his hat and bowed.

Fremont gestured to Don José to dismount and join them. He swung off his horse and handed the reins off to the older scout whose gray-flecked braids nearly reached his waist. Black eyes stared out from crinkled eyes above high cheekbones the color of burnished manzanita.

"Eduarda!" He hurried to her, kissing her hand. "My dear, it is so good to see you." Looking up at Don Julian, he said, "You too, Julian!" The men embraced and slapped each other on the shoulder.

All the Foxens shared looks of bewilderment at the surprising turn of events.

"José, what brings you here?" asked Don Julian.

Don José deferred to Fremont, who said, "He was arrested three days ago in San Luis Obispo for violating the terms of his parole. Had it not been for the pleas of his wife and the intervention of prominent citizens, he would have been executed by a firing squad." Fremont nodded to Don José. "Proceed."

"It's only by the grace of God that my fourteen children are not fatherless." Putting his hand on his heart, he said, "I made a most regrettable mistake and allowed myself to be pressured into taking part in an attack near San Juan Bautista. I can assure you it was not out of loyalty to the

14

Mexican government." Turning to Fremont, he said, "I owe the commandante my life. In return for his mercy, I have promised to be his faithful servant. I pray that God will use me to convince General José Maria Flores to accept a peaceful surrender." With hat in hand, he bowed in Fremont's direction.

Doña Eduarda dabbed her eyes with a handkerchief. "Señor Fremont, on behalf of my extended family, I wish to thank you for sparing the life of my godmother's son. May God bless you, señor." She made the sign of the cross in Fremont's direction. Spreading her hands widely, she said, "You are most welcome to whatever we have."

Arching his eyebrows in alarm, Guillermo glanced at Angel.

Don Julian put one arm around her narrow shoulders. "I join my wife in thanking you for saving Don José's life. We owe you much in return. Please come in for some refreshment."

"Thank you. I would be honored." Turning to Don José, Fremont said, "By all means, you are welcome to join us. I am sure you and the señora have much to talk about."

There were smiles all around. Doña Eduarda led the way. "Martina, take the younger ones to the dining room so we can visit, por favor?"

Don Julian gestured for Fremont and Don José to follow his wife into the adobe. The men stomped their feet on the wooden steps to shake the mud from their boots.

Turning to her brother, Martina exclaimed, "Can you believe this? Mamá's cousin is riding with the Americanos? What a surprise!"

Glancing over at the Indian scouts, Guillermo whispered, "I don't know. I'm worried Fremont's going to use that favor to his advantage and persuade Papá to give him some of our horses. You saw how Mamá treated him like royalty."

"It's true. Family is everything to her. I can hear her say now, 'Horses can be replaced, people cannot.'"

His sister was right, which was all the more reason to worry.

Panchita tugged on her big sister's arm. "What about my heifers?" Her godparents had given her a dozen cows the previous spring for her First Communion.

"Don't worry," Martina said. "Guillermo and Angel won't let anything happen to them. Will you?"

"They'll be fine," said Guillermo, though he had a nagging fear one of them had already been slaughtered along with her calf. Either way, he'd spare his little sister the pain for now.

Martina gave her sister a reassuring pat on the head as they turned to leave. Over her shoulder, she said, "Don't worry, Panchita. They know what needs to be done." She winked at her brother and Angel, lifted her skirt and side-stepped the puddles as she tiptoed into the house.

Angel looked toward the Indian scouts who were waiting nearby on horseback and whispered, "Shall we go find my father?"

"Sure, why not?" Guillermo shrugged. "My parents welcomed Fremont into our home like he's family. We've nothing to fear from the enemy. It's our neighbors I'm worried about. Wait till they find out we're supplying the enemy with livestock. Ay, caramba." Guillermo identified himself as a Californio. He did not welcome the Americanos as his father did. He did not trust them.

They tipped their hats to the Indian scouts and rode off in search of Angel's father, Sal. He'd know what to do about the horses.

CHAPTER 4

When Guillermo returned to the hacienda, the visitors were gone. The low-slung adobe sat huddled in the winter's dampness. Except for a wisp of smoke curling from the chimney, it appeared deserted. Despite the lateness of the day, no candlelight shone through its windows. The household routine had been disrupted by the day's events.

He needed to confront his father about the horses, but he was in no mood to risk another tongue-lashing. It was frustrating trying to second-guess what his father expected of him. It seemed often that he fell short in some way. He wanted more than anything for his father to be proud of him.

After removing the saddle and blanket from Benito's back, Guillermo gave him a rubdown in the corral. With each brushstroke, he thought about how he and the crew would have to break six to eight mustangs to replace the cow ponies they were surrendering to Fremont. It took months to properly train one. His father didn't understand the extra work it would mean for the crew. Though the ex-seaman was now a ranchero, he was no caballero.

"Why did Captain Dana have to send the Yankees here?" Guillermo muttered. He suspected the former New Englander secretly favored an Americano takeover and had directed Fremont to Don Julian's doorstep to find out if rumors of an ambush at Gaviota were true. This put his father in a dangerous predicament! Helping the enemy was treason! Guillermo squatted and brushed off the caked mud from the horse's front legs. Benito nickered and playfully knocked Guillermo's hat onto the ground. Guillermo chuckled and retrieved it. "Aren't you the wise guy? Maybe I should let the Yankees take you. How would you like that?" Benito nickered again, one of his big, soft eyes meeting Guillermo's. "You know I'm only kidding. I'd never let that happen."

As he was finishing, he heard dogs barking. Glancing around, he spotted his father making his way across the yard.

A few moments later, Don Julian rested his arms on the corral railing and said, "Good. You're home. When you're done here, meet me in the patio. Something I need to talk to you about, mijo."

"Yes, Papá. I'm almost done."

A knot formed in Guillermo's stomach as he put away the grooming tools and made his way to where his father waited by the firepit. Most of the rancho's business was conducted here. Don Julian propped one foot on a tree stump that served as a chair and relit his pipe. Exhaling, he said, "You're probably confused about why I welcomed Fremont."

Guillermo shrugged while he studied his foot. He scuffed the dirt, unsure how to respond.

"Look at me, mijo. You need to look a man in his eyes whether you want to hear what he has to say or not."

Ay, yi, yi…he had yet to utter a word but had already managed to displease his father. When Guillermo raised his eyes, worry lines etched in his father's forehead warned him something serious was coming.

"Your mother and I intended to remain neutral on the issue of war, but that changed today when we learned her cousin was taken prisoner. The long and the short of it is... we've decided to help the Americanos."

"Help the Americanos!" Guillermo gasped. "Papá, how can you side against our paisanos?"

Don Julian held up a hand in defense. "This isn't about opposing them. It's about losing faith in the Mexican government to fulfill its promises. The constant turnover in governors has created chaos. Favors are passed out to their cronies while the rest of us are left to fend for ourselves against outlaws, wild Indians, and grizzlies...with little in the way of ammunition or supplies. Alta California needs skilled tradesmen like carpenters, blacksmiths, coopers, and an impartial justice system, not to mention schools."

He paused and relit his pipe. "It's still the same backwater frontier as when I came ashore fifteen years ago. Without a real army or navy to protect us, it's inevitable we'll be invaded by a more powerful country. The final outcome of the war isn't in question. It's just a matter of time before the Americanos take back Santa Barbara and Los Angeles. Soon as Fremont meets up with the southern forces waiting for him, General Flores' army will see they're outnumbered and outmatched militarily. My prediction is that they'll surrender within a couple months, but for that to happen, Fremont has to get his men over the mountains. With two cannons, that poses a problem. Since the Refugio Trail is so steep, he was planning to cut through the Gaviota Pass. Dana warned him about the rumors of an ambush there and suggested Fremont come see me in hopes I could advise him."

"What did you tell him?"

"The last I heard, the rebelistas were planning an ambush at the Gaviota Pass, but that was over a week ago before the storm. Now that the gorge is impassable due to the mud and debris, it would make more sense for them to be waiting at the Ortegas' instead." The Ortegas were a distinguished family whose hacienda sat strategically in the canyon where the alternate route, the Refugio Trail, led down to the coastal plain. "That's why Fremont's considering a third, seldom traveled route, the San Marcos Trail. No one would suspect he'd make the crossing there, so he'd have the advantage of surprising the Barbareños. He's asked me to be his guide, and I agreed."

Guillermo's eyes widened in disbelief. "Why can't you just draw him a map? Why do *you* have to guide him when La Nochebuena is almost here? It's not fair for him to drag you away now."

"War doesn't take a break for holy days. Don't you think those men out there would rather be with their families than camped out in the cold? There are times in life we have to make sacrifices, mijo, and this is one of them. The San Marcos Trail is little more than a cow path." He shook his head and gestured with his arms dismissively. "You know that. We traveled it last summer. He needs a local guide who's familiar with the mountains and canyons. A couple months ago, he nearly lost one of his companies in the same area when they were forced to flee the presidio in that uprising we heard about."

"You'll be branded a traitor! You swore an oath to defend the Mexican province from foreign invaders."

"Guillermo, back when I made that pledge, everyone believed that supplies and aid would improve under Mexican rule, but conditions are worse now than during Spanish rule! Mexico continues to neglect us, and due to political corruption, there's no hope of things improving. Mark my words, in time neighbors like Gutiérrez and Davila will switch their allegiance from Mexico to the United States just like Don José Pico. Since he's related to half the population in the province, he'll be very influential."

Guillermo wanted to believe that. "When are you leaving? Tomorrow?"

"The day after. In the morning, the battalion will move up the canyon half a league to new grazing land. It'll give the animals and men time to rest. We'll leave the following day. You're coming with me."

"I am?"

"Aye. I'm taking you along. It'll be good for you to meet some Americanos. They're going to be your fellow countrymen before long. Fremont invited me to their camp tonight to meet with the scouting party. Thought you'd like to come along."

"Uh, yes! I'll have to saddle up another horse so Benito can rest. I rode him hard today."

"I suspect you did. Been rounding up horses with Sal?"

"When Angel and I told him the news, he figured you'd want the belle mare and the best cow ponies hidden away, so we drove them out to Rattlesnake Canyon. Felipe and Chico will camp out there with them until the army moves on."

Don Julian nodded. "Aye, but I think we should take a few of the other horses with us as a gesture of goodwill." He gazed to the north where smoke from the battalion's campfires hazed the dimming sky. "This has been one whale of a day. The last thing I expected was for the Yankee army to come this direction. I'm not one given to high-falutin' ideas, but I'd say destiny came calling today."

Guillermo digested this. If his father was siding with the Americanos, what would keep them from claiming their rancho for themselves?

21

CHAPTER 5

By the time Guillermo and his father reached the Americano camp, night had fallen, as had the temperature. The soldiers would awaken the next morning to a world covered in a blanket of frost. As they approached the final bend in the trail, they encountered two mounted guards blocking their way.

Don Julian touched the brim of his hat. "Good evening, gentlemen. I'm Benjamin Foxen, owner of this rancho, and this here's my son. Colonel Fremont invited us to pay a visit to Company H."

"Yessir. See you brought along some horses," said a bull-necked man. "We're in sore need of fresh mounts. They've been dropping like flies the last week. Not enough grass to keep 'em going." His horse sagged under his bulk, a roan that Guillermo noted bore his grandfather's Rancho Tepusquet brand. Guillermo struggled to keep his expression neutral.

The other sentry was a younger fellow whose cheek was swollen with a wad of tobacco. Neither man seemed surprised by the social call.

"Keep left," said the first man. "Company H should have a flag. If not, ask someone."

They moved out of the way so the Foxens could pass. Guillermo's jaw clenched at the indignity of being granted permission by these strangers to proceed on his family's land.

Upon entering the meadow, Guillermo was taken aback by what he saw. The previously cheerless camp had been transformed into a nearly festive scene. Dozens of campfires illuminated the moss-draped oaks that bent over the weary travelers like eavesdroppers. The hollow-eyed soldiers stared at the Foxens with a mixture of curiosity and envy. One gaunt-looking man called out, "Howdy there, sir! If you're lookin' fer the colonel's tent, it's yonder." He pointed his pipe to the western edge of the field.

"We're headed for Company H. Do you know where that might be?" asked Don Julian.

"Yep. It's not far from the colonel's tent. Just keep heading thataway. That sure is a fine horse you have there." He gave Joaquin an appraising gaze. "What color you call that?"

"Retinto, a brown-black. Where you from, soldier?"

The rawboned man stood up, friendly-like. "Me? Pennsylvania, where we have rolling hills like this but with trees shoulder to shoulder. My friend here," he pointed to the hatchet-faced man next to him, "we was just speculatin' 'bout what kinda wild cats you got in these parts. Panthers, cougars?"

"Call 'em pumas. Tawny colored, like the hills most of the year. Lose at least a dozen calves a year to 'em," said Don Julian.

"Any wolves?"

"Some. Not as many as there used to be. Keep warm now."

"That's what I'm aimin' to do."

Don Julian and Guillermo turned their reins toward the edge of camp. They hadn't gone far when they were intercepted by a handsome man in his twenties wearing a buckskin coat that reached midthigh. He removed his hat in a courtly manner. "Good evening, sir. It's Mr. Foxen, correct?"

When Don Julian nodded, the greeter chuckled. "Who else would be roaming the countryside on a cold night like this? I reckon this young fellow is your son. Welcome, gentlemen. I'm Lieutenant Edwin Bryant, assistant to Captain Jacobs, the head of Company H. We've been expecting you." He reached up and heartily shook their hands.

"A pleasure to meet you. As you can see, we brought along some horses."

"Sturdy ones at that. Much obliged," said Bryant. "This march has taken a toll on the livestock. We've covered more than two hundred miles in some mighty foul weather with little feed." He pointed to a clump of trees nearby. "Your son can tie them up with the others over yonder."

Don Julian handed the ropes off to Guillermo and motioned for him to take them to where Bryant indicated. "I'll come get you when I'm done. Don't expect it'll take long."

Guillermo took the reins and led the horses up a slight rise to where a picket line was strung between two oaks. He tethered the horses to it and rubbed their foreheads. "Adiós, mis amigos." He patted a newly broken yearling on the rump. "You be good now."

He leaned against one of the trees and stared out at the encampment from the shadows. It was hard to imagine such a mass of humanity finding its way to this isolated meadow. The trampled grass and patches of earth worn bare by hooves and boots would recover in the weeks to come, but would some nonphysical imprint remain? Would echoes of these voices linger, and like Petra with her ancestors, would he be privy to their calls?

His father was right. This had been a remarkable day. Here he was, in the Americano camp, feeling surprisingly safe. The Yanks he had encountered so far had been friendly.

Looking out on the two cannons across the way and the abundance of rifles everywhere, he understood why his father was convinced this army would succeed in retaking the pueblos of Santa Barbara and Los Angeles. The Californios, with their lances and pitifully few rifles and pistolas, were no match for these well-armed Yanks. He was overcome by a wave of sadness for his paisanos. Perhaps his uncle's death was an omen. Would his family, like the Chumash who occupied this area before them, lose their land as well? Who would be the greater threat in the end, the paisanos his father was betraying or these friendly Yanks?

CHAPTER 6

The morning of December 20, 1846 dawned clear and bright. The trees and ground were cloaked in sparkling, white frost. As the sun rose over the hill, filling the canyon with light, excitement was building to a fever pitch in the Foxen household. Fremont's cavalry of more than four hundred would be marching past the hacienda!

The girls staked out a space for themselves on the veranda and waited anxiously for a glimpse of the procession. They were bundled in their heaviest shawls, woolen stockings, and mittens. Rebozos framed their pink faces.

Ramona was the first to catch the movement down the trail when she returned from releasing the geese from their night enclosure. Jumping up and down, she squealed, "They're coming! They're coming!" The dogs barked and danced in circles.

Guillermo and his father waited at the trail as the procession made its way down the canyon. Fremont led the way, flanked by the Indian bodyguards who had accompanied him to the rancho the previous day. Pack mules, wagons, and men on horseback, riding two abreast, trailed behind them. When Fremont came up alongside, he touched his hat and said crisply, "Good morning, gentlemen."

"Good morning, sir," said Don Julian. "I'll escort you to a spot down the canyon that will provide you with some good grazing land."

"Thank you, Mr. Foxen. I'm much obliged. Pasturage is a precious commodity to a cattleman, and I appreciate your generosity."

"You're welcome. We've been lucky to have early rains. I wanted you to meet my son, Guillermo, before he heads off to round up some steers. He'll be accompanying us on the march tomorrow, if that meets with your approval."

"Nice to meet you, young man," said Fremont. "How old are you?"

Guillermo hadn't expected to be addressed directly by the commander and was caught off guard. "Th-thirteen, sir." He cringed as the word "sir" came out in an embarrassing croak, underlining his youth. Heat crept up his neck to his peach-fuzzed cheeks.

Fremont nodded. "Pleased to have you along, son."

Guillermo flooded with relief at having passed the scrutiny of Fremont's piercing blue eyes. He doubly appreciated the colonel's good grace in not so much as blinking at hearing his voice crack.

Fremont turned his attention to Don Julian. "On behalf of my men, I want to express our appreciation for your kind hospitality. Besides our livestock needing feed, my soldiers need meat to keep up their strength."

"We're pleased to be of service." Turning to Guillermo, he said, "Best be on your way, mijo. I'll send Manuel and Juan ahead to the encampment to butcher them."

Guillermo nodded, clicked the reins, and caught up with Angel, who was posted on a hill to the east. Besides rounding up strays, he was keeping an eye out for scouts who might wander in the direction of Rattlesnake Canyon.

When Guillermo told him about accompanying his father on the march, Angel sniffed. "He's taking you? Better keep your head low and stay out of the way."

"You're just rankled because I'll have a story to tell when I get back."

Angel crowed and galloped off.

Sighing, Guillermo shook the reins and followed.

That evening, following a supper of pozole and tortillas, the household gathered in the dining room for prayers. A narrow table covered with a crisp, white linen served as the altar. An engraved crucifix and a picture of the Blessed Mother stood on top of it, and flickering candles on either side cast the room in a golden glow. Doña Eduarda led the kneeling worshipers in the rosary. Prayers were dedicated to the protection of Colonel Fremont's army and a peaceful end to the Mexican-American War. A special blessing was asked for Don Julian and Guillermo.

After the vaqueros and Indian servants retired to their quarters for the night, the family settled around the stone fireplace in the sala, the living room. Don Julian sat in his oversized cowhide chair opposite Doña Eduarda, who rocked Alejandro. Like bookends, Ramona and Martina sat on either side of the red velvet settee. Juanita sat between them, clutching her rag doll, and Panchita lay sprawled on the Oriental rug, idly twirling her long, chestnut-colored braid.

Guillermo was left to squat on a stool that he had outgrown months ago. He leaned forward, resting his forearms on his thighs and whittling a piece of willow over a brass bucket. The knife blade momentarily reflected firelight on an ancient carbine that hung from a peg on the wall. On the adjacent wall, a painting of the Madonna and Child gazed down benevolently on the family.

"Papá, what if you're not home for La Nochebuena?" asked Panchita.

"We'll celebrate when we return."

"It won't be the same," said Ramona.

The mantel clock groaned as it did when a storm was on the way. Guillermo's thoughts turned to the soldiers bivouacked up the canyon, far from the comforts of hearth and home.

"Now girls, sometimes we have to make sacrifices," said Doña Eduarda. "Papá and Guillermo will return as soon as they can. Let's enjoy the evening. Guillermo, how about you choose the story tonight?"

Lost in thought, it took Guillermo a moment for his mother's words to register. "Uh…a tale about King Arthur would be good." He shrugged.

"You always choose one about him." Panchita whined.

"It's been months since I've listened to a story." The story had yet to begin, and already his sisters were annoying him. His mother cocked her head and gave him an encouraging smile. He could see in her soft, brown eyes that this evening meant much to her. Since the previous spring, he had taken to spending his evenings with the three Gonzalez brothers after evening prayers. They entertained themselves playing Monte, throwing knives, and strumming the guitar. There was always a reata handy to lasso anything within reach.

Don Julian cut off the bickering and began the story like he always did. "Long, long ago, in a land far across the sea…" In a deep voice that still resonated with an English accent, he told about how the young knight pulled the sword, Excalibur, from a stone. Of all the brave knights in the court, Arthur proved he was the rightful heir to the throne. The tale had always appealed to Guillermo. A young knight being anointed king was the stuff of dreams.

29

Despite his reluctance, it didn't take long for Guillermo to be caught up in the story. He imagined himself being welcomed home as a conquering hero to a cheering crowd. Paisanos would regard him with honor and esteem. Their daughters would vie to be his dancing partner at fandangos. Angel and the other vaqueros would treat him with the respect he deserved. He would no longer be at the bottom of the heap.

A pop from the fire broke the spell. Guillermo straightened and blinked as if waking from a dream. He became aware of how ridiculous he must look, sitting with his knees nearly touching his chin. Ay, caramba! He was past the age of being expected to join his sisters and baby brother for these family evenings. His father had been thrown into the company of salty, old sea dogs when he was not much older.

"Papá, when you were a little, did you ever see the king and his castle?" asked Ramona.

"No." Don Julian chuckled. "My family lived far from the likes of the king. Being born a commoner meant owning land was out of the question. I went to sea to escape that hardscrabble life. Didn't realize that I was trading one kind of servitude for another. Wasn't till I became a sea captain that I felt I was my own man, but that was after many years serving under the command of others." He took a puff from his pipe. "When I ride over the hills of our hacienda, I feel like a lord overseeing my manor. I marvel at my good fortune. Wish my father could see how far I've come," he said wistfully.

A hush descended upon the room, punctuated by the rhythmic ticking of the clock. It was getting late, and Guillermo sensed his mother was about to call it a night.

Panchita piped up. "What's a commoner, Papá?"

30

Guillermo groaned inwardly at the obvious delay tactic. He rested his chin in his hand and rolled his eyes.

"It's a person whose parents are common folks, like most people in the world. Back in Europe, much is made of the class a person's born into. Think of a ladder, and at the top is royalty. Below that is the aristocracy, also part of the ruling class. Everyone else is born into one of the lower rungs. The higher you are on the ladder, the more privileged you are. As you know, your mother's parents came from the ruling class, which makes you one-half blue blood."

"Half our blood is blue?" asked Juanita.

Martina, who had been quiet all evening, said, smiling, "No, no. That's just an expression. Think of it as being sprinkled with fairy dust." She sprinkled her sister's head with imaginary dust, eliciting a giggle.

Not to be trifled with, Ramona asked, "How did your family really get to be blue bloods, Mamá?"

Guillermo had never questioned why his grandparents were treated with extra courtesy by the padres at the mission. At church services, they were seated in pews near the front. Paisanos like the Davilas and Janssens sat in the middle section, and Indians stood in the back. That was the way it was.

Speaking softly because the baby had fallen asleep, Doña Eduarda said, "A long time ago, my ancestors were brave hidalgos. They helped drive the Moors from Spain. The king rewarded them with a title and land. In a special ceremony, he laid his sword on their shoulders and pronounced them noblemen. My father's family was from a part of Spain near the ancient city of Alhambra. I have been told it's one of the most beautiful cities in all the world, with a magnificent castle. My great-grandfather was related to the

31

Count of Osuña and inherited a grand estate. My mother's family was descended from the old Galician family of Lugo y Cota. The province was named in their honor. She used to boast that my father's family had a village named in their honor, but hers had a province."

"Mamá, why did your grandfather leave Spain?" asked Martina, cocking her head quizzically.

"Well, some men have a taste for adventure," she said, winking at her husband with a dimpled smile. "They aren't satisfied until they've discovered what lies over the horizon. Your father came from England, my grandfathers from Mexico, and my great-grandfathers from Spain." She turned to Guillermo. "Hopefully, mijo, you will not feel the need to seek your fortune elsewhere."

"Why would I ever leave Rancho Tinaquaic?"

"Indeed, why would you?" She smiled.

Lying in bed that night, Guillermo thought about his ancestors who had fought for the king of Spain. What would they think of him helping to guide infidels over the mountain to retake one of the original Spanish settlements in Alta California? Would this bring dishonor to his family name or turn out to be an act of valor? What if his family lost Rancho Tinaquaic because they supported the wrong side in the war? Dear God in heaven, did loyalty to country trump family ties? Hearing about his hidalgo ancestors, there had been a stirring within his heart, a call to duty, but instead of defending the land of his birth from the enemy, he had been recruited to help them!

CHAPTER 7

The following morning, Guillermo and his father left the hacienda while it was still dark and frosty. They had said their goodbyes to the family the night before, but Doña Eduarda and Concha, their cook, insisted on rising early to see them off. Fretting, Concha had packed carne seca and fresh tortillas for their journey. "I doubt those gringos will provide you with decent food, so I packed plenty."

Doña Eduarda kissed them. "Vayan con Dios, mis queridos." *Go with God, my loved ones.* She and Concha stood on the veranda, waving their handkerchiefs in farewell.

Father and son had not gone far before they heard a faint melody coming from up ahead. "What's that?" asked Guillermo.

"A bugler's playing 'Reveille,' announcing it's time for the soldiers to get up. At night, 'Taps' is played," Don Julian said.

Dawn was breaking as they approached the encampment. A pink streak lit up the eastern sky, and smoke from numerous campfires shrouded the canyon in a haze. They wove their way to the advance guard's station that was assembling twenty yards from Fremont's tent. A collection of Indian scouts and buckskin-clad mountain men were saddling their horses and stowing supplies in their saddlebags.

Bryant strode over to meet the Foxens. Under his long coat, he wore a uniform of dark trousers, a flannel shirt with a star on each tip of the collar, and a red kerchief tied around his neck. A brace of long-barreled pistols and a knife hung from his waist. He held up a gloved hand. "Good morning, Mr. Foxen and Ghee-yair-mo. Did I say that right?"

"Yessir," Guillermo croaked.

"Welcome. Captain Jacobs, head of the scouting party, should be here shortly. He and the other company commanders are receiving their orders for the day from the colonel. While we're waiting, may I offer y'all a cup of chicory brew?"

Guillermo declined, but his father said, "Sounds good."

Bryant called to a Negro boy who brought over a steaming cup. While the men made small talk, Guillermo glanced around the camp. There was a general sense of weariness among the grim-faced men who readied themselves for the long day's march. Many of the horses and mules stood hipshot, one leg bent to ease their pain. How would these poor creatures make it over the mountains?

"Good morning, Mr. Foxen! Glad you're here!" A man in his twenties approached with a jaunty air of confidence. Guillermo gathered this was Captain Jacobs. "We've been ordered to lead the procession to the Santa Inés Valley. Fremont ordered a foot march for the rank and file due to the lameness of the animals. It's going to be a long day, so we best be off." Jacobs swung onto his horse and adjusted the reins.

"Captain, this here's my son, Guillermo. You didn't have a chance to meet him the other night. I decided to bring him along. He's handy with a reata and can help round up horses."

"Welcome to Company H, young man," Jacobs said, touching the brim of his hat. Turning to the men on horseback, he called, "Our orders are to find a campsite about fifteen miles ahead and round up fresh mounts if there are any to be found. Since Mr. Foxen is familiar with the area, he'll lead the way."

Don Julian, Jacobs, and Bryant made their way to the trail that followed the creek. Guillermo followed, the rest of the company riding in pairs behind him.

His father chatted amiably with the officers as they trotted along. "Where you chaps from?"

"From Kentucky. Edwin's from Louisville, and I'm from Lexington."

"Hmm, long way from home. Took you what, five, six months to make the journey?"

"From the jumping off point at Independence, about four months," said Jacobs. "We were lucky. We had a good guide. The east is all abuzz with talk of opportunities out west. Our fathers are political friends with Fremont's father-in-law, Senator Benton, and they encouraged us to make the trip. Benton's an advisor to President Polk and a big proponent of westward expansion. Arranged for Fremont to be assigned the job of mapping out trail routes. He's a surveyor for the US Topographical Corps."

"Who happened to be exploring in the province when war with Mexico was declared," Don Julian said good-naturedly.

"Indeed," Bryant said. With a sly smile, he said, "It was fortunate that a scouting party was able to summon him back from the Klamath area in Oregon Territory."

"And that you're here as well," Don Julian said. He held up a hand in defense. "Don't get me wrong. We Anglos are mighty relieved the United States finally made its move. We were afraid the French, Russians, or Brits would beat you to it."

"No loyalty to Mother England, I take it?"

"Been away too long to be subject of a monarch again."

While his father chatted with their new companions, Guillermo thought about the crew guarding their remuda back in Rattlesnake Canyon. If only Angel could see him now. Riding with the advance guard was like being on a noble quest. They rode a league through the winding canyon, eventually passing La Laguna's deserted-looking hacienda. The corral was empty, and its gate hung open at a crazy angle, swaying back and forth in the wind. An eerie emptiness had settled over the land.

"From the looks of things," Jacobs said, "whoever lives here was warned to drive off his livestock."

"Its absentee owner lives in Santa Barbara with his family. His crew of vaqueros must have driven the livestock back into the hills," said Don Julian.

They ascended the steep Zaca Ridge that skirted the mysterious dome-shaped mountain. Its lake was sacred to the Chumash, who believed it to be bottomless—a doorway to a spiritual realm. It was also the roosting site of condors so large they could carry off a newborn lamb.

They rode on until early afternoon when Jacobs called a noonday rest under a stand of sycamores. The horses and pack mules were watered and allowed to graze while Guillermo and his father shared Concha's provisions with the officers. The Indian scouts squatted in a circle, passing around their own victuals. A few gringo scouts lay sprawled on the ground with their hats covering their faces. These grizzled men were cut from the same buckskin cloth as his father's friend, Ike Sparks, who bought the Foxens' mercantile store when they moved to their rancho. No doubt their survival skills greatly surpassed those of their well-bred commanding officers. Guillermo envied their ability to relax at will to catch up on much-needed sleep.

"This sure hits the spot," said the soft-spoken Bryant.

"Haven't tasted anything this good in months!" Jacobs said as he polished off his second tortilla stuffed with savory beef and green chilies.

"I'll be sure to pass that on to our cook," Don Julian said, wiping his mouth with his kerchief. He pointed off in the distance. "Look at that! Must be the platoon that went searching for horses. Looks like they found a whole herd!"

"It's Captain Finley! By golly, will you look at that!" exclaimed Jacobs.

A short time later, a soldier rode up to explain how he and his men captured the horses: they encountered an Indian who told the search party where they could find some horses hidden in a canyon on Rancho Casmalia. Finley was upset with how he'd been treated by his ranchero's crew at Rancho Guadalupe. Thanks to the tip, Finley and his men were able to round up sixty-five horses and drive them east to intercept the battalion. He said, "They can graze while we wait for you to catch up with us. I'll go back and let the others know you're headed that direction." He rode off to rejoin his men.

"Well, that should help. We're not much of a cavalry when half our horses are lame," said Bryant.

Don Julian said, "Since we don't know how many of them are suitable for riding, I could have Guillermo help with singling out the ones that can be saddled. He's good at sizing up horses. The last thing some poor soul needs, who's footsore from carrying a saddle on his shoulders, is to be bucked off a mustang."

"You're right," said Jacobs. "Think you can do that, Guillermo?"

"Sure. Papá's right. Some may be good only for carrying packs. I'll be happy to have a look at them to help sort them out."

Reclining on the ground, Jacobs said, "That's the Santa Inés Valley out there." A hilly valley studded with oaks stretched below them.

"Yes, it is. If you look closely in that direction," Don Julian pointed to the west, "you can make out the mission's bell tower. El Camino Real passes over the mountain behind it. The ocean lies on the other side, as does the hacienda belonging to a clan of rebelistas—the Ortegas. It's situated up the canyon from one of the most protected coves on the coast. Was an outpost for smuggling merchant ships when trading with foreigners was banned. The French pirate Bouchard ransacked it 'bout thirty years ago. The patriarch was a scout with the Portola party and was one of the first commandantes of the presidio in Santa Barbara. His sons and grandsons are spread out in a dozen canyons."

"The main road goes over that wall of mountain?" asked Bryant. "Good Lord! It's gotta be four thousand feet high! I can see why the rebelistas would expect us to take a detour. Wish we had a way of communicating with Naval Commander Robert Stockton to get one of his ships anchored offshore for protection. Where's the pass where the ambush is supposed to take place?"

"Gaviota Pass is to the northwest. There's a trail that cuts off from the main road to the north of the mission." Don Julian pointed to the right with his pipe. "It passes through hilly terrain before it winds through a narrow gorge barely wide enough for a cart. Rocky overhangs make it treacherous in bad weather, and it's prone to rockslides. When the creek's running, it's impassable. Last I heard, rebelistas were planning to dislodge boulders and roll them off the cliffs onto the file of marchers below. Local rancheros and their vaqueros would be posted to shoot those attempting to flee."

"In other words, we'd be sitting ducks," said Jacobs. Scanning the valley, he asked, "Where's this shortcut Fremont is considering?"

Guillermo pointed to the southwest. "It's out in that direction. It's shorter in distance but will add an extra day or two because of its poor condition. It's seldom used except to drive cattle to and from Rancho San Marcos, which is tucked back in those hills. My grandfather used to manage it for the mission padres."

The men squinted off in the distance. "Looks like a gradual climb," said Bryant. "Think there'll be enough grass for the livestock?"

"There should be good grazing up to the rancho, but beyond that, the brush gets thick," Don Julian said. "The crest of the mountain is exposed sandstone, slippery even when it's dry. Have to say I'm mighty concerned about those cannon wagons."

Jacobs and Bryant rolled their eyes. Bryant said, "Shore would be nice to know if there's an ambush waiting for us. We could request that Fremont send a group of us to go scout it out. What do you think of that idea, Mr. Foxen?"

Guillermo stiffened. Didn't Bryant recognize the risk that would mean for him and his father? If they were spotted anywhere near Gaviota with Yankee scouts, they would be charged with treason. He held his breath, waiting for an answer.

"To know if there's an ambush, we'd have to approach Gaviota from the ocean side, and the only way to do that would be to cross over the Refugio Trail and then head north. Even if we managed to get past the Ortegas without them knowing, it would take two days at least to circle back and rendezvous with the waiting battalion. However, if you were to cross over the San Marcos Trail, you'd be in Santa Barbara by then. It's a matter of how much of a hurry Fremont is in."

Jacobs sighed heavily as he stashed his tobacco pouch in his jacket pocket. "Guess we'll have to wait and see. Better get going. We've got maybe four hours of light left." He signaled to the scouts to saddle up.

Guillermo took in a deep breath. If Fremont chose the treacherous but faster trail, they would be putting themselves in grave danger.

CHAPTER 8

ompany H continued its march toward the west, leaving
the cover of the hills and entering the valley. Everyone
was on high alert for a chance encounter with a vaquero
herding cattle or a rebelista scout. Guillermo's heart raced
at the prospect of being spotted. He warily scanned the hill-
tops, momentarily startled a couple times by the silhouette
of a grazing cow. The windblown countryside had an empty
and deserted feel about it. He was struck by the expanse of
green, but recent storms had left a scar on the landscape,
shearing branches and toppling trees. They passed a knoll
where the splintered remains of a black oak stabbed the sky.
A battle of the elements had been fought here.

It was late afternoon when they caught up with the herd
of stolen horses grazing in a hidden swale along the Alamo
Pintado Creek. After some discussion, Don Julian suggested
it was as good a place as any to set up camp for the night.
The low-lying hills offered a measure of protection from the
wind and spying eyes. This was the western edge of Rancho
Corral de Cuati, three leagues south of the Foxen rancho
and belonging to the rebelista Gustavo Davila. What would
he think if he were to discover his neighbor had foiled the
Californios' plot of ambushing the Yankees?

Guillermo helped his father set up their makeshift
shelter under a sprawling oak. They draped a battered

41

canvas sail over one of the lower limbs and staked it in the ground. Before Guillermo left to assess the horses, he gathered firewood. It was gratifying to discover the day's sunshine and wind had partially dried out the damp wood. Two Indian scouts stood guard while the cook and his crew prepared supper.

The brand on the horses confirmed they came from Rancho Guadalupe, which belonged to Antonio Olivera, his grandfather's elder brother. Losing a herd of this size would be a significant loss. Half were well-trained cow ponies, while the others were common work horses of varying quality. The four mules would be valuable for carrying packs as well as riders.

It was dusk by the time Fremont arrived in camp, followed by exhausted soldiers carrying saddles on their shoulders. Their lame horses came hobbling behind. It was a pitiful sight. Men collapsed on the ground, too weary to pitch a tent.

Fremont's servant erected the colonel's tent and then unloaded his personal belongings from the pack mules. Among them was a massive bearskin robe that Guillermo was told served as Fremont's bed. A portable desk made of mahogany also disappeared inside the tent. A hand-painted Americano flag, a shabby substitute for Mexico's proud eagle and serpent, was mounted above the door flap.

Stragglers continued to limp into camp as different companies arrived at the night's destination. The mood was grim, with scant conversation. Men huddled in blankets around scattered fires, cleaning their guns and smoking. Supper was a simple fare of stewed beef and chicory coffee.

Needing something to do with his hands, Guillermo found a stick and began whittling. A full moon had risen over the mountains, casting an iridescent glow over the peaks. Guillermo and his father kept company with a French trapper named Archie. He had a beak nose and a black mustache and beard, and he wore his long, matted hair loose, giving him a wild-man look. His eyes glittered with excitement as he told a tale about a Yankee military messenger who rode horseback from the pueblos of Los Angeles to Yerba Buena.

"It all started a few months back when a company of American navy men were left behind by Stockton to enforce martial law in Los Angeles for a few weeks. The citizens cooperated until they became outraged at the restrictions imposed by a Major Gillespie. They staged an uprising and ousted their occupiers from the garrison. The Americans tried retreating to the harbor at San Pedro, but their cannon got bogged down in the mud. It ended up being captured by horsemen with, ah, how you say...?" Archie made a swinging motion over his head.

"Reatas!" said Guillermo, on the edge of his seat.

"Ah, oui! Re-a-tas! Anyway, Gillespie and his men barricaded themselves on a hill with few provisions. Their fate was looking mighty grim. Time was on the side of the insurgents, who merely needed to wait them out, but when all hope seemed lost," he snapped his fingers in the air with a flourish, "a private by the name of John Brown attempted the impossible! He managed to sneak through enemy lines and escape his pursuers by riding five hundred miles in five days!" Archie punctuated this amazing feat by spitting a stream of tobacco juice into the fire, making it sizzle.

"Five hundred miles in five days?" asked an incredulous Don Julian. "How many horses did he ride?"

"Who can say? Many! He keeped stealing fresh ones every twenty miles or so. Who knows, maybe you supplied him with one and didn't know it."

Guillermo and his father traded looks. "When was this?" asked Don Julian.

Archie rubbed his chin. "Late September, I reckon."

Guillermo shrugged, indicating it was possible. "What happened? Were they rescued?"

"By the time a ship arrived with reinforcements three weeks later, it was too late. They'd already surrendered to Flores' army and were allowed to return to the harbor after their weapons were confiscated. Was a humiliating defeat. When we arrive in the pueblo of Los Angeles, who knows, we could be looking down the barrel of American guns!"

A burly, red-faced man seated around the fire spoke up. "Grew up hearin' 'bout another freedom rider. Raced through the back roads of Boston Town to warn the citizens the Brits were comin'. Paul Revere was his name, but this ride you're talkin' about makes that look like a Sunday stroll in the park."

Shouts rang out down by the creek, and Guillermo's heart jumped in his throat. "Maybe some rebelista spies have been spotted?" He still feared that their paisanos would soon overtake the determined Americanos.

CHAPTER 9

"**S**ounds to me like someone's hurt," said Don Julian. He hurriedly emptied his pipe into the fire, jammed it in his hip pocket, and took off in the direction of the commotion.

Guillermo hesitated, trying to decide if he should hide. Curiosity got the better of him, and he followed in his father's wake and came upon a group of onlookers encircling a figure lying on the ground.

"Been kicked by a mule! Looks like his leg's busted!" yelled a hollow-eyed man with a handlebar mustache.

Don Julian made his way through the crowd and knelt beside the grimacing boy who looked to be in his late teens. After examining him, Don Julian said, "Aye, it's busted all right. Mijo, hand me that stick you've been whittling. Anyone have something we can wrap his leg with?"

There was some scurrying around, and three kerchiefs were donated to the cause. Someone brought a lantern and held it aloft so Don Julian could see as he ripped open the seam in the boy's trousers to expose the injury. Guillermo's stomach lurched at the sight of the unnaturally bent leg.

"Neely! What in tarnation happened to you, lad?" cried a stocky man who pushed his way through the crowd.

"The d-dag gum mule k-kicked me, Pa," Neely moaned. "I knowed y-you told me n-not to walk behind it…but I was so p-p-plum tuckered out, I j-just fer-fer—got."

Neely's father removed his woolen jacket and laid it over the boy.

Still kneeling, Don Julian extended his hand. "Name's Benjamin Foxen. It was my rancho you camped at the last two nights. Sorry to say but looks like your son's leg is broke. I can set it. Had plenty of experience in my time. Ex seaman."

Wiping the sweat from his brow, the man said, "Be much obliged to ya. Tell me what I kin do to help."

"How about holding onto his knee to steady it for me?" After manipulating the leg and applying a splint, Don Julian said, "Well, this is the best I can do for now, but he needs to keep it still so it can properly heal. He can't do that here. I can take him back to my place. My wife and servants will take good care of him."

The man rubbed his face, which was nearly obscured by a tangle of reddish whiskers. "Do hate to impose on your hospitality, but don't see how there's any way around it. Mighty fine of you to help."

A young man cleared his way through the crowd. "Pa! What happened? Neely!" He joined them on the ground as the man recounted the accident.

Turning to Don Julian, the older man said, "Oh, by the way, McNab's the name, Angus McNab. This here's me other lad, Logan. We're recent settlers to California from Ohio."

Like his father, Logan was compactly built, fair skinned, and freckled.

Don Julian raised stiffly and put a hand on Guillermo's shoulder. "Mijo, I'm gonna need to take him back home. I'll let the colonel know and catch up with you tomorrow. You'll have to take my place tomorrow guiding them across the valley toward the river."

"But Papá…" He resisted the urge to plead *don't leave me*. Why did his father always have to be the one to volunteer to help others?

McNab said, "Don't worry none about your lad, Mr. Foxen. Logan and I'll watch out for him. That's the least we kin do."

After his father left, Guillermo returned to the shelter and checked on Benito, who was picketed nearby. He found him contentedly nibbling on grass. As he brushed the gelding's reddish-brown coat, his mind grappled with the peculiar circumstances that had conspired to leave him stranded in the midst of the enemy's camp. While deep in thought, he was startled by a hand on his shoulder.

"Comó estás? Long day, no?" asked Don José Pico, smiling broadly.

Guillermo sighed. "Sí. At least we got to ride. Feel sorry for those on foot had to carry their saddles. They're exhausted. Why can't the battalion take a rest so they can recover?"

"It's my understanding that the forces in the south have been waiting for Fremont's army for weeks. He feels he must push on to give them support."

Guillermo whispered, "Don't you feel guilty being here?" Gesturing around, he said, "They're the enemy! They'll probably want to steal our land after we help them!"

"No. On the contrary, I'm grateful. If it hadn't been for Fremont's mercy, I'd be resting in a grave right now. I no longer view these men as our enemy. They're liberating us from a neglectful Mexico."

Guillermo couldn't believe what he was hearing. It was one thing for his Anglo father to express such disloyal sentiment, but his mother's cousin? "What about our paisanos? We'll be branded traitors when they find out that we helped Fremont."

"These are trying times. You have to be strong." Pico gently pounded Guillermo's chest with his fist. "I promise you our paisanos will change their minds in time. I care more about the welfare of my family. My children will have a better future as Americanos. Rest assured your father is helping the right side. He's a forward-looking man who sees the future. An American future."

Guillermo gave a half nod, unsure how to answer.

Pico said, "We should be turning in. It's getting late. If you need anything, I'm camped across the way. Buenas noches." He turned, headed across the field, and faded into the mist like an apparition.

Guillermo declined offers to sit around the campfire and retreated inside his shelter. He had much to think about. Using his saddle as a pillow, he stretched out on the ground, pulling the blanket up under his chin. Someone struck up a plaintive tune on a harmonica, bringing a lump to his throat, and he stared at the shrouded moon that passed through a gap in the canvas roof. It was the same moon that shone down on Rancho Tinaquaic. He imagined how, in a few hours, the household would be bustling with activity, attending to the injured soldier. There'd be much curiosity about him. He envisioned his sisters being shushed so the guest could sleep. How strange that he had swapped places with a Yankee soldier.

The bugler signaled the day's end. Those who had been lingering around the campfires called it a night. Except for the occasional low murmur, some snoring, and the exhaling of horses, it was quiet under the stars.

Guillermo thought about Fremont snug in his bearskin robe. This was Fremont's third expedition west, having left Washington, DC, more than eighteen months before—an eternity. These invaders were far from home. Like Jacobs and Bryant, most were new arrivals to the province. How long had it taken the Kentuckians to get over their homesickness? A few days, weeks, months?

An owl hooted from somewhere across the meadow. It was hard to believe that only the night before, he had been sitting in front of the fireplace at home, chafing at the indignity of being forced to spend an evening with family instead of playing Monte with Angel. Now here he was, missing the sound of his sisters' prattle. Unlike the Yankees who were headed on to Los Angeles after Santa Barbara, he was grateful his duty would be over in a couple days. He'd be free to return home then with a few good stories to tell for his trouble, but he first had to lead the battalion across the valley and hope against hope he wouldn't be spotted by a rebelista scout. He closed his eyes and prayed his father would return before the river crossing.

CHAPTER 10

It was still dark when Guillermo was startled by the half-hearted call of the bugle, followed by groans. As he struggled to make sense of where he was, a sense of dread enveloped him and he remembered. He lay on the cold ground and listened to the camp come to life: a pot clanked, men yawned, and horses whinnied. Without his father, he was reluctant to emerge from his tent and join the strangers, but duty prodded him to his feet. The last thing he wanted was for Jacobs to send someone to roust him out of bed.

He arose, stiff with chill, and began dismantling the shelter. When he had rolled up the canvas and secured it with leather thongs, a gravelly voice came from behind him.

"Here, kid. Take this." A puffy-eyed Logan extended a tin cup of steaming coffee. "It'll warm you up." He nodded in the direction of the campfire. "We can thaw out over there."

They squatted on the damp ground and nodded to a half-asleep man staring at the fire. Warming his free hand over the crackling flames, Logan said, "Zeke, this here's Guillermo. His father's the one who took Neely back to his rancho. Zeke's from Tennessee," he said, as if that should mean something.

All Guillermo knew was that a vast country belonging to a land-grabbing people lay over the distant mountains.

These gringos had illegally swarmed into Mexico's province. Nevertheless, good manners dictated that he offer a hand to the stranger.

Zeke's Adam's apple bobbed prominently when he croaked a greeting. He looked like he hadn't had a decent meal in months. "Pleasure to meetcha. Ghee-yair-mo, is it? What's that in English?"

"William. I was named for my father, William Benjamin Foxen."

"That's a good Anglo-Saxon name. I knowed a William once. Went by Bill. Told me what his name meant, but darned if I kin remember now," Zeke said, scratching his head.

"Bill?" The word felt peculiar to Guillermo's tongue and lacked the dignity of his given name.

Zeke asked, "Guillermo, I'm guessin' your neighbors around here are insurgents, right?"

"You mean rebelistas?"

"Yep. Must be hard on yer pa to secretly be hopin' fer an American takeover but forced to pretend he don't."

Guillermo shrugged. "Sí." It was too early in the day to try to hold his own in a conversation about name origins and politics. He glanced around the camp, now teeming with activity. "Where did these men come from?"

"All over." Hooking a thumb toward Fremont's tent across the meadow, Zeke said, "Company A's mostly mountain men and French fur trappers who came out from St. Louis with Fremont. That Frenchman I seen you talking to last night, Archambeau, he's one of 'em. He's one heck of a hunter. Can foller the tracks of a lizard on a rock. Saw him in action near Rancho Santa Margarita a week ago.

"Then there's Companies B through L, made up of settlers from frontier states like Ohiya, Kintuckah, Missourah, and Tennessee. There's more of us from Tennessee than any other state." Zeke took a swig of coffee and wiped his mouth on the grimy sleeve of his buckskin jacket.

"What about your father, Logan?" Guillermo asked. "Is he English, like mine?"

"Close enough. Came over from Scotland with his brother when he was a lad. What about yours?"

"Born in Norwich, England, and left home at sixteen to join the Queen's navy."

Zeke nodded. "Company G has quite a few Brits. It's a motley crew if there ever was one," he said, shaking his head. "Runaway sailors…Negroes…Germans…men on the run from the law. Its commander is Captain Buford Hell Roarin' Thompson, a professional gambler, so they say. He's the only one who can keep 'em in line." He lowered his voice. "A bit of advice. Steer clear of them—no tellin' what they might steal off ya. Always keep yer piece loaded by yer side."

Guillermo cringed. He hoped he wouldn't be asked about what he carried, because unlike some boys his age, he didn't have a rifle. Because of the US embargo, weapons were hard to come by. "What about the Indians? Where did they come from?" he asked.

Logan picked up the line of conversation. "As I understand it, the Delawares came from back east with Fremont. The Cosumnes come from the foothills of the San Joaquin River, near the Sierras. Mostly horse thieves, but Fremont's taken a liking to them. Now the Walla Wallas, they's from the Oregon Territory. I heard that on Fremont's second expedition, he stayed with them on the Columbia River. Had some skirmishes with other tribes in the area and had to hide out from the hunters and trappers workin' fer the Hudson's Bay Company. Wild country up there. They lost some of their best men in an ambush by the Klamath Indians. The Walla Wallas think of Fremont as a great white chief. They'd do anything for him, and he thinks highly of them. Trusts them with his life. They're warriors."

"You mean like knights?"

"Knights fought for a cause, like in the Crusades. Warriors don't need a cause. They fight cuz that's what they do. My pa says the Delaware and Walla Wallas couldn't care a whit about who controls California. They're just loyal to Fremont. He won't go anywhere without his personal bodyguards, Sagundai and his nephew William Chinook. Took the young one to Washington, DC, last winter to live with a Quaker family. Learnt himself to read and write."

Dawn was streaking across the pale sky when Archie signaled to Guillermo it was time to head out, so he bade his two companions adios as he made his way to where Company H was assembling. Jacobs announced they would split up: Guillermo would go with him, leading the way across the valley, and Bryant would backtrack and round up stragglers and pack animals that had given out the day before.

The groups parted ways, and Guillermo led his group in a southwesterly course across the valley.

Don Julian returned midafternoon, reporting that the injured soldier was recuperating at the rancho. He had already spoken with the McNabs, updating them on Neely's condition. He brought more of Concha's tortillas and carne seca with him, which cheered Guillermo and Captain Jacobs.

After riding four leagues, they bivouacked along the Santa Inés River, which was still foamy with run-off from the mountains. The Santa Inés Mission and El Camino Real were only a league away. Guillermo felt a mixture of nervousness and excitement to be camped so close to where they might be observed.

After they had set up shelter, Don Julian and Don José Pico were asked to escort Jacobs and a few scouts to the mission to have a look around. Guillermo stayed behind with the McNabs and others in the battalion. Would Padre Jimeño think his father was on a divine mission or a fool's errand?

A couple hours later, word spread that a ranchero had returned with the scouting party and was meeting with Fremont. Don Julian returned later and joined Guillermo and the others at the campfire, filling them in on developments. Curious men drifted over to hear the news. José María Covarrubias, one of the grantees of the Santa Inés Mission, claimed most of the men in the valley had left two days before, and he stayed behind to protect the mission and his family. He made no secret of the fact he was honored to meet Fremont, whose father was a Frenchman like Fremont's. Covarrubias had emigrated to the province from France by way of Mexico. He offered to ride around the countryside to recruit volunteers, though it was doubtful there were any to be had.

"You're sure he's not a spy?" asked Angus McNab.

"José's no spy. He's a shrewd chap who knows which way the wind blows and has no intention of going against it. Probably hoping to get in Fremont's good graces so he can position himself for a plum appointment in the new government. Heard someone say they expect Fremont will be appointed governor by President Polk," said one of the chaps in the battalion.

"I heard that rumor too. Mr. Foxen, did this Covarrubias think there was an ambush waiting for us at Gaviota?"

"All he knows is that the local rebelistas gathered at the Ortegas' and haven't returned," said Don Julian.

"If Fremont asks your opinion on whether to proceed through Gaviota, what will you say?" asked Zeke.

"I'll tell him that chances are there is no ambush, but since he's responsible for the lives of his men, it all comes down to how much he wants to avoid the possibility of bloodshed."

It was a relief knowing the locals had left the valley. "Taps" was sounded, and they called it a night. Guillermo hoped Covarrubias' friendly visit was an omen of good things to come.

CHAPTER 11

The following morning, the camp awoke to a cold rain. It was December 23, and La Nochebuena was one night away, but the dreariness and fatigue warded off all hints of festivity.

Fremont ordered the battalion to veer away from El Camino Real and proceed toward Rancho San Marcos, which was on the mountain separating Santa Inés Valley from Santa Barbara. Murmurings of "coward" and "harebrained plan" rippled from company to company. An ugly mood descended on the troops.

Company H was the first to set out. Its orders were to lead the battalion across the river and proceed toward the summit of the mountain. It would be a grueling day. Guillermo and Bryant followed Don Julian and Jacobs. From the set of Bryant's jaw and grim expression, Guillermo figured he was none too happy to be heading away from the Refugio Trail.

"Tell me about this San Marcos Trail," said Bryant. "When was the last time y'all went over it?"

"Last summer. It's an old Indian trail, barely wide enough for one man on a horse. Going up isn't as bad as going down the other side. Fog can be so thick it's hard to see a hand in front of your face," Guillermo said.

Bryant gave Guillermo a sidelong glance and raised an

eyebrow. "Well now, that makes me feel a whole lot better. Guess it's a good thing we have y'all to guide us over."

"But…"

"But what, Guillermo?"

"But if it's clear and dry, you won't need help getting down, right?"

"Let's hope not." He was quiet for a few moments. "I plumb forgot. It's nearly Christmas, and y'all want to be home with your family. Let's hope the weather is good and we can make our way down the mountain quickly."

They rode on in silence until they reached the ford in the river. "Looks like a herd of horses was driven across here recently by several riders," Jacobs said, pointing out the fresh hoofprints in the sandbar. The river was fifty yards across.

"They were in a hurry, judging by the depth of the prints," Don Julian said. If he suspected, like Guillermo did, that they were made by Augustin Janssens, a local ranchero, he made no mention of it. Janssens was the military commander of the district and well connected in social circles in the Santa Barbara and Santa Inés area. Guillermo admired his calm demeanor, which was different from the hot-headed paisanos who raced around the countryside stirring up unrest.

They proceeded across the river and noted with some concern that the current in the deepest part of the channel was swift. Jacobs decided that two scouts would remain behind to assist in transporting the wagons across. If the rain continued throughout the day, the river could rise quickly.

As they made their way along the south side of the river, two Indians were spotted coming out of Quichuma Canyon.

As soon as they saw the riders, they turned and fled. Jacobs and two scouts galloped in pursuit. Guillermo hesitated for a few moments and then joined the chase. Benito took off at a gallop and overtook the Indians in no time. Loosening the looped reata hanging from the saddle horn, Guillermo gave it a few twirls. He easily lassoed one of the men, who fell to the muddy ground, his arms bound to his side. His companion cowered in a squat, seeing that he was overpowered. They pointed to where they had seen horses. This was good news. Guillermo looked to Jacobs, who gave the okay for them to be released. The Indians clambered up the hill and out of sight.

"Handy with that rope of yours, I see," said Jacobs.

"It's what I do every day—round up livestock."

Jacobs nodded in admiration and announced they'd be splitting up. Most would go with him to see about capturing the horses, and Bryant, Archie, and Guillermo would proceed to Rancho San Marcos.

The trio crossed several streams before they arrived at the rancho. It lay on a rambling meadow about a league up a gradual slope. The adobe bunkhouse and corrals were deserted. There was no main house because the rancho was managed by a crew of vaqueros. Skulls from longhorn cattle were mounted on top of sprouted willow poles to keep out predators, two-legged and four.

"No sense waiting for them out here in the rain. May as well go inside. Could be the last time we have a roof over our heads for a while," said Bryant.

They corralled the horses and sought shelter in the bunkhouse. The rain continued to fall steadily. Guillermo pitied the exhausted marchers who were wading across the river with saddles stowed across their shoulders. Runoff from the mountains could cause the usually dry arroyos to rise quickly.

Guillermo led the way into the adobe. It took a few moments for his eyes to adjust to the darkness. Glancing around the room, he saw pallets stacked along the perimeter for beds. Two reatas hung from pegs in the wall. Something skittered in the ceiling, and he figured the leaky roof was home to a nest of mice. The room smelled dank and musty. The only evidence of recent use was ashes in the hearth. His spurs jingled as he dragged them across the hard-packed earthen floor. He pulled out a crude bench near a rickety table and set about scraping the mud from the bottom of his boots with his knife.

Bryant sat across the table from him and removed from his saddlebag a tobacco pouch, a leatherbound book, a bottle of India ink, and a quill pen. After lighting his pipe, he began writing.

Archie sprawled on one of the pallets, leaning his back against the crumbling adobe wall as he prepared to smoke. He rolled a cigarette into a thin tube of paper, licked it, and let it dangle from his mouth. Bending forward, he struck flint to the insole of a worn boot. It took half a dozen strikes before he caught a spark. Shielding the weak red glow from the draft, he succeeded in sending a curl of smoke toward the low-beamed ceiling. He leaned back. "This is prime land, that's fer shore. River flowing through it…when settlers discover it, squatters'll be thick as fleas."

"Squatters?" asked Guillermo.

"Settlers who decide to claim a piece of land simply by occupyin' it. They're attracted to out-of-the-way places like this."

"That can't be legal."

"If land's unoccupied, squatters can file a claim, but even when it is, that don't stop squatters none. Landowners have been known to up and leave their land or mysteriously disappear." He winked. "If you know what I mean." He held up a hand in defense. "Now don't get me wrong. Most settlers are law-abidin' folks, but new land also attracts an element who can sniff out easy pickins like a hound dog trackin' a lame coon and her brood."

"Archie." Bryant sighed. "Don't go cluttering the boy's head with notions like that." He said to Guillermo, "Your father looks like he can handle himself just fine. No one's going to mess with him, and you have a crew of vaqueros, right?"

"Yessir, there are seven of us." That included Old Fernando, who spent his days tending to the hacienda. It was doubtful that with his dimming eyesight he could still hit a target, but at least he could hold a rifle and maybe scare off intruders.

Both men nodded in approval. "Guillermo, can't help but notice you're not carrying a rifle," Archie aid.

Bryant shot him a look. "I apologize for his lack of manners. Not everyone has the good fortune to be raised properly like you."

Archie scrunched up his eyebrows. "What'd I say wrong? Just statin' an observation, sir."

Guillermo held up his hand. "That's okay. With the embargo, arms have been in short supply."

"Well, won't be long 'fore that's over," said Archie. "Then your pa kin make shore everyone on your rancho is armed."

"Arch-ie." Bryant groaned. "That's enough." He lifted his glasses and pinched the bridge of his nose.

"Yessir, I'm just sayin'…"

"I think y'all made your point clear enough."

Jacobs, Don Julian, and the scouts came riding up forty minutes later with two dozen fresh mounts. Jacobs said, "Found these in a box canyon. We'll put them in the corral for now. The colonel should be arriving within the hour."

"Well done!" shouted Bryant from the doorway of the bunkhouse. "In that case, we'll saddle up and see how much farther up the mountain we can go before dark. Come in out of the cold and rest a spell. When we see you later, we'll have supper going. With the cloud cover, we won't have to worry about our smoke being spotted."

While gathering their saddlebags, Guillermo asked Bryant, "Sir, do you write in your book every day?"

"I try. I record daily events. Used to be a newspaper reporter back home. May end up writing a book someday."

"You don't say?" Until this trip, Guillermo hadn't seen his limited ability to read or write as a liability. No one in his mother's family had learned, but if the province was being taken over by these brash Americanos, he would have to learn some new skills to compete with them, and if he was anything, he was competitive. He wanted to be one of the best at whatever he did.

CHAPTER 12

The trail steepened as the advance guard veered away from the river and headed into the foothills. It wove its way through scrub oaks and crossed several small streams before coming to a meadow dotted with several large valley oaks.

Bryant said, "Looks like the remains of a vineyard over there."

"You're right," said Guillermo. "It used to produce wine grapes for the padres at the mission in Santa Barbara, but when the church's land was taken away and sold to private citizens, there was a shortage of labor. With no one to tend it, it was abandoned."

"What you're sayin' is if there's no Injun labor, work doesn't' get done." Archie sniffed. "A perfectly good vineyard is abandoned cuz it's beneath Californios to do manual labor?" He leaned out of the saddle and spat on the ground in disgust.

"My father thinks nothing of toiling in the hot sun to plant a field of wheat, but he's different that way. The blue bloods like my grandfather say it's not the order of things. A gentleman does not do manual labor. That's for peons." Guillermo saw no point in adding that he was inclined to agree. Horsemen did not walk if they could ride. Guillermo was of the old-school caballeros who preferred ranching to farming.

They continued to climb farther up the trail. A light drizzle fell, but patches of blue peeked through the leaden sky. Looking back at the valley, Guillermo noticed that the clouds had parted and a ray of sunlight shone down on Mission Santa Inés. It looked like a beacon from afar. The next day, parishioners from surrounding ranchos would gather there to celebrate La Nochebuena. Holy Mass would follow a procession commemorating Mary and Joseph's search for a place to spend the night of Jesus' birth. Guillermo had always taken shelter for granted, but with each plodding step up the mountain, he yearned for the comfort and familiarity of home. Only one more night in the cold, and he and his father would rejoin the family, their duty fulfilled.

Below him, a steady stream of men and animals trekked up the winding trail to Rancho San Marcos where most of the battalion would be bivouacking for the night. The advance guard would leave them behind to clear the trail of rocks and deadfall for the second leg of the journey up the mountain. It was grueling work, and Guillermo was relieved when Jacobs announced in the late afternoon that they were done due to a lack of visibility. Fog spilled over the ridge from the seaward side, enveloping them in a heavy mist that muffled voices and the clomping of hooves. They had cleared half a league beyond the rancho. The next morning they would push on to the summit.

Camp was set up at the foot of a huge sandstone boulder.

"You know, we're in the heart of grizzly country now," Don Julian said between puffs on his pipe. "These hills are packed with them."

"Oo-wee! How'd you talk your wife into moving so far from civilization in the first place?" said Archie.

"Well, after retiring from the sea, I opened a mercantile store in the port of Santa Barbara. I ran that for a few years but got restless. Thought I'd like to try my hand at ranching, and she gave me her blessing. All the prime land had been snatched up along the coast and in the Santa Inés Valley, but there were two adjacent grants available in the backcountry. My father-in-law suggested we apply for them so our families would be neighbors, and thataway we could help each other out. Least that was the plan."

"What happened?"

Don Julian drew deeply from his pipe and exhaled, squinting through the smoke. "With lots of help and hard work, we saw our dream come true. My father-in-law had been superintendent of several mission ranchos, including this one, San Marcos, and he handpicked a crew of vaqueros to work for me. He provided the Indian labor to build our home, outbuildings, and corrals. My mother-in-law insisted my wife's childhood servant come live with us and help with the children. Our herds had multiplied many times over, but one day, my wife's only brother, Ausencio, was killed in an accident on our land. He was riding back to his parents' place and dismounted to chase a horse that had gotten loose. Stepped in a squirrel hole and broke his leg. Swelled up so fast he couldn't get it out. Laid like that for three days before I discovered him. Vultures had been circling the area, and I went to investigate, but by then, blood poisoning had set in, and he was near death." Don Julian paused and tapped his pipe against the heel of his boot.

Jacobs shook his head in sympathy, along with the others gathered around the campfire. "Frontier living is perilous that way. All it takes is one misstep, but thousands of emigrant homesteaders will come west, pouring into the territory, eager to take the same risks for their hundred-sixty-acre homestead."

"Captain, is it true that your president promised to honor our land grants?" asked Guillermo.

"Yes, it is. President Polk declared that so long as men like your father can prove ownership with proper documentation, they have nothing to fear."

"You have done well for yourself, Mr. Foxen. You've got your own little kingdom tucked away in the hills," said Archie, spitting a stream of tobacco into the fire.

"I've been lucky, that's for sure," Don Julian said, crossing his legs at the ankles and warming his feet to the fire.

"You're too modest. Can tell you're a man of action and a shrewd one at that." Archie said and winked. "You married well." Something in his jeering tone raised the hackles on Guillermo's back.

"Aye, I did. She's got enough faith in divine providence for the two of us. As for me, well, I put my trust in the barrel of a gun. In dangerous country like this, a man is responsible for defending his family and property. Now that you Yankees are taking over, hopefully it won't be long before we have some law and order."

"There'll be a transition period before civil systems are put in place. It'll take a while for the old guard to accept the new authority. Fremont plans on appointing former Mexican citizens to political and civil posts to foster a spirit of cooperation and goodwill, though I doubt those in Santa Barbara will benefit from his generosity. He's determined to get revenge for the townspeople chasing Lieutenant Talbott's company into these mountains and setting fire to the brush. He's talked repeatedly about burning down their homes."

Guillermo shot his father a worried look. "Tell him, Papá..."

"Someone needs to tell him it wasn't the Barbareños who did that. I've heard from my friends that it was a posse of rebelistas that rode up from the south, fresh off a victory in Los Angeles. Most citizens of Santa Barbara are resigned to a US takeover, and all of us Anglos welcome it," Don Julian said.

"I'll be sure to pass that information on to Fremont," said Jacobs.

Guillermo was relieved to hear that. His grandparents lived in the pueblo, as well as other family and friends. Now all he had to do was pray that nothing dangerous impacted the descent down the trail the next day.

CHAPTER 13

The next morning, the fog burned off early, revealing a brilliant blue sky. Guillermo's spirits soared. It had been decided that a small party would push on to the summit before the others. Captain Jacobs, Archie, Delaware Charley, and Tom Hill would accompany the Foxens. It was good to be back in the saddle instead of walking and clearing the trail.

They rode into a headwind that grew stronger as they approached the summit. Yucca plants taller than a man sprouted from the rocky landscape like white torches. The higher they climbed in elevation, the spindly oaks, sycamore, and mesquite gave way to the hardier madrone, buckthorn, and pine trees. The final leg was mostly exposed sandstone, scoured smooth by erosive winds and rains. Boulders were strewn about haphazardly as if tossed by a giant, while some were stacked in crooked piles.

They reached a low saddle of the mountain in late morning and had their first glimpse of the plain below. It was a serene scene with cattle grazing on green pastureland, beyond it the sparkling Pacific. The group hiked to a nearby promontory that provided a sweeping view of the coastline. A series of bluffs that jutted progressively into the ocean were hazily outlined in the mist. Rust-colored kelp beds floated in coves.

Don Julian offered his spyglass to Jacobs and pointed southwest. "You can make out the mission perched on a knoll out there, and the presidio is between it and the harbor. Don't appear to be any ships anchored in it." The horizon stretched between Santa Cruz and the Anacapa Islands, resembling giant whales surfacing from the depths.

"Looks deserted to me." Archie sniffed. "Locals musta got word we was comin'. Either they're hidin' out or fled." He was referring to the citizens of Santa Barbara. He turned and spit a stream of tobacco juice behind him.

Don Julian pointed out sections of the trail zigzagging its way down the mountain, but it was mostly hidden in dense mesquite and manzanita. The trail was four to six feet wide and dropped off precipitously into a deep ravine, and it was steeper than Guillermo recalled. Debris from recent rains needed to be cleared. Surveying the scene, he had the sinking feeling his father would volunteer him for the job. He undid the sweaty chin strap from his hat and murmured, "Ay, caramba."

"Mon Dieu!" exclaimed Archie. "That's the trail? How are we 'sposed to get artillery wagons down that?"

"I tried telling Colonel Fremont that." Don Julian shrugged. "He was intent on avoiding a confrontation between the Mexican rebelistas and the battalion on the main road."

The head of the cavalcade would be arriving late afternoon. There was no reason to expect the trail down the mountain would be any more passable than the way up. Had his father expected they would help with the descent and not bothered to tell him? This was testing Guillermo's patience and endurance to the limit. As much as he hated to admit it, there was no way he and his father could abandon

68

the battalion now. It was a tossup as to who he felt sorrier for: the weary troops and animals or himself. His hopes of spending La Nochebuena at the mission were dashed, but he fought to hide his disappointment.

Tom Hill sat relaxed in the saddle, scanning the canyon walls with eagle eyes. He seemed untroubled by his leader's folly as he took in the lay of the land.

"Mr. Foxen, how many miles do y'all think it is to the bottom?" asked Jacobs.

"Hmm, I'd call it more than a league, so that'd make it four miles, give or take. Then it starts leveling off. There's a grove of trees at the mouth of the canyon that'll provide some cover."

Jacobs pursed his lips. "We need to reconnoiter the trail to make sure it's passable and well-marked."

As if to dissuade them, a blast of frigid air pushed them back a step or two. Guillermo felt the brim of his hat catch the wind like a topsail, but by the time his hand flew up to grab it, it was gone. "Ay, caramba! My hat!" He watched in horror as it twirled and spiraled down the ravine and out of sight. Turning to his father, wide-eyed, he recoiled at the craggy face contorted in disgust.

"By Jove, don't look for any sympathy from me, lad. That's what you get for being careless." As if in pain, Don Julian scrunched up his face. "Why would you undo your chinstrap inahow?"

Judging from the bewildered expression on his father's face, Guillermo may as well have sprouted a horn on his forehead. He had no explanation. Heat rose up his neck to his face. Without his hat, his humiliation was bared for all to see.

Don Julian asked in a weary tone, "How many times do I hafta tell ya?" He drew out the final words of his chastisement as if speaking to a small child. "You-gotta-learn-to-use-your-ca-bez-a, mijo." He poked the side of his hat with a sturdy finger.

Jacobs glanced the other way while the others fidgeted uncomfortably.

Guillermo said, "I'll ride down the trail a ways and see if," his voice caught, "I can spot it." His chin began to quiver. He had to escape and pronto. Squeezing Benito's sides, he turned the reins and trotted off, not waiting for permission. He felt five sets of eyes on his back but willed himself to control his breathing and stifle the sob that threatened to escape his throat. He had barely rounded the bend when his shoulders heaved uncontrollably and the floodgate of pent-up emotions burst. He had tried so hard to make his father proud of him only to be humiliated by him. It wasn't fair.

He dismounted through a blur of tears and stood at the edge of the trail. The frigid wind forced him to lock his knees and brace his body against its buffeting gusts. Benito whinnied and nudged his elbow, and when that failed to get a response, the horse sniffed at the sweat-stained bandana that covered his head. Guillermo reached back and pushed the horse's head away. "I know, I look strange without my hat." Shaking his head in disbelief, he moaned, "Ay, caramba!" He stomped his foot and kicked a spray of pebbles over the side of the trail. "How could I be so careless?"

It wasn't just any hat he had lost. It had been Tio Ausencio's and was irreplaceable.

He stared out at the panoramic view. The sea shimmered with light, reflecting the sun's rays in constantly changing patterns. In his misery, it seemed spiteful of Mother Nature to show off her radiance. With grim satisfaction, he noted clouds gathering far out on the horizon.

To his left, the sleepy pueblo lay nestled at the foot of towering mountains. Waves rolled into its horseshoe bay, fringing the shore in white. In a few hours, church bells would ring out, calling the parishioners to celebrate Mass on one of the holiest days of the year. His grandparents on his mother's side, Ausencio's parents, would be among them. Little did they suspect the infidels were closing in, about to enter from the pueblo's "back door." The invaders' first act would be to lower the green-and-white Mexican flag, and Fremont's men would triumphantly replace it with the Americano flag. Fremont had vowed the citizens of Santa Barbara would pay for their insurrection of several months back.

Staring at the rugged terrain below, it was hard to imagine the long file of trail-weary men and animals wending its way down the steep slope. Would they make it down safely? Along the trip, Guillermo had come to view the Yanks as decent men, not all that different from his paisanos. Archie, Lieutenant Bryant, Captain Jacobs, the McNabs—they had welcomed him into their circle and treated him with respect. That was more than he could say for his ex-seaman father who treated him like a lowly deckhand.

The mountain on which he was standing bore silent witness to man's arrogant pursuit of dominance. On the plain below, Dos Pueblos Creek crossed the undulating landscape and flowed to the sea. For untold centuries, two Chumash villages had coexisted on opposite sides of the wide ravine. Their inhabitants had masterfully sailed the channel waters in their planked canoes to catch fish and sea otters and trade with the Indians on the Anacapa and Santa Cruz islands, but upon the arrival of the Spanish padres and soldiers, they were forced to abandon their tule huts and labor on mission land as new converts to Catholicism. They were promised the land

71

would be held in trust for them until such time they were trained to use it productively as civilized Christians. In the meantime, their once-thriving population was decimated by disease brought by the Mexicans and, before them, the Spaniards who had come up and established the mission. Rather than return the mission lands to the surviving Indians, the Mexican governors doled them out as favors to their cronies.

Now the gringos were nearing the summit, having journeyed across the vast continent in their quest to expand their borders from sea to sea. The arrogant Yanks believed they had been ordained by God to snatch the paradise from the slack hands of the Californios. Like the ocean tide, there would be no holding them back.

"*Ándale*, Benito. We got a job to do." Guillermo swung into the saddle and started up the trail.

Before he rounded the bend, he heard the jingle of reins and clopping of hooves. Two Indian scouts were heading toward him. The wind had picked up and was blowing swirling dust in the air, and both scouts wore bandanas over their noses and mouths. When he came up alongside Guillermo, Delaware Charley pulled his bandana down and shouted, "Captain Jacobs sent us ahead to clear trail and scout countryside. Archie coming soon on foot."

Guillermo hadn't counted on having to walk, but he saw the logic in it. "Looks like a lot of rocks and debris. After I leave Benito up there, I'll make my way down. There are a few spots where the trail divides up in separate paths. We need to mark those clearly so no one takes a wrong turn. Not Injun style. Easy to read…for gringos."

Delaware Charley flashed a broad smile before he slid the bandana up over his nose. They nodded and went on their way.

CHAPTER 14

Guillermo rode back up the trail to where his father, Jacobs, and Archie were gathered under a stand of pines. They halted their conversation as he approached.

"What I could see was lots of fallen rock. I'll go down and help clear the trail. Maybe I'll find my hat," Guillermo said.

"Think you can remember the way from last summer?" Don Julian asked. "Some paths will lead you in circles."

"I think I can remember it." He said to Archie, "We're going to be hoofing it?"

"Can't take a chance of Old Jacques here twistin' an ankle. This should be a test for our legs. Think you can keep up with this old billy goat?"

"Hmph! I'll probably have to slow down so I don't leave you in my dust." Guillermo removed Benito's saddle and blanket and set them at the base of a pine.

His father came up alongside him. "Here's a shovel. You're gonna need it to clear debris and bigger rocks." Guillermo took it and continued gathering up his things.

Don Julian said, "The shortest way down won't necessarily be the best one for the cannon wagons. They'll need room to maneuver. May have to be dismantled and lowered down in some sections, but hopefully it won't come to that. Make sure the trail is clearly marked. Of course, you're going down with two Indian scouts and a mountain man, so I 'spect they know what they're doing."

He hovered over Guillermo as he stowed his saddlebag in a pile. When Guillermo straightened up, they nearly collided. Don Julian started to say something, hesitated, and stepped back to let his son pass. Guillermo walked over to where Archie and Jacobs were staring out to sea.

Jacobs squinted toward the horizon, "Is that a fog bank out there or storm clouds?" A curtain of darkness had formed behind the islands in the channel.

"The way the wind's picking up, it could be a storm's blowing in," Guillermo said. "Then again, fog's a constant here on the coast. Either way, we need to get a move on."

The pair set off down the trail at a jaunty pace. Guillermo's long legs enabled him to keep pace with Archie stride for stride, and he was relieved to put some distance between himself and his father. Archie chatted on about a variety of topics but was careful to sidestep the earlier incident between father and son. They kicked small rocks off the trail and shoveled the heavier debris over the edge. In a few instances, the rocks were so big they had to use the shovel as a lever to dislodge them. These bounced down the slope for hundreds of feet, shattering into smaller pieces as they went. Forty-five minutes later, they caught up with Delaware Charley and Tom Hill, who were dragging a tree limb off the trail.

Archie said, "Looks like no one's traveled this in months. In places, it's barely wide enough for a horse."

"Let alone cannons," Delaware Charley said. "Captain not happy when he see this."

As the afternoon wore on, the winds picked up. They whipped the brush amid swirls of dancing dirt that stung their eyes and agitated the scout's horses. The sea roiled, and the spray of the whitecaps created a mist over the water. As the islands at sea were swallowed up by the wall of ominous clouds that crept ashore, the rumble of thunder could be heard off in the distance. No doubt about it—a storm was approaching.

An hour later, they halted at a sharp turn in the trail about halfway down the mountain. Delaware Charley shook his head and shouted into the wind, "Too steep for cannons!"

Guillermo pointed to a break in the weeds that looked like a possible detour. He and Delaware Charley followed it and saw where it made a wide sweep, angling downward at a more gradual descent. They swiped at the undergrowth with long knives, and as the brush was thinned, the remnants of a cow path appeared. There were multiple paths that wove their way through the chaparral for ninety feet to where they rejoined the main trail. Tom Hill waited for them at the juncture. He was told the alternate route was narrow in spots, but they thought a wagon could make it through without having to be dismantled.

Archie looked up at the darkening sky and shouted, "Time to head back up! If we leave now, maybe we can beat the rain!"

"You go!" Delaware Charley said. "We finish clearing trail. Look for insurgents."

Guillermo was disappointed he hadn't spotted his hat but agreed it was time to head back. He doubted the scouts would find any sign of the Barbareños from Santa Barbara. The coastal plain looked deserted. His legs rebelled at having to march back up the mountain, but he wasn't about to let Archie widen the gap between them.

They were halfway from the summit when the first sprinkles plunked on his head and shoulders. For the umpteenth time that day, he berated himself for losing his hat. Pulling his poncho over his head, he trudged on. The pungent smell of sage filled the air. Lightning flashed miles out to sea, turning the clouds an ominous shade of indigo. His legs burned with fatigue, and he knew that once he stopped, they would cramp into knots.

By the time they reached the summit, the storm had unleashed its fury. Although it could not have been later than half past three in the afternoon, it seemed much later. The churning clouds coming in off the ocean obscured the plain below. Somewhere out there, Delaware Charley and Tom Hill would be hunkered down, contending with the elements.

Don Julian was waiting for them under a pine where the trail leveled off. He shouted into the wind, "Was beginning to wonder if you'd taken shelter in the caves!"

"Caves?" Archie swung a look at Guillermo. "You never mentioned nuthin' about any caves."

"F-figured you'd rather…get soaked…than come across a grouchy bear…or puma."

Back at camp, Guillermo and Archie were greeted with hearty slaps on the back from Jacobs and Bryant. Three companies had made it to the summit and were scattered among the boulders and trees for protection. The others had sought shelter on the leeward side of the mountain. Fremont's artillery wagons would bring up the rear, arriving the following morning. Due to the darkness and rain, the descent would not begin until dawn. That meant another night on the mountain. Guillermo accepted the news with relief. Don Julian, Jacobs, and Bryant pumped him and Archie for information about the condition of the trail so Jacobs could pass it on to Fremont. Archie told them it was passable, but some sections were nothing more than a rocky shelf with a sheer drop-off on one side.

"It appears we missed a safe passage by mere hours," said Jacobs. "What can we do when the men and animals are bone tired? There's no way of hurrying them along."

"Wall, let's hope we wake up to clear skies tomorrow," said Archie.

Amen to that, thought Guillermo, not looking forward to tomorrow.

CHAPTER 15

Shortly after dawn, in his place behind the battalion, Fremont conferred with his company commanders and Don Julian. It was decided that Company A would begin the descent within the hour, guided by Guillermo! Don Julian would remain behind to organize the staging area, releasing groups of men and animals in intervals. Archie would lead the artillery company.

Putting a heavy hand on his son's shoulder, Don Julian said, "I don't need to tell ya to be careful. I'm concerned about those cannon wagons getting stuck in ruts or going out of control. Avoid taking any steep shortcuts. Better to take it slow and easy."

"What if the trail gets washed out and I can't make it back up to you?"

"Well, ask someone to fire off three shots for you. I'll meet you at the foot of Refugio Trail, near Janssen's rancho, if it is too bad to get back up the mountain."

Archie had been adjusting the saddlebags on Old Jacques a few feet away and interjected. "Don't mean to be nosy, but I think I have a solution to your problem." He turned and pulled out a rifle from a long leather holster. "With your permission, Mr. Foxen, I'd like to pass this here on to your son. It belonged to a friend of mine who got kilt up in Oregon country. Bob would approve of Guillermo having this. Thataway you two can signal each other."

Guillermo turned to his father, and Don Julian's bushy eyebrows arched in surprise. Raising a hand, he said, "Archie, that's mighty generous of you. It's the handsomest rifle I ever did see." Peering at it closely, he asked, "Isn't that one of those buffalo guns?"

Archie nodded and beamed. "Shore is. Called a Hawkens."

Don Julian's mouth twisted in thought. "By Jove, that's one valuable piece. I don't know."

Archie persisted. "Hate to say it, but I suspect it'll come in handy in the days to come. Think of it as repayment for all your help."

Guillermo's eyes pleaded *por favor, Papá!*

"Hmm…suppose you're right." His faded blue eyes softened, and he slapped Guillermo on the back. "Well, mijo, looks like you just got yourself a rifle and a mighty fine one at that!"

Glancing between his father and Archie, Guillermo stammered, "M-muchas gracias! I can't…believe this! It's beautiful!"

That being settled, Archie placed the rifle in Guillermo's hands. "Merry Christmas to you. Hold it up, and let's see how it fits you." Both men slapped each other on the back and shook hands.

Guillermo held it up to his left eye and aimed it at a boulder across the canyon. The length of the polished walnut stock felt like it had been made for him. Standing there in the rain and wind at the top of the mountain, Guillermo felt complete. Even without Tío's hat, he didn't feel like a tagalong kid any longer. Like every other cavalryman, he was armed. Even more importantly, he had earned his father's approval. The hardship and disappointment of the previous few days evaporated.

Guillermo and his father worked out a signal that three shots meant there was a problem. Don Julian said, "Mijo, don't worry about me. I'll be waiting with the horses for you to return, whether it's tonight or tomorrow. I have my spyglass, and I'll keep watch for you. The last of the rear guard will let you know the condition of the trail. If it's impassable, signal me, and I'll meet you at Janssens'. I don't need to tell you to stay out of sight of the Ortegas." The Ortegas were the Mexican rebelista family that lived in the valley below the Refugio Trail, an alternate route over the mountains.

Guillermo nodded.

When the bugle signaled to advance, the rain had stopped, but the dark skies appeared menacing. Fremont ordered the horses and mules be led down the trail by foot. Guillermo chose a roan gelding that had been trumpeting to the other horses and stirring them up. As they proceeded down the trail, the horse balked several times and had to be coaxed with raisins Guillermo had stashed in his pocket. He could have chosen a calmer horse, one who would have docilely followed him, but what would have been the challenge of that? He prided himself on being able to handle spirited horses.

By the time they made it past the first bend in the trail, the gelding showed signs of being a natural leader, stepping smartly over the rocks and debris. He seemed to enjoy being in the lead and responded easily to Guillermo's commands and yanks on the reins, but trouble erupted half an hour later when the winds picked up. Within minutes, they whipped through the canyon and pelted the trekkers with cold rain.

Over the roar of the storm, Guillermo heard Sagundai yell, "Look out! Rocks!"

Guillermo's free arm flew up over his head. No sooner had he ducked than a rock whizzed by, bouncing into the abyss on his right. This startled the gelding, who reared up on his hind legs, pawing the air, his eyes bulging in terror. Guillermo fought to hold onto the reins while trying to reassure him. "It's okay, boy, you're fine." He heard the other horses let out high-pitched whinnies, communicating their fear. This was not good. Widespread panic could break out.

Just as the horse was starting to regain his composure and follow Guillermo's lead, a clap of thunder sent him panicking down the debris-strewn trail. Guillermo raced after him, hoping to slow the horse before he lost his footing in the mud. Just as he was gaining on him, Guillermo's forward momentum caused him to lose his balance. One leg slipped out from beneath him, sending him sliding through a puddle. When he stole a sheepish peek back at Fremont and Sagundai, he was relieved to see that their backs were turned as they were preoccupied with calming their own mounts. He limped down the trail in his soaked trousers, calling to the gelding who was now out of sight. He was relieved to see, around the bend, that a minor rockslide had blocked the horse's way. As Guillermo came up alongside him, the horse looked at him as if to say *where have you been?* He allowed Guillermo to rub his neck and regain hold of the reins. They picked their way through the rubble, Guillermo kicking aside the smaller rocks. "No more antics. You need to set an example for the others. Comprendes?"

The gelding neighed and danced in place while they waited for Fremont and Sagundai to round the bend. Within moments, the clopping of hooves and jingle of reins announced their arrival. Guillermo gave them a wave to signal that all was well and resumed leading the procession.

As the afternoon wore on, the storm gained in intensity, unleashing sideways rain. Guillermo shielded his face in the crook of his arm. In addition to being battered by the storm, his shins ached from the downhill march. His boots were soaked, and his toes tingled with numbness. They continued down the windy trail, wading through endless streams of foaming mud.

Guillermo heard high-pitched screams from horses behind him. When he got to a sharp turn, he glanced back and saw a horse struggle with the soldier who was trying to coax it to step through a river of mud. It backed up, and in the process, one of its hind legs got too close to the ledge. The earth gave way. It fought frantically to regain its balance, but it was no use. Just like that, it vanished! The soldier managed to let go of the reins before he was dragged over the edge himself. Guillermo realized to his horror that the sounds he had heard earlier were horses sliding off the trail behind him.

Sagundai held up four fingers. "That makes four. Hooves sliding right out from under them!" he yelled over the wind.

A wave of nausea engulfed Guillermo, and he felt light-headed. It was a cruel twist of fate that after they began to descend, the storm unleashed its fury. It was too late to turn around; they had no choice but to proceed. The longer they lingered on the mountain, the more vulnerable they were to being swept off.

Shielding his face from the downpour, Guillermo wondered bleakly if this was his father's fault for not refusing Fremont's request to make this journey, but how could he have foreseen the ill weather? He turned and strained to catch a glimpse of the colonel's face. Fremont's chiseled jaw was clenched, and his chin was raised in defiance of the pelting rain. He stared resolutely ahead as if no drama was occurring behind him. If he was second-guessing himself, he showed no sign of it. Was this what a leader was supposed to do, steadfastly persevere in the face of adversity and not let losses deter him from his goal? If so, it seemed callous, yet Guillermo supposed someone had to be unwavering.

There was another high-pitched scream. Guillermo cringed and resisted the urge to turn around. Tears streamed down his face, mixing with the pelting rain. The gravity of the situation overwhelmed him. The torrential downpour seemed determined to drive them back, but there could be no retreat. The only way to safety was through the raging streams of mud.

Could this ordeal be some kind of initiation? He recalled the story Petra told him about the night he was born. Over the course of the previous month, a star with a long tail had been seen lighting up the night sky. Petra proclaimed that Doña Eduarda's firstborn was ordained for a special purpose. Could this be the event that had been foretold in the heavens? Even if he didn't feel brave inside, he'd have to convince the gelding to trust him. He would have to pretend.

He trudged onward, leaning into the wind through blinding sheets of water. As the storm raged, rivers of mud carved ruts in the hillside, undermining the stability of the trail. He tried blocking out the sound of horses and mules screaming. It was madness!

The storm raged another hour and a half as they slipped and slid their way down the mountain. He prayed no men would be lost but knew full well the odds were against it. When the trail finally leveled off to a slight slope, he spotted the welcome sight of a tarp flapping under a sprawling oak. Glory be! They made it! Thanks be to God!

Suspended from a low-lying branch, something dark was swinging crazily in the wind. He figured one of the Indian scouts had hung it there to keep from being washed away. Guillermo's curiosity was piqued, but he had more urgent matters to attend to such as erecting a makeshift shelter. It would feel grand to get out of the wind and rain.

Then it hit him. He tossed the pack on some high ground and ran, sloshing toward the flapping object. His heart raced as he puddle-jumped across the quagmire. Sure enough, the object was dangling by a leather strap!

Delaware Charley appeared from behind the tarp with a broad grin on his face. He plucked the hat from the branch and flung it toward Guillermo, who caught it by its brim. "Found it in bush not far from trail. Barely wet. Fine-quality beaver felt," he said.

Guillermo couldn't believe his eyes. He shook his head in amazement. "Híjole! Gracias! I can't believe you found it!" Examining the hat inside and out, he found it in surprisingly good shape. The silk headband was soaked with water instead of the usual sweat. "Should be good as new when it dries out. This was my tío's. It's my lucky hat."

It wasn't over yet. There were still men and horses on the mountain who needed help. He would return to help them. He and Delaware Charley parted ways when the scout was called by Captain Jacobs.

Guillermo set about picketing the livestock wearing Tío's hat, which for all the world felt like a crown. Now all he had to do was survive the rest of the day unharmed.

CHAPTER 16

Men staggered into the oak grove, seeking shelter wherever they could. Some collapsed in the mud. One bedraggled fellow exclaimed, "Lordy, Lordy! Thought I'd die up there! Never so glad to be on level ground in my life!" He knelt down and kissed the muddy earth.

The first cannon made it safely down the mountain late afternoon, hoisted on the shoulders of Archie and two artillerymen. "Oo-whee!" Archie exclaimed. "This here cannon weighs a ton! Nearly slid away from us several times!"

"Where's the wagon?" asked Guillermo.

"Had to be dismantled. The cannon was lowered over a rocky section to get it past that one steep bend in the trail. Still three pieces of artillery on the mountain. I'm headin' back up after I have me a couple smokes," said Archie.

The job wasn't done. There were still men, animals, and artillery on the mountain, but Guillermo worried most about the animals. A third of the way up, he and Archie encountered two cavalrymen struggling with a horse and pack mule. The procession had come to a halt amid impatient complaints. It was agreed that Archie would continue up the mountain while Guillermo stayed behind to help with the animals.

It turned out the McNabs had lost their best horse, and their remaining animals were frozen in fear, sensing death in the air. Logan fought to calm his horse. Balking, the gray mare stepped backward, coming inches from the crumbling edge. She shook her head wildly, whinnying her protests. Guillermo offered to take the reins, and an exhausted Logan handed them over. Guillermo gently coaxed the terrified horse forward with encouraging strokes on her neck and side. Haltingly, step by tentative step, her knees unbuckled, and she slowly gained momentum. "C'mon, girl, you're doing fine. Let's keep moving."

"You did it!" Logan shouted into the wind.

"Need to keep her moving! Trail narrows up ahead! I'll lead her past it!" Guillermo said.

A gust of wind blasted them, nearly sending Guillermo and the mare over the edge. He dug his heels into the muddy shoulder of the trail and righted himself. A river of water flowed between the horse's legs, threatening to undermine her tenuous balance.

"C'mon girl, you can do it."

A wild look in her eye told Guillermo she was on the verge of bolting. She pulled on the reins, shaking her head in refusal. He frantically searched his pocket for a few remaining raisins, anything to distract her from going into a full panic. To his great relief, he discovered a few sticky globs that he held up like a prize. "Aha! Look what I have!" He waved them in front of her, and it broke the spell. Food! She hadn't had much of it in days. She licked the raisins from his hand, allowing him to pet her forehead with the other. She nudged him for more, and he stepped backward. She followed him, sniffling his poncho. He continued to praise and soothe her, and she took one cautious step forward, then another. When she halted, he pretended to search his pocket for more, and that got her moving toward him again.

They played the game until she forgot her fear. Step by step,
they cheated death.

CHAPTER 17

Guillermo and the McNabs staggered into the oak grove well after nightfall along with other members of Companies C and G. The scene had taken on a different look since Guillermo left a few hours before. Now hundreds of men were spread throughout the area in canvas lean-tos, huddled under trees, or collapsed in the mud. Like ghosts, some skulked about in the darkness. The only light came from the occasional glow of a cigarette, it being too wet for a campfire. The rain continued to fall but had dwindled to a heavy drizzle. The ground was saturated, and water collected in low-lying areas. Puddles were growing into ponds.

Guillermo led the way to his tent. The Christmas night bivouac site was punctuated by snores, hacking coughs, grunts, and whinnies. It took some searching, but he finally located the tent by the limp bandana hanging from one of its poles. He fully expected to find someone sprawled inside, but surprisingly, it was empty.

"Will ya looky here?" Angus pointed out a crude sign that read FOXEN. Guillermo credited Jacobs as being its author. "This here's as good as a reservation in some fancy hotel. Hoo-wee!"

An hour later, a voice in the darkness said, "Is that you, Guillermo? Logan? It's me, Zeke." A figure sloshed toward them in ankle-deep water.

"You're jest now making it down the mountain? I figured you made it down before us," said Logan.

"I woulda, except I got slowed down helping to haul parts of a wagon down," said Zeke. "Most of Company K is down, but there's still some stragglers left up there. I 'spect they'll be spending the night and wait till morning 'fore they head down."

"Did you see my father at the top?" asked Guillermo.

"That I did. He and Bryant have been at the staging area all day. They've tried to keep the trail from getting too crowded, but bein' that it's nearly washed out in places, there's some bottlenecks. Counted a dozen animals go over the side on my way down. Criminy! Back home we have some humdinger gully washers, but I've never seen rain come down sideways like that!"

"As far as you know, no men were lost. Right?" asked Guillermo.

"None as far as I know, but I worry about those poor souls stuck on the mountain. Shore hope none of 'em get swept off during the night. Won't know until the companies assemble tomorrow if any are missin'," said Zeke.

"Dear Lord, please watch over man and beast. Let 'em survive the night," Angus murmured. A chorus of Amens was offered from those within earshot.

The rain let up sometime in the early hours of December 26. When the sun rose from behind the towering mountain, the sky was aflame in a pinkish glow. It heralded a day without rain. Un milagro! *A miracle*. Gradually, the chill of the morning shadows gave way to a sun-drenched day, and the sky was a glorious blue. In the light of day, the dismal camp was a muddy soup. Haggard men struggled to their feet, their clothes caked with mud. The early risers gathered damp wood and fanned their smoky fires. The oak grove was shrouded in a blue-gray haze.

As the morning wore on, those who had been forced to spend the night on the mountain straggled into camp. In the late morning, word came that, miraculously, all men were accounted for. The last of the four cannons had been retrieved, but the bad news was that more than a hundred animals had perished. The count was worse than Guillermo feared. Buzzards circled the canyon that had become a graveyard of horse and mule corpses.

Guillermo was preparing to head back up the mountain to rejoin his father when word spread that a party of Anglos had arrived to meet with Fremont. The atmosphere remained relaxed, everyone too exhausted to feel threatened. Sometime later, Guillermo was summoned to Fremont's tent. As he approached the group of men surrounding the colonel, he recognized his father's friends: Ike Sparks, the general store owner, Lewis Burton, a prominent citizen in Santa Barbara, and Nicolas Den, the son-in-law of Don Julian's godfather. Although they had become naturalized Mexican citizens years earlier, they privately hoped for an Americano takeover.

"Guillermo! Good Gawd, boy! The colonel here tells us you led his army over the trail from San Marcos and in a storm to beat all storms!" exclaimed Ike. All three men slapped Guillermo on the back and shook his hand until he thought it would fall off.

"Your pa's still up on the mountain?" asked Lewis.

"Yessir. I was just getting ready to hike back up. I left my horse at the top since it was too dangerous to lead him down."

"Nonsense!" said Ike. "Let me give you a ride up. Haven't seen your pa in a few months, and we have some catching up to do. Had me another daughter born yesterday!"

Before Guillermo could respond, Fremont said, "I understand from Lieutenant Talbott, the American marine who escaped from Santa Barbara by the skin of his teeth during the insurrection of the rebelistas from the south, that you're a crack shot, Mr. Sparks. I could use another sharpshooter. Appreciate it if you'd volunteer your services for a few weeks."

The look on Ike's face said he was none too happy with the invitation for fear of the retribution he would face from his fellow Mexican paisanos, neighbors, and friends, but he promised to give it some consideration.

Two Indian scouts finally made it into camp and announced the trail was passable but barely. Guillermo's father was waiting for him at the summit. When it was time to depart, Guillermo found it harder to say goodbye than expected. When word spread that he was leaving, a group gathered to see him off. Ike was standing off a ways, and Guillermo could tell the group was curious about his grizzled friend.

"Who's your friend, Guillermo?" asked Archie.

"This here's Ike Sparks, originally from Maine. Used to be a fur trader like you. Now he runs the general store."

Ike took a few long strides forward and greeted them. "Welcome to Santa Barbara! We are mighty happy to see you. It's a Christmas miracle you made it over the old Indian trail in that deluge! No one kin recollect it ever coming down that hard…like in Noah's day. Plumb near thought we'd float away. Pueblo looks like a swamp."

"How long you been in California?" asked Archie.

Ike rubbed his graying whiskers. "Well now, reckon it's goin' on twenty years now. Came out with Jedediah Smith's expedition to hunt beaver in 1826. We all got thrown in jail fer trespassin' on Mexican land. Mexican government wanted to send us back, but eventually we got ourselves hired by Captain Dana, who owns the rancho north of Foxen's, to hunt sea otters, since beaver were all gone. You passed his rancho on the way down here." There were nods of agreement and an awkward pause. Sparks said, "In case you was wonderin'," he pointed to a jagged scar that stretched from his missing right eye to his chin, "got this here in a fight with a grizzly. He weren't as lucky as me. He didn't survive. These hills is teemin' with 'em!"

"That's what Guillermo and his pa told us. Guess they weren't exaggeratin' none."

Guillermo knew the garrulous Ike was just getting warmed up and didn't want to drag out the farewell any longer. Taking advantage of the break in conversation, he said, "Well, guess we better get going. Don't want to keep Papá waiting. Adios, everyone. Good luck!" His throat tightened, and he hoped he'd be able to depart before his quavering voice betrayed his emotions. There were handshakes all around.

As Guillermo climbed onto the back of Ike's horse, Angus came over and said, "Hopefully all this will be over in a few weeks, and Neely will be ready to travel by the time we come back through. See you then."

On the trip back up the mountain, Guillermo learned from Ike that the Barbareños had fled south a few days before to the pueblo of Los Angeles to gather forces with Flores' rebelista army. US Commander Robert Stockton was waiting there for General Steven Kearney's dragoons to arrive from the southwest and Fremont's battalion to help fight the remaining remnant of Mexican insurgents. There had been no ambush waiting for Fremont's battalion after all.

CHAPTER 18

Guillermo tightened the wool blanket around his shoulders as he stared into the blazing fire in the family's sala. He ignored his mother's admonition to change out of his wet clothes. So what if he caught lung fever?

The merry chatter of Ramona and Martina swirled behind him. "Wait till you meet Señor Neely! He's very friendly. He can make shadow animals on the wall with his hands and play the harmonica, and Martina thinks he's very handsome with his blue eyes." Ramona covered her mouth and dissolved into giggles.

"What?" said Martina, rolling her eyes. "You said it first, and I just agreed!"

"Now, girls, let's not fuss. Guillermo will meet Señor Neely tomorrow."

Don Julian, enthroned in his cowhide chair, sucked contentedly on his pipe. Juanita lay nestled in his lap. Doña Eduarda rocked Alejandro, who drowsily studied Guillermo with sober eyes. The clock on the mantel struck nine gongs. Had it only been five days since they had last gathered here? It seemed a lifetime ago.

A wayward gust of wind flew down the chimney and sent sparks flying on the hearth. Guillermo absentmindedly stamped out a couple embers with a damp boot. He thought about Fremont's men huddled around campfires in the battalion's encampment at the base of the San Marcos trail. He pictured Archie stretched out on the ground with his feet to the fire, a cigarette dangling from his mouth.

Boom!

A thud rocked the adobe, making dirt rain down from the beamed ceiling. The engraving of the Madonna and Child that hung on the wall swung back and forth. They all looked at one another in confusion.

"What was that?" asked Ramona.

"A giant oak must have toppled over in the wind. Not surprising. The ground's saturated from all the rain," said Don Julian, his voice groggy from fatigue. "Let's hope no cows were huddled under it." He took a deep draw from his pipe.

"Shouldn't someone go out and check to make sure?" asked Panchita.

"Too dark for anyone to see. Besides, that would be an act of God, and we don't need to interfere in His matters, mija."

"But Papá..." she pleaded. She turned to Guillermo for support.

"Forget it, Panchita. Animals die all the time. That's just the way it is," Guillermo muttered, shrugging. His remark was harsh, but he figured she'd have to face the ugly truth sooner or later. He stared into the fire, feeling several sets of eyes upon him.

A quiet settled over the family. They listened to the wind in silence until Doña Eduarda said, "Now that Papá and Guillermo have returned safely, we'll have our Natividad feast tomorrow. We must continue to pray for the safety of Colonel Fremont's battalion. Now we need to get some sleep. Mijo, you may sleep here by the fire tonight. I'll make sure the children don't bother you in the morning. Sleep as late as you wish." She rose from her rocker and kissed him on his head. "It's so good to have you home again."

One by one, they filed out of the sala until he was alone with his thoughts. Curled up in the blanket, he thought about the tree losing its battle to the elements. Nothing was permanent. He drifted into a state of twilight sleep, repeatedly waking with a start to the scream of falling horses.

The following morning, Doña Eduarda led him, stiff and puffy-eyed, into his bed chamber to see Neely.

"Good morning. How are you feeling?" asked Guillermo.

The soldier's right leg was propped up with pillows and wrapped with strips of cloth. Angry purple and scarlet bruises peeked through. Pale and freckled, he looked younger than Guillermo expected.

"Better. The swelling must be going down because the bandages don't feel as tight this morning. Thanks to your father, I may recover from this without much of a limp, that is if I can keep it still so the bone can knit back together. Never been confined before. The Good Lord must be teaching me patience," Neely said. "What took so long? We all thought you'd be back before Christmas."

Guillermo pulled up a chair and told him about the march down the mountain. He concluded by shaking his head and fighting to keep his voice from breaking. "Don't know if I'll ever get their screams out of my head, and for what? After making it down the San Marcos Trail, turned out there was no ambush at either Gaviota or Refugio beaches. The Barbareños had gone to Los Angeles!"

Neely remained quiet for a few moments. "Did all the men make it over safely?"

Guillermo nodded. "Sí, as well as the cannons. Their wagons had to be dismantled and lowered by ropes in spots where the trail was steep and twisty."

"Sounds like you're being too hard on yourself. Not a man was kilt. That counts for a lot."

Guillermo hung his head. "I suppose so, but it still makes me angry so many animals died. It's not right. It would have been better if the battalion had waited for the storm to pass, but no, we were forced to go down in a blinding storm. Someone should have tried talking sense into Colonel Fremont."

"For all you know, people did but he didn't listen. He was arrogant, if you want my opinion. There was scuttlebutt that the president's going to appoint him governor of California."

"Even if he's not much of a military leader?"

Neely shrugged. "It's all about knowing people in high places. Connections. Just be glad you're back home on your beautiful rancho. I can hear the cows mooing in the distance. Something comforting about that, and you have a great family. You're lucky, Guillermo. Try to put the other behind you."

"Guess you're right." Guillermo slapped his hands on his knees and rose. "Well, it's time I head out. I'll stop by and pay you a visit after supper, if you don't mind. Too bad you can't join us for our big feast. I could bring in a plate for you, and we could eat together. I'll ask if I can join you."

"I'd like that very much." Spreading his arms, Neely said, "I'm not going anywhere."

Guillermo left the room, smiling.

One night in mid-January 1847, Guillermo and Neely played Monte by the light of a flickering candle. The adobe was quiet except for Don Julian's deep-throated snoring that could be heard through the wall. Outside, the wind howled like a banshee accompanied by the barking of the dogs. Occasionally, the tinkling of a bell could be heard between gusts—his father had hung one from the neck of the belle mare, Aleta.

"I'm guessing it's the wind and coyotes that have the dogs agitated," Guillermo said. "It's your turn to pick a card."

Neely cocked his head toward the wall and whispered, "Shh…what was that?"

Guillermo stared at the wall, squinting in concentration. "Something's knocking against the side of the house, and I hear a horse whinnying."

A sudden movement came from his parents' room. A door opened, and as his father passed the bedchamber, he muttered, "What in tarnation is Joaquin doing out of the corral?" This was followed by the front door unbolting and heavy footsteps on the veranda.

Guillermo jerked his head back. "Joaquin's out? How can that be? Juan was supposed to be on guard." As he rose to investigate, he wagged a finger at Neely and said, "No peeking at my cards while I'm gone."

He'd only gone a few steps when he heard his father yell, "Guillermo! Sal!"

Guillermo rushed out of the room and through the sala, unlatching the heavy front door. A gust of wind sent a cloud of dust into the room. He stepped out onto the veranda, and it took both hands to close it behind him. He stared out into the yard, and a tumbleweed bounced across the yard followed by fragments of tree branches. His father's spyglass swung wildly by its leather thong from the oak tree. He raced down the steps toward the corral and saw, to his horror, that it was empty, its gate swinging wide open! Eight horses should have been inside, including Benito. The only one remaining was Joaquin, who his father and Indian servant Juan were saddling.

His father's words came in bits and phrases. "Horses… stolen! Get rifle!"

Guillermo stumbled back into the house, pulled on his boots, threw a poncho over his head, and returned with his rifle and powder horn. His father was hoisting himself into the saddle, his hair standing on end in the wind. Guillermo stood on the edge of the veranda, trying to pour gunpowder into the barrel, but it blew back into his face, stinging his eyes. Ay, caramba! He should have been more patient and readied his rifle inside the house. He rammed whatever gunpowder made it into the barrel and stuck a cap in the chamber.

Don Julian reined Joaquin over to the steps and yelled for Guillermo to hand him the rifle and hop on behind him. Had any other horse besides Joaquin been left behind, they would not have been able to ride tandem. Joaquin's large stature was well suited to Don Julian. Guillermo wrapped his arms around his father, and they galloped across the hacienda yard with the dogs racing alongside them.

A nearly full moon was high in the sky, casting the canyon in a silvery light. A cluster of tracks led across the field and up the trail to the north. They sped through the winding canyon. Joaquin needed no prodding to pursue the herd. The intelligent stallion was the dominant horse in the remuda and had managed to break away from the horse thieves to get help. He had pawed and neighed at Don Julian's bedchamber window to sound the alarm.

"What do you want to bet the Tulares took 'em!" Don Julian hollered over his shoulder.

They caught a whiff of acrid smoke. The canyon opened up to a plain where the tracks led them into the wide riverbed. Water ran in a shallow channel on the north side.

The dogs took a shortcut and sprinted ahead, barking for them to follow. Around the bend in the river, a group of Tulares huddled around a campfire. The stiff legs of a horse protruded from dancing flames.

"Please, God, not Benito," Guillermo whispered.

Some of Rancho Tinaquaic's cow ponies were drinking from the channel. Joaquin trumpeted a call, and they raised their heads, sniffing the air at the familiar scent.

Pointing to the Tulares, Don Julian ordered, "Fire over their heads!" He handed the rifle back to Guillermo.

Guillermo cocked it, aimed, and fired high, sending the Tulares scrambling for cover in the nearby gulley. Three of the six stolen cow ponies scattered in different directions like buckshot in a bale of hay. To Guillermo's dismay, he didn't spot Benito. The two herding dogs needed no command to round up the horses. They circled the wide perimeter and herded them into a tight band.

"I'll try getting close to Aleta so you can lasso her. You can jump on her back, and the rest will follow you home!" Don Julian yelled, trading Guillermo the reata for the rifle. "I'll make sure the Tulares don't return!"

Which horse had they slaughtered? The charred remains gave no clues. Guillermo loosened the lead on the lasso and swung it over their heads, letting the loop get larger with each pass. On the fourth revolution, he tossed it over Aleta's head, jerking on the slack as it slipped over her neck. He handed the reata off to his father, slid off Joaquin's rump, and ran over to calm Aleta. She didn't fight the rope and let Guillermo approach her. Joaquin backed up slightly to keep the reata taut as Guillermo reached out to calm her. The stallion nickered reassurance to the jittery horse.

Don Julian kept one eye out for the Tulares and the other on Guillermo and their valuable belle mare. "Whoa, girl, you're okay now. It's just me," Guillermo said.

She lifted her head and sniffed. Within moments, she allowed him to swing his lanky body onto her back and danced in a circle while he petted her neck. Though she wasn't used to being ridden bareback, she responded to his commands. "Good girl. You're fine now. Vámonos!" He squeezed her sides and leaned to the left to point her toward home. Glancing over his shoulder one last time, he scanned the area. "Benito! Benito!" he called into the wind. A bitterly cold gust blew his words back in his face.

"*Ándale*, Guillermo! Head on home! I'll keep an eye out for him!"

Don Julian didn't waste any more bullets scaring the Tulares. He had made his point and had no intention of using unnecessary violence. Guillermo headed Aleta back down the sandy riverbank. The two others followed, flanked by Don Julian and the dogs.

The following morning Neely hobbled out of the adobe on crutches, fashioned from branches of a sycamore found along the creek. He joined the crew of vaqueros gathered at the corral, discussing the previous night's raid. He squeezed in beside Guillermo and nodded at the tired-looking men. Angel, shot him a look of *What are you doing here?* Neely pretended not to notice.

"Those Tulares is getting bolder," said Sal. "Stealing our best cow ponies from under the nose of a dozing guard."

"That's a first. Never had a raid like that before. If it hadn't been for Joaquin, we'd have lost 'em all," said Don Julian, shaking his head in disbelief. "Took the bell right off Aleta's neck and hung it from the corral gate. Mighty clever."

"What do you wanna bet, Neely, what we thought were coyotes calling were really Tulares? No wonder the dogs were going loco," said Guillermo. "If only I'd gone out to check sooner..."

"Jefe, something's off about all this. Why would the Tulares risk stealing the remuda in the corral when they could have captured the other horses that were grazing a safe distance away?" Sal asked.

"I agree," said Don Julian. "It doesn't make any sense."

After a few moments, Guillermo said, "Only if they were determined to take our most valuable stock."

"When have Tulares cared about the quality of the horses they steal? Horse meat all tastes the same," said Chico, the middle Gonzalez brother.

"Papá, he's right. What if they were recruited by some angry rebelistas to harass us, to punish us for helping the Americanos?"

"Hmm, the timing would fit. By now word has spread. Even if this was a coincidence, I think we need to post two guards to guard the corral," said Sal.

"Excuse me, Mr. Foxen, but that's something I'd like to volunteer for." All heads swiveled in Neely's direction. "Since I'm not herding cattle during the day like the rest of you, I'd have an easier time staying awake. It's the least I can do to help out."

Don Julian took off his hat and scratched his thatch of graying hair. "Appreciate that, son. We could use an extra hand. The rest of us will take turns keeping you company. Thataway we just have to give up one night a week for guard duty. Think we can manage that?"

Nods were directed toward the pale young man. Compared to the bronzed skin of the vaqueros, Neely was a pale salamander color.

"Now that we got that settled," said Chico, "I say we quit standing around jaw jacking and comb the area for tracks. I think a couple of us should head west."

"West? You mean toward Ranchos La Laguna and Corral de Cuati?" Don Julian looked to Sal. "What do you think?"

Sal shrugged, "May as well. They can round up strays along the way."

"Okay, Chico. Take my spyglass," Don Julian said. "Avoid a confrontation by not making any accusations, you hear? I want Benito and the other two back…but I also don't want to stir up any trouble with our neighbors. Got that?"

"Me? Stir up trouble?" Chico laid a hand on his chest. "Jefe, you know me better than that."

"Exactly. That's why I'm sending someone along to accompany you. The rest of us'll return to the riverbed." He glanced at Neely. "How 'bout you take up a post on the veranda while we're gone, but keep that leg propped up?"

"Yessir!"

Guillermo, Don Julian, Sal, and Angel saddled up and headed north to the riverbed and the site of the previous night's encounter. They had no trouble finding footprints in the wet sand. One set led east toward a fork in the river. The Sisquoc River served as a trail for the Tulares though the rugged backcountry. The farther east they rode, the more likely they were to encounter bands of hostile Indians. That assignment was given to Sal, who headed upriver while Guillermo and Angel searched the immediate area of the abandoned campfire. A pair of turkey vultures perched on a piece of driftwood fifteen feet from a pack of coyotes fighting over the carcass. Their ugly red heads atop ruffled necks bobbed as they watched the action.

Within a few minutes, Angel yelled, "Jefe, there's hoof-prints heading up Tepusquet Canyon!" He pointed across the river.

"Good!" Don Julian hollered back. "Guillermo! You two follow the tracks! I'll hang around here and wait for Sal. Fire a shot if you need help!"

The two young vaqueros galloped up the riverbank, kicking up sand and gravel. Guillermo rode a newly broken gelding. Sudden movements and sounds made him skittish and quick to bolt, so Guillermo was forced to soothe him with pats on his neck and verbal assurances. They followed the creek to the mouth of the canyon. Two sets of hoofprints led them to a mesa where a pair grazed leisurely under a stand of oaks.

As they approached the horses, Guillermo sighed. "Ay, caramba. Benito's not here. Where could he be?" He and Angel easily lassoed the horses and led back to the riverbed.

Sal had returned. "No luck," he said. "Lost the tracks in gravel a ways upstream."

At this point, the rolling hills of Rancho Tinaquaic gave way to a rugged terrain of sparse vegetation. The region was the domain of the giant condor that soared on his twelve-foot wingspan on thermals high above craggy peaks and contorted sandstone formations. It was a no-man's land that separated the coastal valleys from the vast plain that lay to the east. If Benito was a captive of the Tulares, there was a good chance he wouldn't survive the long journey.

CHAPTER 19

D on Julian and Sal led the two horses back to the rancho's corral. Guillermo and Angel remained behind to
search the oak grove for Benito. They retraced the route
they had taken a few weeks earlier when they discovered
Fremont's encampment.

"Think the Yankees will return this way when the war's
over?" Angel asked as they threaded their way through the
woods.

"Heard Fremont and his officers will return to Monterey
by ship. Settlers like Neely's father and brother will be on
their own to return to their farms up north. One of these
days, they'll be passing through to get him. In the meantime,
it's good to have a rifleman guarding the corral."

"Hmph! What makes you think he can shoot? Just
because he has a rifle don't mean he can hit anything. Only
a tenderfoot walks behind a mule." Angel scoffed, spitting
off to the side.

"Don't be so quick to judge. He marched fifteen miles
that day with a saddle over his shoulders. I'd like to see you
do that. One gets careless when exhausted. Besides, he told
me they had to fight off Shawnees back where he came from.
I believe him when he says he can shoot." Guillermo heard
the defensiveness in his voice.

"Well, at least he can keep watch over things while

we're gone. Even if he sits on the veranda like a scarecrow," Angel said.

Guillermo opened his mouth to counter the remark but caught himself. There was no point trying to defend Neely when nothing he said would change Angel's opinion. Until Neely left Rancho Tinaquaic, Angel would be critical of him.

They rode through dappled light, scanning the shadows for any sign of Benito and calling out his name. Guillermo's hope of finding his horse faded with each passing hour. Self-pity over the randomness of life enveloped him as he rounded a bend and made a startling discovery. A massive oak lay toppled over, diagonally crossing the creek bed and blocking their way.

"Híjole!" exclaimed Angel. "This was standing last time we came through here! It's huge! Its trunk's gotta be eight feet around!"

"This is what caused the loud thud a couple weeks ago, "said Guillermo. "Papá said a giant like this can be heard a long ways when it falls." They stared at the tree in awe.

"When this is chopped into firewood, it'll get us through two winters easily," said Angel.

"Better yet, we could get beams from it for a roof on a new stable. I think last night taught us we need more protection for our horses than just a corral," said Guillermo.

Seeing the huge clumps of dirt still clinging to its roots was like coming across a corpse. Its collapse seemed to mark the end of an era—of what Guillermo wasn't sure. It was yet another example of how the elements won in the end. He felt powerless and small. Benito was nowhere to be found. "Vámonos. I don't reckon we'll find Benito here. He doesn't like this place any better than I do."

"You don't *reckon*? Now you're talking like a Yankee?" Angel sneered, rolling his eyes.

"What's wrong with you? Ever since I got back, it's been one jab after another. You think I wanted to ride with the Americanos? Well, I didn't, but I figured I'd make the best of it, and you know what? I made some friends along the way. It didn't matter that I was a Californio or a muchacho. They didn't look down on me, and they didn't give me a hard time about what I said or did!" He slapped his hand on his thigh and sputtered. "Ay, caramba! Those strangers treated me better than the crew I ride with every day!"

Angel stared at Guillermo for several moments. "You're right, but that's because I wasn't going to give you a chance to brag about it. Your father told us all about what you did the morning after you returned. Guess I was afraid you'd get a swelled head." He took off his hat, rubbed the sweat off his brow, and shrugged. "Besides, you know how it is… we all give each other a hard time. I suppose you get the brunt of it, being the youngest of the crew and all, but you never said it bothered you before."

Guillermo cocked his head and gave Angel a skeptical look. "Now it's my fault? C'mon, you know it'd be worse if I let on it bothered me. Never heard you complain either."

Angel's voice rose in intensity. "You think my brothers' comments don't get under my skin? It gets old being the youngest and expected to hold my own against them." An awareness crossed his face, and he spread his arms as if to say *why do I treat you that way when I don't like being treated that way?* He had a comical way of twisting his mouth and widening his eyes when he was perplexed. "Guess I pass the favor on to you."

106

Guillermo shook his head and cracked a weak smile. Feeling the steam go out of him, he slumped in the saddle, drained. "I'd probably do the same thing if I had a brother older than Alejandro to keep in place."

Angel took a swig of water from his water bag and offered it to Guillermo. "Do you want to tell me what happened on the mountain?"

Guillermo took a deep breath and sighed. "For now, I'll just say they were the worst days of my life, yet in another way, they were the best." He shook his head in confusion.

Angel considered this for a moment. "Let's go back to the hacienda for something to eat, and you can tell me all about it. Vámonos! I'll race you home!" He tugged on the reins and galloped out of the oak grove with Guillermo close behind.

Benito was still missing. With each passing hour, Guillermo's hope of ever seeing his trusty cow pony again faded.

CHAPTER 20

When Guillermo and Angel rode into the yard of the hacienda, they were puzzled to see the family, vaqueros, and servants gathered on the patio. There was much smiling and laughter as if a fiesta were underway. Even Petra, who seldom ventured out of the adobe, was bouncing Alejandro on her hip and moving her head animatedly.

Guillermo and Angel tied their mounts to the hitching post and joined the revelers.

"Finally! Been waitin' for you two!" bellowed Don Julian, waving them over with his pipe in hand.

Neely hobbled out on his crutches to intercept them. "The war's over! You're Americanos now! Isn't that great, y'all?" He slapped Guillermo on the back.

Angel bristled and made a beeline for the outdoor kitchen where his sister was tending a pot of beans.

Brothers Felipe and Chico sat at the outdoor table, surrounded by members of the Foxen and Gonzalez families. They hunched over bowls, eating with gusto and taking turns telling how they came to hear the momentous news. Their mother, Concha, stood off to the side with her arms folded atop her ample stomach. Over her shoulder, she ordered her daughter, "Rosita, más tortillas, por favor!"

Chico wiped his mustache on a sleeve when he spotted

Guillermo and flashed a wolfish grin. "'Bout time! We found Benito! He's in the shed being tended to by Juan."

Guillermo stood dumfounded for a few moments. "Really?" He took off his hat and slapped it against his thigh, so relieved he had no words.

Chico held up a hand to calm him. "Nothin' wrong with him that won't heal in a week or so. He's fine."

There were cheers and exclamations of delight from both families and Neely. Guillermo's knees buckled, and he sank to the ground and covered his face in his hands. "O Dios mio! Gracias!"

Ramona and Panchita ran to him and hugged him around the neck. "Isn't it wonderful? Benito's back!" they squealed.

He opened his arms and hugged them both.

"Got all our horses back except for the spotted filly!" Don Julian said. "I'd say we were mighty lucky!"

Guillermo rose to his feet and swiped away a few tears.

Angel came around the beehive-shaped oven and joined the others. "Bravo! See, I told you he'd be found! Where'd you find him?" he asked, tearing off a bite of tortilla.

"Along Zaca Creek, this side of the mesa," Felipe said. Turning toward his father, he said, "Good thing you sent us to check it out, Papá, otherwise we would've headed off in the other direction. Chico wanted to stop by La Laguna, but I talked him out of it." He jabbed his younger brother in the ribs. "See, aren't you glad you listened to me?"

Chico made a face and said between bites, "Once in a blue moon, you're right. Lucky for Guillermo, this happened to be one 'em."

"Seems you always have an excuse to go over there," said Sal wryly.

"It's cuz of Luisita. Right, Chico?" Angel said.

"Cállate, little brother. You don't know what you're talking about," said Chico.

This brought a round of teasing and jeers.

Impatient to hear about Benito being found, Guillermo said, "Where'd you find him?"

Felipe held up a hand. "Hold on, I'm getting to it. We stopped at the creek to water the horses, and who do we find? Paco Fuentes and Enrique Rios, Gustavo Davila's vaqueros, with Benito! They claimed they found him wandering loose on Corral de Cuati land and were on their way here to return him. Could tell they were surprised to see us but tried hard not to show it."

Guillermo's eyebrows furrowed. "Híjole! How did he wind up down there?"

"You're right. It didn't make any sense, and they knew we was suspicious," Felipe said, "but they was cool as skunks in the moonlight. When I told 'em about the Tulare raid, they shook their heads and said, 'That's the problem with your land being a crossroads. Tulares is used to traveling across it. They consider what's yours as theirs.' As they was saddlin' up, Fuentes called out, 'Did you hear the news? Flores and Fremont signed a peace agreement.' We said, 'When was that?' They said a messenger told Don Gustavo it was signed a few days ago.'"

"That didn't take long," said Guillermo. "The rebelistas must not have put up much of a fight."

"Aye," said Don Julian, "they probably took one look at Fremont's riflemen and cannons and decided they had no choice but surrender. Every Yankee who comes west is well armed. Has at least one rifle and revolver. Right, Neely?"

"Yessir, Mr. Foxen. Even a poor man's got a piece if not two."

"Fremont probably promised political favors to José Maria Flores, head of the Mexican rebelistas, and his lieutenants to sweeten the deal," Don Julian said, taking a draw on his pipe.

"Do you think Don José Pico will be released to return to his family?" asked Doña Eduarda.

"In time, but for now, he's valuable in helping Fremont establish relationships with the most influential men in the province."

"Señor Neely, soon your father will be coming for you. Es muy importante your leg be strong enough for the ride home. Do not walk too much," she said.

"No, ma'am, I won't. I can feel it's getting stronger every day." Neely's fair skin had pinkened from its first exposure to the sun in more than three weeks.

"Well, the war's over, and the horses have been found. Now life can return to normal. Come along, mijas. We have chores to finish," said Doña Eduarda.

The men exchanged glances and lingered behind. Concha placed a bowl of beans in front of Guillermo, but he waved it off. "No, gracias. I need to check on Benito."

Concha scowled and was about to say something when Don Julian interjected. "No, mijo. Sit down and eat. Benito can wait."

Concha flashed an *I told you so* look and shook her finger. "Your papá's right. You need to eat. Get some fat on your bones."

Guillermo tilted his head toward the sky and sighed. He swung a leg over the bench and plopped down across from the brothers. Something in their eyes told him they had more to tell. When their mother was out of earshot, Guillermo whispered, "What's going on? Are you sure Benito's okay?"

"Don't worry," said Chico, putting up a hand to reassure him. "He's fine except for some rope burns on his neck. Juan's washing him down and putting salve on it."

"Rope burns on his neck? If Fuentes and Rios found him wandering on their Corral de Cuati, how did his neck get rubbed raw in that short amount of time?"

"Ex-actly," said Felipe. "Their story doesn't add up. What we didn't say in front of the others was that Paco Fuentes made a threat. After he told us about the treaty, he said, 'According to rancheros in the valley, just because some ink was scribbled on paper don't mean the war's over. In out-of-the-way places like this, laws can't be enforced. For now, Yankee sympathizers should expect to pay for their traitorous acts.' Then they rode off."

"Ay, yi, yi," Guillermo groaned, tossing his spoon into his bowl of beans. "Do you think they could have had something to do with last night's raid?"

Chico nodded. "Let's put it this way—since they weren't surprised about it, we think they probably know something about the Tulares being recruited and bribed to steal our best horses."

"I don't trust those hombres," said Sal. "Don't believe their story about finding Benito so far away. From now on, we need to keep close watch over the corral. Who wants to be on guard duty tonight with Neely?"

"I will," said Angel. Looking at an astonished Guillermo, he said, "Don't worry about Benito none. I'll take care of him."

"Gracias. You're sure?"

"Sí, no problema. Neely and I'll keep an eye on things. Won't we?"

"You betcha." Neely winked. "No one's going to mess with the horses tonight."

Angel snapped his fingers. "Oh, I nearly forgot, jefe. We came across a giant oak that toppled over in the oak grove. There's enough wood to keep us in firewood for a couple years."

"I was thinking, Papá, we could use some of it to build a stable," said Guillermo. "There's enough wood for some strong roof beams."

Don Julian stroked his chin. "Aye, we do need a better shelter for the horses. Probably should wait until spring before we start chopping it up. Let it dry out some."

Spring seemed a long way off. A lot could happen between now and then, but the major news was that the war was over, and now Guillermo was no longer a Mexicano but an Americano! That was a strange notion. More pressing, he worried the previous night's raid was the beginning of harassment by avenging paisanos for helping Fremont. It seemed as soon as one problem was solved, a new worry replaced it.

CHAPTER 21

Before Guillermo's eyes adjusted to the darkened shelter, he was greeted by Benito's whinny. Neely followed behind on crutches. The cow pony limped forward, nuzzling his blazed forehead into Guillermo's chest.

"Welcome back, mi amigo. You had me worried." Guillermo ran his hand along the horse's sleek neck, careful to avoid the raw red marks.

Juan leaned against his rake and said, "He's been waiting for you, Señor Guillermo. He heard you outside and has been stamping his hoof."

Guillermo stroked Benito's nose and crooned. "I'm sorry, amigo. I wanted to come sooner but got held up." Turning to Old Fernando, he asked, "So who is that for?"

Fernando's hands worked independently, yanking tight on the taravilla, a tool he used for separating the strands of tanned leather. "I'm making a reata for this young man," nodding toward Neely. "This here'll be an eight strand, sixty yards long. A couple of these will hold down a young bull so he can be branded, yet it's flexible enough to rope a heifer. Figured as a new settler to the province he needs at least one."

Neely stared in awe at how swiftly Fernando's hands twisted and yanked on the rawhide. "Thank you very much! How old were you when you made your first one?"

"Ay, caramba. I was the assistant to the assistant of the reata maker when I was a boy. I used to tend the big vat where the leather would soak for days to get it soft enough to work with. Another boy and I stoked the fire and scraped off all the hair and fat. Smelly job. Wasn't until my late teen years I was allowed to cut it into strips. That was a big step. Then took another five years or so till I was trained to braid it. Vaqueros are particular about the weight and length of their reatas. Some like them light, others prefer heavier ones. Maybe Guillermo will show you how to work one." To Guillermo, he said, "What do you think?"

"Sure, I'd like that. Maybe by next week you'll be allowed to get on a horse again."

"That would be great!"

The following week Neely joined the crew in herding cattle. He wanted to see if his leg was strong enough to handle being on horseback a couple hours, and he wanted to try his hand at lassoing a longhorn cow. Riding southeast toward Zaca Mountain, a league south of the Foxen rancho, he paused and took in the scene. The foot-high grass on the rolling hills billowed in the breeze like waves in the ocean. "Lord have mercy!" he exclaimed. "This is beautiful! It's as green as Eden! 'The mountains and hills will burst into song before you, and the trees of the field will clap their hands.'"

"I like that. Did you just make it up?"

"Oh, no. I can't take credit for that. It's from the Bible. The prophet Isaiah said it a long time ago. Doubt that what inspired him could compare with this."

Guillermo smiled and sat back in the saddle contentedly. "Yessiree, I like that…'the trees of the field clapping their hands'…it's like they're celebrating your recovery."

115

"I agree." Neely closed his eyes and inhaled deeply. "Funny how being laid up with a broken leg makes me realize how fine it is to breathe in fresh air and feel the sun on my face. It's like being reborn, but I wouldn't trade this time for anything. I'm going to miss Rancho Tinaquaic and its rolling hills, the oak trees, the sound of the cows lowing, and your cozy home, but most of all you and your family."

"Thank you. We're going to miss you too." Guillermo dreaded the thought of Neely leaving. He was especially enjoying their late afternoon target practices.

During one of their last shooting sessions together, Neely said, "Your technique's getting better. You're learning to make adjustments for your gun, and that's important, but we gotta get you so you react quicker, without thinking. You have to be aware of your surroundings, the animal sounds and silences. Scan the countryside, searchin' for something that doesn't belong. Always be on alert, vigilant."

"You make it sound like my luck's going to run out."

"Because one of these days, it will. I've been watching you, and you can't go daydreaming cuz you're bored. Make it a game to always be asking yourself why a flock of birds have left their tree, the jays have stopped squawking, or the deer are standing at attention. Observe the animals around you, cuz they'll sense danger before you do. You need a mule around. They're always the first hoofed creature to know something's amiss. Watch their ears—they'll tell you a lot."

Neely took a swig of water from his water pouch. "If an outlaw has you in their sight, it's best to jump off your horse and get low. Learn to shoot both lying on your stomach and sitting down. If you're waiting for a target to get within range, it's important to learn to keep your arm from shaking. You gotta be able to hold your gun and stay relaxed at the same time. Here, I'll show you how." He slid off his mount and unholstered his rifle. As he was demonstrating, Guillermo focused hard on remembering the technique. Perhaps one day his life, or someone else's, would depend on it.

CHAPTER 22

The McNabs and Zeke arrived one gray afternoon at the end of January 1847, after the Treaty of Cahuenga was signed in which General Flores ceded to Colonel Fremont and the Americanos Alta California from north of Yerba Buena to San Diego. Their reunion was marked by much laughter and backslapping.

Despite hobbling about on his crutch, Neely showed off his new lassoing skills. He tossed the reata Fernando had made for him over the head of a bewildered sheep who happened to graze too close to the adobe.

Delighted at seeing the surprise on the visitors' faces, Ramona and Panchita insisted that Neely show how he could rope a cow. While the men stood around scratching their heads, the giggling girls disappeared around the corner of the house. Moments later, they returned holding long-horned cow skulls atop their heads They trotted around the yard, and mooed. The dogs joined in the fun, nipping at their heels and long skirts. Neely lassoed the girls from ever-increasing distances.

Guillermo stood off to the side, watching with his arms crossed, pleased with the results of his roping lessons. It had helped that Neely was an eager student who practiced hours on end while guarding the hacienda.

"To think I was feeling sorry for you, recuperating with

a broken leg and all!" Angus exclaimed. "May have to go into the cattle business to put your talents to use!"

After the trail-weary travelers were served a hearty meal of beef stew, frijoles, and fresh tortillas, the menfolk retired to the patio. Sitting around the fire pit, the visitors recounted the march south following their harrowing descent of the San Marcos Trail.

"We rested in Santa Barbara for several days," Angus said, "then continued on toward Los Angeles. Took us ten days to get to the mission at San Fernando. Didn't have no opposition to speak of, just a lot of posturing on the part of the Californios. As we marched down the narrow coastal plain, they observed us from the ridgeline of the steep hills." Flames reflected off his eyeglasses as he recalled the scene by pointing his cigar into the night air. "They made an impressive sight, lined up on horseback with their lances pointed to the sky. Opposite them was the navy gunboat *Julia* that escorted us down the coast as far as Buenaventura."

"Pa, tell 'em how at El Rincon we saw whales spouting when we marched on the beach at low tide," said Logan, who was cleaning his rifle. He said to Neely and Guillermo, "Picture this. On one side we have the Californios, and on the seaward side, a gunship and a group of whales! It was like we was in some kind of parade!"

Zeke said, "The Californios pointing offshore caused us to take notice. They was enjoying the show as much as we was!"

"After Buenaventura, south of Santa Barbara, we separated from our naval escort and headed inland along the Santa Clara River," Angus said. "Those same horsemen followed us, careful to stay out of rifle and cannon range, taunting us by prancing back and forth and yelling. Between them and the wind, we was harassed every step of the way. Sand and gravel from the riverbed blew everywhere so thick there was times we couldn't see our hands in front of our faces. Tumbleweeds made faster progress than we did." He spat, causing the hot coals to sizzle and smoke. "Traveled two days like that. Passed a deserted adobe in the middle of nowhere. The wind finally calmed down when we camped at a grove of willows. In the moonlight we saw the silhouettes of the Californios posted on the hills around us like a flock of crows. When they wasn't yipping, they howled like coyotes across the canyon. Kept it up for hours. We rotated the watch so there was always two companies on guard." He tapped a curling snake of ash from the end of his cigar into the fire and then took a deep drag.

"That land along the Santa Clara River belongs to Don Carlos Carrillo," said Don Julian. "Probably had his crew of vaqueros and relatives watching you."

"Then he has a big crew and lots of relatives. There was at least sixty, seventy of 'em. Figured they'd be joined by their compadres any day, and we'd have ourselves a real battle. We continued up the Santa Clara Valley another couple days until the trail led us over some rocky barren mountains. High desert country. We split into two groups to protect the artillery wagons, then joined forces as we descended into the valley of San Fernando. We expected to encounter the main contingent of the rebelistas but turns out they'd been occupied with General Kearney and Commodore Stockton's Americano forces sent by President Polk farther south at San Gabriel. They ended up having the biggest battle in Alta California at San Pasqual near San Diego. We had no problem proceeding on to the mission at San Fernando where there was good pasturage for the animals. We hadn't been there long when two messengers for the Californios brought word that their generals wished to meet with Fremont, so he and the prisoner we took at San Luis Obispo rode off to meet with them."

"Ah, yes, that prisoner was my wife's cousin, Don José Pico. They're related to General Pio Pico, a rebelista like Flores," said Don Julian.

"Seems like everyone's related in these parts," said Zeke between sips of brandy.

"That they are," said Don Julian. "I learnt years ago to be careful what I say about so-and-so, because chances are I was chatting with an in-law if not a blood relative."

"Well, in this case, it most likely helped matters," Zeke said, "cuz a peaceful surrender was negotiated quick-like." He snapped his fingers. "Turns out the insurgents suffered a humiliatin' dee-feat jest days before we arrived. They must've realized they was outmanned, especially with us closing in. The peace treaty was signed on the thirteenth at a deserted rancho called Cahuenga, ending the war…leastways here in Alta California. Don't know if the other poor fools is still fighting it out in Texas and Mexico. The following day, we marched to the pueblo of Los Angeles as victors. Was hoping to see some perty señoritas, but they must have been hidden away from us infidels. 'Twas a disappointment, I tell ya."

Don Julian grinned. "I promise you they was whisked away by relatives to be protected from foreigners like you. Californios are a proud and gracious people. Generous to a fault, but when it comes to their womenfolk, they're mighty protective." He squinted through the haze of smoke and pointed a stout finger at Zeke. "And shrewd. You have to have more to offer than jest your good looks and genteel ways." Everyone had a good chuckle at that.

"Guess I better start workin' on betterin' myself," Zeke said, his Adam's apple bobbing like he'd swallowed an egg whole.

"Was there talk about who the governor of California will be? Will it be Fremont?" asked Don Julian.

"Think that's what he was counting on," said Angus, "but seems he jumped the gun and didn't clear the terms of peace with Stockton or Kearney before signing the treaty. They were hankering for some kind of retribution for the twelve men lost at a battle at San Pasqual and for the siege in Los Angeles, but Fremont wanted to end things peaceable-like. Granted amnesty to the insurgents and promised protection of life and property to all Californios. Being politically minded, cuz we know he sure ain't no military man." He spat into the fire. "He was looking to make allies out of the Californios." He shrugged and took a swig of brandy. "I was just glad to have it over with so we could all go back to living our lives. I have acres waiting to be plowed so I can plant wheat and barley come spring."

Zeke blew a smoke ring from his cigar. "The joke among the rank and file was that no sooner had the war with the Californios ended then it broke out among the Yankee commanders! Both Fremont and Kearny claimed they was appointed by President Polk as military commander. Poor ol' Stockton was stuck in the middle, not knowing who his superior was!" He slapped his knee and crowed. "Don't that jest beat all?"

Guillermo's ears had perked up at the mention of the treaty. "Papá, if life and property are protected, we don't have to worry about Fuentes' threats, right?"

Don Julian said to Angus and Zeke, "My crew came across a couple vaqueros from a neighboring rancho who informed them that traitors, meaning us, can expect retribution for failing to do our part to defend the province from invaders." The smiles slid from the guests' faces. To Guillermo he said, "The thing is, just because something's written on paper don't mean it's the law of the land immediately. Unfortunately, it takes time. Law has to be enforced for it to have power."

"Yer pa's right. You need a sheriff and deputies to enforce the law," Zeke said, "and judges and juries to mete out justice, and those take time to establish."

"Don't look so glum, mijo. Knowing how impatient Anglos are about changing things, it won't take long before things start to feel civilized, even in out-of-the-way places like this. So long as I have proper documentation, which I do, our land grant will be honored. No one can take that away from us. If we have squatters, we'll run them off. Simple as that."

Angus said, "Yankees don't let grass grow under their feet, that's fer sure." He snapped his fingers. "Before you know it, California will be Americanized." Having settled the matter, he sighed and patted his belly with satisfaction.

"I think a toast is in order," said Zeke. He lifted his glass. "Here's to the Foxens and their piece of paradise! May it be passed down for generations to come!"

Glasses were clinked all around, followed by shouts of "Hear, hear!" Don Julian said, "And may we all prosper under the red, white, and blue!" The ritual was repeated with lots of smiles and cheers.

The festive mood continued late into the night. Guillermo strummed his guitar, and his father led them in his favorite sea chanties that echoed through the remote canyon. Like Angus, Guillermo hadn't felt so lighthearted in weeks. The music and laughter worked their magic. As strange as it was, he pitied Neely for having missed out on their ordeal on the San Marcos Trail. The shared hardship had forged a special bond with the others. Death had been their companion that day on the mountain, and they had survived only by the grace of God.

The next morning, Guillermo and Angel escorted the visitors to the Sisquoc River, flowing from the eastern mountains separating the coastal valleys from the Tulare Valley. When it was time to say goodbye, Guillermo guided Benito next to Neely's horse and shook his hand. "Adios, mi amigo. Vaya con Dios. If you come this way again, you're always welcome."

"Likewise. If you ever make it up to northern California, ask around for us. You'll always have a place to stay and a meal. Remember, aim low and to the left." He nodded to Angel, who returned the gesture.

Zeke called out, "Take care, Ghee-yair-mo! So long!" He started to turn away and then pointed a gloved finger in the air. "Oh! That reminds me! Plumb near rode off without tellin' ya! Finally came to me the other day what William means. It's protector. Seems fittin' in view of your present circumstances. With that new rifle of yours, you can help yer pap defend yer land." He waved his hat in salute and galloped off.

A lump formed in Guillermo's throat as he and Angel watched the foursome ride away in the river channel. Chances were he'd never see them again. That left a hollowness in his chest, but they had left behind valuable gifts that could fortify the Foxens' hold on their land: Sadie the mule and shooting lessons. Whether the meaning of his name was a coincidence or not, he chose to accept it as ordained from above.

CHAPTER 23

In the weeks that followed, other members of the California Battalion stopped at the Foxens' hacienda on their way north after being discharged in Los Angeles. Disbanded from commission, Edwin Bryant and Lansford Hastings were among them. They brought news that Fremont had asked Jacobs to accompany him to San Diego after learning he had been replaced as governor by Colonel Mason of Kearney's dragoons, who fought in the battle at San Pasqual.

Don Julian said, "It's looking like the territory is experiencing the same kind of unstable leadership as in the Mexican and Spanish days." He took the news about Fremont in stride, though Guillermo struggled to make sense of it. It was unfair that the person responsible for recruiting them to help his army was now unavailable to protect them from the retribution sure to follow.

The heavy rains produced abundant grass in the winter of 1847. Spring followed with a bumper crop of wildflowers. South-facing hillsides were ablaze with orange poppies and fields of blue and white lupine that formed a waving checkerboard pattern in the breeze.

With the longer days came increased outdoor labor. Don Julian supervised Juan and Manuel in planting fields of wheat and corn. When that was done, the giant oak that had fallen in the storm was chopped up and the logs hauled in the lumbering oxcart. Firewood was stacked in neat piles by the outdoor kitchen. They set aside a long section from which boards were hewed for the rafters of the new stable. When that was done, they set to work making hundreds of adobe bricks for the walls. The new stable would enlarge and enclose the current open-air shelter adjacent to the corral. When completed, it would be large enough to protect the belle mare and the best cow ponies from horse thieves.

One day in late March while Guillermo and Angel were riding the range, they spotted buzzards circling an area to the west and heard cattle bawling in the distance. Upon investigating, they discovered one of their bulls lying in a field, surrounded by a dozen heifers and calves. The cows retreated a few steps as they approached. The fallen beast raised his head and let out a strangled bellow before letting his head loll back on the ground, his tongue protruding from a foaming mouth.

The boys circled him, and Guillermo said, "Look, there on his shoulder."

A hole the size of a peso seeped with blood that ran down the bull's side and puddled on the ground. Members of the bull's harem stretched out their necks and bawled in distress as their leader lay panting with glazed eyes, his dirt-encrusted nostrils flaring.

Angel pushed his hat back and fumed. "Some low-down scumbag shot him and left him for dead. Poor fellow. Wonder how long he's been here."

"We were here yesterday, so it happened either last night or this morning. Who would have done this?"

Angel said, "What do you want to bet it was Fuentes and Rios? Other than La Laguna's crew and Antonio at La Zaca, they're the closest for miles around." Antonio Palchaljet was a former mission Indian. A favorite of the padres, he was granted a modest parcel of land to farm. Staring down at the wounded animal whose side heaved with each labored breath, Angel said, "Takes one demented hombre to leave an animal like this. How about we fan out and see if we can find any tracks and see where they take us? Before we do, you want to finish him off, or shall I?"

Guillermo pulled out his rifle from its holster. "I'll do it." The feverish eye of the beast focused on him as he raised his rifle, cocked it, and aimed. The blast reverberated through the canyon, startling the heifers and their calves. The bull's head slumped for the last time, his sightless gaze fixed on his former harem. The buzzards squawked and flew out of formation.

The boys split up, searching for tracks. Angel canvassed the field for signs of churned up grass, and Guillermo headed down to some willows by the creek. It didn't take long for him to find what looked to be two sets of hoofprints in the moist dirt. "Angel! Over here!"

Angel galloped over and studied the tracks. "Looks like two riders spent some time here recently." Looking around, he said, "They'd have the cover of the trees and a clear shot of the bull grazing. Let's see where these take us."

They followed the tracks a ways west until they became obscured by cattle prints. They headed back to the corral where Sal and Chico were breaking a mustang. Sal was leaning against the corral fence when Guillermo and Angel came galloping into the yard.

"Papá! A bull's been shot! We found it out near Alisos Canyon," said Angel.

"What? A bull shot?" Sal rubbed a stubby brown hand over his mustachioed face as he took in the bad news. "Where?"

Chico had been walking a haltered horse around the corral. He called out, "What's the matter?"

"We was telling Papá how we found a bull shot in the shoulder."

"Judging by the pool of blood," said Guillermo, "we think it happened early this morning…maybe last night. We finished him off. Found some tracks down in the creek. We're thinking it was Fuentes and Rios. They could have easily cut across La Laguna land."

Chico threw his hat on the ground and fumed. "This is getting out of hand! Something's gotta be done to put a stop to this. I say we ride out to Corral de Cuati, have a look around."

Sal held up his hand. "Hold on, no one's going anywhere. I'll talk to el jefe and see what he thinks. He's supervising Manuel and Juan down in the wheat field." He swung onto his horse and galloped off to inform Don Julian of the latest attack.

"We're gonna need to round up the cattle so they're not anywhere near La Laguna's boundary," said Chico.

"I agree." Guillermo nodded. "But cattle can smell water from a league away. It's going to be hard keeping them from wandering back there, because that's where the best watering hole is. This could make the dry season especially long and difficult if we have to worry about our cattle drifting off to Alisos and Zaca Creeks."

"We have no choice but to keep the herd to the north, closer to the Sisquoc River," said Angel.

"Well, there's no denying it now," said Guillermo. "Someone's declared war against us."

So much for the peace treaty. The Californios were still out for blood.

CHAPTER 24

That night after evening prayers, Guillermo and Angel worked by candlelight in the blacksmith shed, molding bullets to increase the rancho's arsenal of ammunition. A growing pile of round balls sat on the workbench. In hushed tones, they discussed the day's events. The bull's killing meant the harassment was escalating.

Angel was pouring molten lead into the cast iron bullet mold when Guillermo detected the telltale aroma of his father's tobacco and whispered, "Here he comes."

Don Julian's bulky silhouette filled the doorway. Puffing on his pipe, he asked, "How's it coming? Looks like you got about…what, three dozen bullets made?"

"Uh-huh. This is number forty," said Guillermo. He clamped the scissor-like handles of the bullet mold, held them for a count of ten, and released them.

While the bullet sat cooling, Angel piped up. "We're down to the bottom of the barrel, el jefe. At this rate, we're going to be out of lead in another month."

Guillermo cringed at Angel's blunt delivery of the bad news.

"How in tarnation can that be?" Don Julian erupted, scratching his head in confusion. "I was counting on that lasting us until late spring." That was when he made his annual trip to the Tulare Valley for matorral weed, the ash of which made his Castile soap, and lead ore. His eyes narrowed. "I know you've been shooting a lot of coyotes lately. How many rounds you shooting a day?"

There it was. The dreaded question. "I limited it to five a day. Neely told me I should be practicing at least double, triple that, but I told him we didn't have the lead to spare. I've been working hard to make each shot count so if I'm under pressure, I'll have more confidence in my aim." Guillermo gulped and waited for his father's reaction.

Don Julian stared at his son and nodded several times, twisting his mouth as he considered his response. He took a deep breath and exhaled slowly. In a surprisingly mild tone, he said, "I see. I appreciate that you're trying to conserve ammo. Given the circumstances, it makes sense that you're trying to improve your aim. Lord knows we need protection around here, not just from the coyotes." Shifting his weight, he cocked his head and asked, "What I want to know is when you were planning to tell me? When we plumb ran out?"

"I'm sorry, Papá. I should have told you sooner." Shrugging, Guillermo said, "I don't know how it happened. One day I looked in there," he pointed to the barrel, "and couldn't believe how much it'd gone down. I kept waiting for a good time to tell you…but…" He remembered to meet his father's eye. "That was a mistake. Now I've put us in a bind. I'm sorry."

"There's no way I can make a trip to the Tulare Valley during calving season," said Don Julian. "I'll have to go soon or wait a couple months until after the roundup and matanza. Then it'll be hotter than blazes. We're spread mighty thin as it is, trying to keep the livestock out of the barley and wheat fields and make bricks for the new stable. Always more work than hands to do it." He took a deep breath, standing with his arms akimbo, taking in the situation. Guillermo sensed a heavy weight on his father's shoulders as Don Julian rubbed his chin whiskers. "I could probably trade some lead with the Olivera's crew at Tepusquet in exchange for the peach brandy I've set aside for the padres at the mission. We're going to have to use the Sisquoc River water this summer to keep the herd from wandering south, and I don't want to impose on them any more than I have to. Never know how long the dry season will last."

"I'm sorry, Papá."

"Well, no crying over spilt milk. I almost forgot the reason I came. Juan and Manuel skinned the bull, and the hide is stretched out to dry on the matanza field. The distraught cows followed them out there and were bawling something fierce. They're away from Alisos Canyon for the time being, and the whole herd needs to stay to the north. I don't want any wandering onto La Laguna Rancho. Consider it your number one job each day to check morning and late afternoon for strays. Let's think of that area as no-man's land. You hear me?"

That section of the Gutiérrez's' U-shaped land grant was narrowest near where the bull had been shot, separating Rancho Tinaquaic from Corral de Cuati by a mere half league.

Don Julian left for Tulare Valley three days later, taking with him Juan and Manuel, two pack horses, and Sadie. They would follow the Sisquoc River east through the rugged wilderness that stretched for twenty leagues. Some years earlier, he came across a small rancheria of Tulares who inhabited the western edge of the valley. They had been stricken with smallpox, and one family was near death. Don Julian stayed with them for several days, nursing them with herb poultices for their festering sores. They all survived, and in gratitude to the gringo shaman, each year they harvested the matorral weed and burned it, collecting the alkaline ash for his Castile soap. When he came on his annual trip, they exchanged it for various tools, dried fruit from the Foxens' orchard, and other supplies.

They also persuaded other Tulares not to harass their friend. When they learned that some other gringos discovered a mine back in the arid hills, they showed a curious Don Julian where it was. The miners had abandoned a vein of lead ore that when refined, provided him with lead for bullets.

Ten days later, Don Julian returned with four barrels of matorral ash, lead ore, and sobering news. Sitting around the campfire, he shared with the Gonzalezes and Guillermo what he had discovered. "My Tulare friends informed me that two vaqueros from this area had recruited a band of hostile Tulares to attack a gringo ranchero."

There were gasps of "I knew it!" as their suspicions were confirmed.

"When I asked why, they told me the bad ranchero had helped another gringo (Fremont) who was leading a large army. Because of him, the province would be overrun by many foreigners. Many will come in covered wagons over the eastern sierras and steal their land. The bad ranchero, meaning me, needed to be punished, so his horses were stolen, but he and his son caught up with them and rescued his horses."

"What do you want to bet those vaqueros were Fuentes and Rio?" said Guillermo.

"Sounds like it. My Tulare friends became alarmed at the news and feared they were targeting me. I reassured them all was well, but they noticed I took home double the lead ore from last year. I asked that they not tell anyone that I paid them a visit. The last thing I want is to involve them in my troubles. After I share some of the lead ore, we should have enough to get us through summer. When the hides and tallow are carted to Santa Barbara, I'll trade them for more lead at Ike's mercantile store. Until then, we all need to ration the lead so there's enough in case of an attack."

Heads nodded around the campfire. The threat was heating up. Who knew what Fuentes and Rios would do next to harm the Foxens?

CHAPTER 25

In the weeks following Don Julian's return from the Tulare Valley, Juan and Manuel were kept busy making adobe bricks for the stable. Each week, the walls of the stable grew higher. The servants hewed beams for the roof and boards for the door. Guillermo and Angel processed the lead ore so the refined metal could be molded into bullets. Rancho Tinaquaic was being fortified against future attacks.

The spring of 1847 heralded fields as lush as those of Don Julian's boyhood home in England. On the hillside behind the hacienda, a profusion of orange poppies opened their umbrella-like blooms each morning to catch the sun's rays and closed as the sun sank in the late afternoon. Dainty violets lined the trail, and jackrabbits bounded through the mustard, pursued by stealthy foxes. Coyotes skulked in the shadows as does with their fawns ventured into the fields to graze on the abundant forage.

As Easter approached, the Foxen girls excitedly planned for their first trip to the Santa Inés Mission since the previous summer when Alejandro was baptized and Panchita received her First Communion. It was decided that the Gonzalezes would break tradition; rather than attend Easter service, they would remain at the rancho with Juan and Manuel. The Foxens and Petra set out in a caravan midmorning on Saturday for the journey of seven leagues to the mission. The girls chattered about who would be in attendance. The men rode mainly in silence, preoccupied with the weightier matter of how they would be received by their paisanos.

When the group trotted onto the mission grounds at sunset, they were struck by its rundown appearance. In the intervening months, the arches of the long corridor had further deteriorated from the winter rains. Birds nested in the exposed rafters where the roof was exposed to the sky.

Upon seeing the Foxens, Padre Jimeño hurried out to meet them, calling, "Hola, Don Julian! Doña Eduarda! Bienvenidos!" His round face lit up as he took in the six Foxen children. "My, how you've all grown!" He adjusted his arms in the bell-shaped sleeves of his gray robe and said, "Eduarda, you will be happy to know your parents arrived a few hours ago. They've been anxiously awaiting your arrival. Mateo, my helper, will show you where they are camped."

Don Julian said, "Go ahead, dear, I'll be along shortly."

Doña Eduarda thanked the padre and followed the Chumash boy to where her parents were camped. Guillermo stayed behind with his father, hoping to hear news.

Slapping his saddlebags, Don Julian said, "Brought along some of my Castile soap and peach brandy for you and Padres Moreno and Sanchez."

"Ah, muchas gracias, Julian," said Father Jimeño. "You're always so kind to remember us. They're hearing confessions now. Tomorrow the three of us will celebrate Mass, and afterward there will be a fiesta. Do hope you'll stay for that."

"Well, we'll see how we are received and go from there. We've been waiting for tensions to subside before coming here."

"I understand. The Americano takeover has been a bitter pill for many of the paisanos, especially the old-timers.

As you can imagine, naturalized citizens like the Janssens and Covarrubias have a hard time concealing their elation. Those who think they will profit are pleased, and those who fear they'll lose status under the new regime are gnashing their teeth. Hopefully in honor of our Lord's resurrection, people will be willing to set aside their differences. How have you been faring otherwise? Heard you had several horses stolen in a raid some months ago. I was sorry to hear about that."

"Recovered all but one. The Tulares are getting sneakier. Had to resort to posting guards at night. Hard to stay awake at night and then herd cattle the next day. Could use a few more hands." Don Julian looked around. "From the looks of it, you're shorthanded as well."

"It's hard to believe there was a time we had more than a hundred thousand head of livestock and nearly two thousand novices. So many have died from disease that we're down to fewer than twenty Chumash, and most of those are old and infirm. The able-bodied ones sign on with the ranchos. With only a few vaqueros to tend our herd, it's shrunk to a few hundred head."

"How can that be? You have prime valley land along the river!"

"It seems our calves are rounded up by neighboring ranchos before we have a chance to brand them." Padre Jimeño shrugged.

"I see. So the greedy are taking advantage of your circumstances."

"Sí, tis true, I'm afraid." Padre Jimeño sighed.

They parted ways, and Guillermo and his father rode to a large pasture behind the church where several families had pitched tents and were relaxing around campfires. They

136

spotted the rest of the family encircled by jubilant relatives under a sprawling oak. When the Oliveras noticed the new arrivals, they rushed to greet them. Señora Olivera, Guillermo's grandmother, wept with joy. "My goodness, I can't believe how tall you've grown!"

Guillermo was taken aback by his abuela's shrunken appearance as she leaned heavily on her cane. Like its intricately carved ivory handle, her face was a net of wrinkles perched on a birdlike neck. As he bent low so she could plant a kiss on his cheek, he was enveloped by the fragrance of gardenias. A flood of happy memories washed over him as he recalled the frequent visits between their families when they had been neighbors, but Tío's tragic accident had ended all that when she had insisted they return to the safety of the pueblo. The death of her eldest son had taken a toll on her body. Outwardly she had aged a decade in less than two years.

In addition to his grandparents, women and children from various families swarmed around his mother and sisters, welcoming them with smiles and squeals of delight. While the females socialized, Guillermo helped his father unload the animals and set up camp. He was keenly aware of the Cota and Aguirre men glaring at them from across the way.

While their womenfolk visited, the former rebelistas observed the goings on without offering a nod or a wave in greeting. A year ago, they would have sauntered over and greeted his father with hearty "Bienvenidos!" Now they remained smoking on their tree stump seats, brooding at having a traitor in their midst. Don Julian busied himself with the task at hand and showed no sign of being bothered.

For the umpteenth time, Guillermo wondered if his friends Alfredo and Marco from the mission school would hold it against him for helping Fremont's army. Their reactions would probably mirror those of their fathers. If that were the case, Marco was more likely to give him the cold shoulder, as his family, the Carrillos, were ardent rebelistas.

It wasn't long before the church bells gonged five times. "Better hurry up if we're going to make confession," said Don Julian.

The girls scurried about freshening up from the long ride, washing their faces in a basin and donning lace mantillas atop their braided heads. Their father prodded them, saying, "Come along, girls. The padres will be heading off for supper within the hour."

The family set out across the field toward the church, Don Julian leading the way with long strides. The girls half ran to keep up while chattering about being reunited with their friends. Guillermo envied them. Until that happened for himself, he couldn't relax. Both Alfredo and Marco attended the seminary school in a two-story building adjacent to the courtyard of the church. It was a stone's throw from where he was now, and the prospect of running into them caused his stomach to knot.

As the family proceeded down the corridor, their footsteps echoed on the red tiles. When Don Julian reached for the heavy double door that led to the sanctuary, it swung open, and the Palchaljets emerged. The two families hadn't seen each other for nearly six months, not since the arrival of the Indian family's seventh child in the fall. The Foxens huddled around the infant girl who was held by her mother, Juanita. The baby stared with solemn, black eyes at the sea of smiling faces. Meanwhile, her brothers and sisters chased one other in circles around the nearest bougainvillea-vined arch. After visiting for a few minutes, Doña Eduarda excused herself and led the girls into the church. Guillermo lingered with his father in the corridor chatting with Antonio Palchaljet, while his wife and children returned to their campsite.

Antonio said, "I want to thank you again for pulling that infected tooth. Oo-whee! I've never had such pain! Whole side of my face was out to here." He held his hand a few inches from his bronzed cheek.

"Think nothing of it. I was happy to oblige," said Don Julian. "You'll be happy to know those pomegranate cuttings have sprouted into saplings, and I expect fruit next summer. Eduarda and the children can't wait."

"Good to hear. When are you planning to hold your cattle roundup?"

"I'm figuring in another six weeks, mid-May. What about you?"

"I'll wait until yours is over. Count me in. I'll bring along my oldest son to help."

"Thank you, Antonio. Appreciate your offer. I fear we could be shorthanded this year on account of hard feelings over me helping Fremont. I'm guessing you heard about that."

"I did, and I don't hold it against you none. Just between us, I'm hopeful about the takeover, though I have to pretend otherwise. It's no secret there are paisanos who resent me owning land. Perhaps the Yanks will protect my claim."

"So long as you have the proper documents, your land should be safe."

"I'm counting on that."

Glancing at Guillermo, Don Julian said, "We better be going, mijo. It wouldn't do for us to miss confession." Turning to Antonio, he said, "I'm sure there's a lotta folks who think my soul's in jeopardy of perdition for what I did. I'm not opposed to letting them think I'm repenting for my sins, though I'd do it again tomorrow if I were asked. My conscience is clear on that front. Well, it's been good chatting with you, Antonio. Have a good evening."

As they parted ways, Guillermo whispered, "It's a relief to know we can count on him to help us. Now we just have to wait and see about La Laguna's crew."

"Aye. Wouldn't hurt to say a prayer that Octaviano Gutierrez will be as generous as Antonio."

"Of course." Guillermo needed no prompting for that petition. More was at stake than getting help with the roundup. The loss of his friendship with either Alfredo or Marco would be painful, as the fun they had at roundups and fiestas were the highlights of Guillermo's year.

The following morning, Guillermo awoke to church bells joyously announcing Easter Sunday. The cloudless sky promised a mild spring day, fit for a celebration. The girls dressed with care, eager to wear the frocks they had carefully chosen for the occasion. When it came time to fix their hair, they lined up like a staircase with their mother at the top and Juanita at the bottom. Doña Eduarda quickly braided Martina's dark tresses with nimble fingers, forming coils of braids on either side of her head, tied with yellow ribbons. Meanwhile, each girl attended to her younger sister's hair: Martina fixed Ramona's while she worked on Panchita's. Panchita labored on Juanita's, sticking out her tongue in deep concentration as her small fingers struggled to twist the long strands of hair. "Hold still, Juanita! I can't do this if you keep moving."

"Ouch!" cried Juanita. "You're hurting me!"

"Now, girls, let's not fuss. We're almost done here, and Martina will finish up for you, Panchita."

Just as Martina was fastening the lace mantilla to Juanita's head, Don Julian called, "Come, ladies! You look beautiful. If we don't hurry, we'll have to stand."

Guillermo's stomach lurched as he tugged on the ruffled cuffs of his white shirt so they peeked beneath the wrist of his silver-trimmed black jacket.

"My, don't you look handsome!" His abuela gushed when she spotted him again. "It nearly takes my breath away how much you resemble Ausencio."

He flashed a dimpled smile and kissed her on the cheek. "Gracias. I wished I shared his confidence. Nothing seemed to bother him."

"Ah, give it time, my dear." She chuckled. "At fourteen, he was no different than you."

Guillermo chewed on that surprising tidbit while he combed back his wavy hair and tied it into a short pigtail with a leather thong. As he turned to go, he took a deep breath. The time of reckoning was upon him. Soon he would find out if Alfredo and Marco were still his friends.

His parents and grandparents led the way across the field to the mission quadrangle. Alejandro balanced on his father's broad shoulders, and the females lifted their long skirts to keep them from dragging in the dirt, while their fans swung by straps from their wrists. The family made a handsome sight, all decked out in their finest attire. His sisters' excited chatter revealed they shared his nervousness for what was to come. As they entered the arched corridor, they saw up ahead families filing into the sanctuary. Another couple glanced their way and offered friendly waves before disappearing inside. Hopefully those small gestures were a good omen.

Doña Eduarda gazed up at her husband. "I'm happy to be here. My heart is full."

The church bells rang for a final time, prompting the men to herd their families through the doors into the sanctuary. Whereas his mother and sisters had been treated with courtesy, Guillermo was under no illusion it would be the same for him and his father. He removed his hat and took a deep breath as he prepared to face the paisanos he and his father had betrayed. His old self would have jumped at the chance to beat a hasty retreat to postpone the inevitable, but he wasn't that scared rabbit anymore. He had faced worse danger and prevailed.

"So...are you ready, mijo?" asked Don Julian.

"Sí, I just want to get this over with."

A twinkle escaped Don Julian's pale eyes, and he nodded. "Remember, stand up tall and hold your head high. You have nothing to be ashamed of."

Guillermo thought that over. He would have preferred slipping in the back door to avoid being noticed by the whole congregation. Not because he was ashamed, he just didn't want to appear cocky. He prayed the Easter Mass would heal any enduring bitterness festering in the hearts of his paisanos.

CHAPTER 26

One by one, the Foxens and Oliveras filed in, taking turns kneeling in the center aisle and making the sign of the cross. Don Tomás led them to an empty row of benches five rows back.

Guillermo felt dozens of pairs of eyes follow him as they passed the De la Cuestas, Janssens, Ortegas, Carrillos, Villas, and Davilas—all families whose haciendas were in the vicinity of the Foxens'. One man glared at Don Julian with undisguised contempt, but his wife smiled weakly at Doña Eduarda, her mother, and the girls. Murmurs rippled through the church. There were a few demure smiles from other women and their daughters, but mostly the expressions were somber on this holiest of days.

A line of young men and boys sat in the front row, arranged according to height. The older ones, in their late teens and early twenties, were seminarians who hoped to be ordained in a few years, but most were twelve to sixteen— sons of wealthy rancheros, who had come there to study. Guillermo spotted Alfredo Gutíerrez, Diego Villa, and the Cabrera brothers. Marco Carrillo was not among them.

Guillermo followed his family to a bench and knelt to pray. Afterward, he sat and stared straight ahead at the altar. Beyond it stood a statue of Saint Inés holding a lamb, a crown of fresh flowers adorning her head. Above the altar, a gold, eight-armed chandelier hung from one of the massive beams in the thirty-foot-high ceiling.

The back doors to the sanctuary swung open, and the congregation shuffled to its feet as the choir sang the opening procession. Two seminarians in white albas were the first to make their way down the aisle. An acolyte followed, and to Guillermo's surprise, it was Marco. It was so strange to see his friend dressed in a long white alba, hatless, his hair slicked down, and his somber eyes focused straight ahead. It was impressive that he had been chosen for such a coveted role among the students. Next came the three friars with the portly Padre Sanchez leading the way, holding a silver crucifix on a long pole.

When the group reached the front of the sacristy, Marco knelt, rose, and lit the two altar candles, which filled the apse in a golden glow. The two seminarians swung censers on chains, dispersing the incense smoke over the altar.

Padre Sanchez, began the Mass by reciting the Creed. Voices from the choir loft repeated the refrain, "San-to Dios, San-to Fu-erte, San-to im-mor-tal, Li-bra, nos Se-ñor de to-do mal." *Holy God, holy stronghold, holy immortal, free us from all evil.*

The theme of the Mass was sacrifice. Padre Sanchez exhorted the parishioners to be willing to sacrifice that which they held dear in order for the kingdom of God to be realized on earth.

Ay, caramba, Guillermo thought. Did Padre really mean that he was supposed to be willing to give up his family, Benito, and Rancho Tinaquaic? How could losing any of those further the kingdom of God? As Guillermo saw it, it would only serve to make him angry at God.

At the conclusion of the service, Padre Sanchez said, "As the school year draws to a close, we want to thank God for the school's third year of existence. As the only one of its kind in the province, families in the area are blessed to be able to send their sons here to receive a formal education. However, our dwindling herd of cattle is hard pressed to supply sufficient food for thirty students. I'm humbly asking every family to donate as many heifers as they can. This sacrifice will enable us to continue to do God's work in preparing our young men for the future." He made the sign of the cross, blessing the congregation.

There was an undercurrent of grumbling among the rancheros. Guillermo assumed Padre's plea for donations was a result of greedy neighbors stealing the seminary's calves before they could be branded. His father would respond to the plea with several heifers, even though he wasn't able to afford the three hundred dollars in tuition to send Guillermo to the boarding school.

The congregation stood as the procession of friars, altar boys, and the acolyte made its way down the aisle to the back of the church. Guillermo nodded to Antonio Paljalchet, who was standing in the back with his wife and children. Like the other Chumash in attendance, his lowly status dictated that he occupy the rear portion of the church despite being a landowner.

Martina gave a little wave to Carmelita Cota, daughter of Don Pablo, who returned the greeting with a furtive smile. Carmelita's father had passed without acknowledging Don Julian, who was posted by the center aisle and had also been snubbed by the Villas. The Dens and Janssens bestowed warm smiles on the Foxens as they filed out. That was encouraging. One by one, the benches emptied as families filed out of the church, spilling into the courtyard and milling about, chatting with friends and family. Occasions such as this provided the paisanos the opportunity to socialize and catch up on news.

Before Guillermo was able to set off in search of his friends, he heard girlish squeals behind him. "Martina! Ramona!" called out Alfredo's younger sisters.

"Chatta! Arcadia!" exclaimed his sisters.

The four girls jumped with delight, hugging their friends they saw so seldom. Panchita looked on with hopeful eyes. After a few moments, Chatta turned to her and said, "Panchita! How pretty you look in your dress."

Panchita broke into a broad smile at being included.

"Cómo estas, Guillermo?" the girls said.

He muttered a greeting and excused himself to seek out the girls' brother. Through the crowd, he could make out a banquet table laden with baskets of fruit and sweets in the shade of the corridor. Sure enough, Alfredo was hovering nearby. As he popped something into his mouth, Marco Carrillo clamped him in a headlock from behind. They playfully scuffled, and Alfredo managed to slip away but not before sticking out a lanky leg to trip his attacker. Two señoras in charge of the refreshments shooed them away from the table like pesky mosquitoes. As if their lack of decorum wasn't enough, their croaking laughter branded them as adolescents. They contrasted sharply with their pious counterparts, the seminarians, who huddled in quiet chats with the friars.

As Guillermo made his way across the courtyard, two sprite-like figures darted out in front of him. He halted abruptly but not in time to avoid colliding with one and stepping on a delicate slipper.

"O perdóneme!" he blurted. He tipped his hat to a pretty raven-haired girl and her companion, Carmelita Cota. "I'm so sorry. Hope I didn't hurt you!"

Carmelita's friend said, "Oh no, I'm fine. We should have been more careful. My apologies!" She cleared her throat and cast Carmelita a look.

Carmelita said, "Guillermo, I want you to meet my cousin, Maria Estefana."

He bowed slightly. "It's a pleasure to meet you."

"It is mine as well," Maria said, peering up at him with velvety-lashed eyes. "You're not one of the students, are you?" The fringe on her shawl swayed as she dusted herself off from where they had bumped.

"No, I'm not."

"Maybe we'll see you at the fiesta this afternoon, no?"

"Uh, I'm not sure we're staying for it. Maybe."

"Well, let's hope so."

"Hasta la vista!" Carmelita called out as she dragged Maria away.

Guillermo heard them giggle as they were swallowed up by the crowd. He was still reeling from the encounter when Señoras Den and Janssens had turned around and smiled. Rosa Den, the eldest daughter of Don Julian's godfather, Daniel Hill, said, "You're Eduarda's son, aren't you? I almost didn't recognize you. You've grown so tall."

The best he could manage in response to the lovely señora was a shrug and a nod.

She smiled. "So glad your family was able to come. We're looking forward to visiting with your mother. It's been a while." She fluttered her ivory fan and gazed up at him with kind eyes. Her friendly words helped relieve his anxiety as he stood in the semi-hostile crowd.

"We're happy to be here too. We've missed coming to church."

"I can well imagine you have," said Señora Janssens. "Go help yourself to the refreshments. Lent is over, and now we can indulge. I'm sure a growing boy like you has quite an appetite."

"Sí, muchas gracias."

He did not recognize the man standing behind her, staring at him through narrow slits. The hawk-nosed señor seemed to ignore the conversation of his compadres as he blew smoke from his cigar in a deliberate manner. Two creases between his thick eyebrows gave him a menacing look aside from the long-barreled pistol strapped to his leg. *Ay caramba, another aggrieved paisano,* Guillermo thought.

Eager to escape the stranger's glare, Guillermo bobbed and wove his way to his friends. As he closed in on them, he noticed that Alfredo had grown gangly during the intervening months and was sporting a wispy mustache.

Marco, a few inches shorter, strutted about with his usual swagger, chest out and shoulders back. When he turned and spotted Guillermo approaching, he put his hands on his hips and announced, "Well, look who's here! If it isn't Fremont's guide!"

CHAPTER 27

uillermo cringed and froze in his tracks. He glanced around sheepishly, wondering who had heard. A group of rancheros standing nearby halted their conversation and stared. The women in charge of the food table huddled behind their fans.

"Hola. So you heard." Guillermo batted a fly that buzzed around his hot face. "It was just something I got roped into." Eager to deflect the conversation away from himself, he said, "Almost didn't recognize you, Marco, in your white alba and pious look. All you were missing was a halo."

"Like you, it was something forced upon me by my father. He told Padre Sanchez he wanted me to begin training to be an altar boy, so this year I started as an acolyte. Lucky for him but unlucky for me, it happened to be my turn in the rotation this Sunday."

Shaking his head, Guillermo chuckled. "Fathers. Always trying to mold and shape us." He asked, "How's the year been going?"

Alfredo shrugged. "It's been easier than last. My Latin's getting better, but if you ask me, we should be learning English." He popped a couple purple grapes into his mouth.

Marco cocked his head in disbelief. "Speak for yourself! I have no interest in learning the language of the infidels! Let them learn Español!"

"You live in a dream world," said Alfredo, spitting out grape seeds. He leaned down into Marco's face. "We lost the war. Remember? Like Father Sanchez said, the defeated are absorbed into the dominant culture. That's the way it works in war."

Marco covered his ears. "Basta! Stop the preaching. Lighten up." He dropped his hands and looked around. "I don't know about you, but I'm ready to cut loose and have some fun. The fiesta should be starting soon. Are you staying for the fandango, Guillermo?"

"Maybe. I hope so."

Marco's eyebrows arched in surprise. "Your father took a risk showing up today. Attending Mass is one thing, but staying for the fiesta? Are you afraid there could be some trouble? You're surrounded by men like my father who still consider themselves loyal Mexicans."

Guillermo glanced back at his father, who was chatting with Augustin Janssens and Nicolas Den. "You're right, but some are willing to put aside their political differences. For today, anyway."

"Hmph! Easy to do for men like Janssens and Den who were foreign-born like your father. Their ancestors didn't sacrifice to settle this Spanish colony like ours did."

"Maybe not, but they've worked hard to build their ranchos," said Guillermo.

"So? They wouldn't have gotten their land in the first place if they hadn't taken an oath of allegiance."

Alfredo glared. "Hey, c'mon. Don't be like this. We haven't seen Guillermo in months."

Guillermo held up his hand to Alfredo. "He's right. My father did take a risk in coming here, but we haven't been to Mass since last fall. How long are we supposed to stay away?" He glanced over at his sisters in a circle of chatting girls and smiled. "My sisters have missed their friends." He paused. "Just so you know, Marco, my mother's cousin, Don José Pico, was mercifully taken prisoner by Fremont instead of being executed. My father intended to remain neutral, but circumstances forced him to take sides. My mother didn't want her cousin to possibly march into an ambush at Gaviota. It all came down to loyalty for family over politics, simple as that."

Before Marco had a chance to respond, Alfredo said, "Come on, Marco, don't hold his father's actions against him. Ay, caramba, I forgive you all the time for being…you." He playfully jabbed Marco in the stomach with his elbow, causing him to flinch.

"As if you're perfect!" Guillermo made a fake move to punch Alfredo in the stomach, causing the other boy to flinch. Marco smirked.

José Covarrubias came up from behind Guillermo and slapped him on the back. "Good to see you, mijo! Heard you were quite the hero up on the mountain, coaxing terrified horses down in that storm to beat all storms. Good for you!" The portly Frenchman held up two glasses of el fresco and said, "Heading back over to catch up on the news with your father. So glad your family was able to make it today!" As he turned his head to go, he set off an explosion of swinging dangles on his wide-brimmed hat and disappeared into the crowd.

Marco's face had gone dark as he sneered. "My uncle forgets that many of our horses were stolen. Wonder how many of them died as a result?" He spat on the ground in disgust.

"Hey, that reminds me!" Alfredo said, his eyes brightening, and he hooked a thumb toward the corrals. "How about we get out of here and show Guillermo El Loco?"

"Hmm." Marco nodded. "That's an idea."

Grateful to have the subject changed, Guillermo slapped Marco on the back. "Sure, show me this El Loco."

"I will, but first I need something to eat." Marco stepped over to the banquet table and snagged a peach empañada. Guillermo and Alfredo winked at each other behind his back, and Guillermo mouthed, "Muchas gracias."

Alfredo waved him off, mouthing in return, "Por nada."

Marco turned and started to make his way through the crowd. Alfredo grabbed two empañadas and handed one to Guillermo, smiling. "I'm glad you came today." They hurried to catch up with Marco, bobbing and weaving their way around señoras and their boisterous husbands.

Guillermo caught a glimpse of his father in conversation with Nicolas Den and José Covarrubias. Don Julian looked relaxed as he puffed on his pipe, nodding to Den and smiling. His sisters had moved to a corner of the courtyard, standing in a cluster of girls, their eyes merry with delight. His mother was sitting nearby on a bench visiting with her mother and aunt, Señora Cota. As for himself, he was relieved to be reunited with his friends.

Marco swaggered past Carmelita and Maria, touching his hat and acknowledging them with a gallant, "Hola, señoritas!"

They smiled and nodded at him from behind their fans. When Alfredo and Guillermo passed, they cooed, "Ho-la, Alfredo. Ho-la, Guillermo."

Intent on seeing El Loco, the boys returned curt greetings and continued on their way. Alfredo arched his eyebrows and said, "Maria's pretty, no?"

Guillermo grinned and flashed his dimples. "Ay, yi, yi! Sí." A realization hit him. "Let me guess who her father is." He craned his neck, scanning the crowd. "Is that him over there, talking to Pablo Cota? With the pistola hanging from his waist?"

Alfredo glanced in Cota's direction. "That's him all right. Why?"

"He glared at me earlier. Now I know why."

"If I were you, I'd steer clear of his daughter."

"Sure you're not trying to scare me off so you can make a move?"

Alfredo grinned broadly, raising a hand. "I swear. I'm just looking out for you, amigo!" He winked.

CHAPTER 28

Alfredo led Guillermo to the stables and corrals behind the mission courtyard. Marco was leaning against the rail of a corral where a group of vaqueros was whooping and hollering, and the shrill sound of a whinny came from inside the pen.

Guillermo asked, "What's the story with this horse?"

Alfredo said, "We're guessing he was left behind by Fremont's army, because his brand isn't from around here. He's been spotted roaming the valley and hills for weeks now. Attached himself to the mission's caballada and was finally lassoed last week, but he turned out to be soured. Won't let anyone near him. He's dangerous, so that's why he's called El Loco."

They squeezed in beside Marco, climbing onto a horizontal rung in the fence to view the action. Guillermo's stomach knotted when he spotted Fuentes in the center of the corral with a whip in one hand and a rope looped around the Appaloosa's neck in the other. Rios was chasing the horse, trying to get it to halt. Every time it changed direction to avoid him, the whip was cracked near its haunches. The vaqueros' brutish actions only served to work the animal into a frenzy.

"Show him who's boss!" yelled Marco.

Guillermo shuddered. Unlike some caballeros who

154

handled horses with a heavy hand, Guillermo believed in winning them over through trust rather than fear.

"Padre Sanchez is offering him to whoever can ride him," said Alfredo. "He's had to be corralled by himself."

Loud cheering came from the adjacent field where a rider waved a silver coin in the air. One of the vaqueros' favorite pastimes was to gallop across the field at full speed, lean far out of the saddle, and pick up a coin amid the dirt, dust, and hooves.

Guillermo turned his attention back to the Appaloosa. "He's a beauty. Powerful looking with those muscled flanks and hind legs. How tall would you say he is, sixteen hands at the withers?"

"At least. Much larger than the typical cow pony, that's for sure," Marco said. "I heard if he can't be saddled and rode, he'll be shot."

Alfredo said, "From the looks of his scars, he's had a tough time of it in the wild."

"It's surprising he survived as long as he has," said Guillermo. "He likely came west with the settlers who traveled across the plains. His owner was probably recruited by Fremont and forced to abandon him when he went lame. Either that or he was stolen from a rancho up north. The horses were in sorry shape by the time they arrived here in the valley. He appears to be limping slightly on his right hind leg. Scarred up pretty good."

The Appaloosa changed directions abruptly and headed toward Fuentes, who yelled, "Ghee! Ghee!" He threw up his hands to stop the horse from his mindless pacing. El Loco reared up and pawed dangerously close to Fuentes' head with his sharp hooves. Fuentes narrowly ducked out of the way, letting go of the rope. He scrambled to safety over the corral fence amid jeers from onlookers.

Rios chased after the trailing rope and grabbed hold of it, but with bulging eyes, the Appaloosa reared and kicked at him too. Rios released his end of the reata and fled for safety over the corral rails. This brought on a new wave of jeers and yells from onlookers. The horse circled the corral, foam spraying from his muzzle. He shook his long, white mane and snorted as the rope dragged in the dirt behind him. His high-pitched whinny declared him the victor of that round.

Another cheer went out from across the way as a rider waved a coin in his hand.

Fuentes threw up a hand in disgust. "He's a hopeless piece of horse flesh! I've always said a light-colored horse was good fer nothin'! He's proved my point! If you boys want to waste yer time, be my guest!" He gave Guillermo a smirk and spit in front of where he was perched on the railing. "Hope you went to confession jest in case." He flashed an evil grin and jumped down from the fence.

Laughter rang out at Fuentes joke, and it was clear he enjoyed his role as the ringleader of the group. His cohorts shared swigs from their flasks as they ambled away on bow-legs to watch the competition at the adjoining field.

The boys leaned against the railing and watched the horse pace around the corral, whinnying and shaking his mane. Alfredo groaned. "Great. Now they've got him all riled up, and they leave him with a rope around his neck. Ay, caramba."

"Let's give him time to calm down," said Guillermo. "Eventually Fuentes is going to want his reata back, and the more he drinks, the uglier his mood will get. Let's hope we can get the rope off El Loco before he returns."

Alfredo looked at him askance. "We? If you think I'm going in there, *you're* loco. What about you, Marco?"

"Um...maybe." Marco's dark eyes followed the Appaloosa as it high-stepped around the corral.

El Loco's pacing slowed, and he backed into the corner opposite from where the boys were perched. He shook his mane and snorted at them. To Guillermo's surprise, Marco swung his leg over the top railing and jumped into the corral.

Alfredo called out, "Ay, caramba, Marco! What are you doing? Want to get yourself killed?"

"Re-lax. You're acting like an old woman, Alfredo," said Marco. He picked up the whip and slowly approached the horse. He hadn't taken five steps before the Appaloosa whinnied and pawed the ground. Instead of heeding the horse's warning, Marco proceeded toward him.

Guillermo whispered, "What's he doing?"

The horse charged. Marco raised one hand and cracked the whip with the other, striking the horse on his shoulder. He tried jumping out of the way but stumbled and fell backward, and the agitated horse reared as Marco rolled on the ground, curling himself into a ball.

"Dios mio!" Guillermo muttered in disgust. He leaped over the corral railing, waving his arms to distract the horse, enabling Marco to scramble to safety. He stood still, speaking softly to the horse. El Loco charged, reared, and pawed the air above his head. Guillermo backed up a few paces but held his ground. Puzzled, the horse shook his head and snorted. Seeing it as a good sign, Guillermo turned his back on El Loco and sauntered along the fence line. When he reached one corner of the corral, he did an about-face and walked slowly but confidently toward the horse. When he got fifteen feet from El Loco, he did another about-face and retraced his steps.

"Be careful," Alfredo whispered. "His tail's swishing, and his ears are back. I'll let you know if he charges."

The Appaloosa whinnied and pawed the ground, warning him to stay away. Guillermo rounded the pen and slowly approached from the other direction. He stopped several yards away and began rooting through his pocket. El Loco stepped back, bumping his rear into the railing. He eyed the intruder warily. One ear was up, the other pressed against his head. He trumpeted a warning and shook his mane. Guillermo noticed the horse's left eye was cloudy. He took several steps to the right and extended his hand, offering some panoche, a kind of sugar. "It's okay, boy. I'm not going to hurt you."

The horse studied him with his good eye and sniffed the sweet treat. Attracted to the smell, he stretched his neck toward Guillermo's hand.

"C'mon, I know you want some."

The horse stamped, warning Guillermo not to come closer. Guillermo backed up, giving the skittish horse his space.

"Just drop it on the ground and let him get it on his own!" called Marco.

"What's wrong with you, Marco?" asked Alfredo. "You act like you want him to balk."

Of course he did. Guillermo knew the last thing Marco wanted was for him to get credit for saddling El Loco. The two friends were fiercely competitive, and every time they saw one another, they parted ways with the loser chafing at the bit to redeem himself at their next contest.

Two outings ago, Guillermo had burned with humiliation after Marco baited him to ride a newly broken mustang. Knowing Guillermo couldn't resist showing off in front of the group, Marco secretly hid burrs under the saddle blanket before Guillermo mounted. He'd been thrown off horses plenty of times, but that time was different. He'd heard his father use the term "hurricane deck" to describe the severe bucking of a bronco but never understood it until that day. He managed to remain in the saddle for two bucks before being catapulted through the air and landing in a heap on the ground, the wind knocked out of him. When he managed to gulp some air, a sharp pain in his side told him a rib had been cracked or broken, but the memory of Marco belly laughing and comparing him to a rag doll as he flew through the air hurt worse than his ribs or pride. It fueled Guillermo's determination to work all summer long to settle the score, despite his lingering pain.

Chico Gonzalez devised their stunt and worked tirelessly with Guillermo and Angel to perfect the timing of the reata throw. He had Angel stand like a scarecrow holding a knife, the blade pointing skyward, with just enough room on the handle for the reata to fit between the top of his hand and the hilt. When the big day came, by all accounts Guillermo executed the throw perfectly, but it came at a price. When he jerked the lassoed knife out of Angel's hand, its sharp blade grazed Angel's cheek. Six stitches were needed to close the gaping wound.

This latest competition was bound to drive a wedge between them, but better that than allow the horse to be brutalized by Fuentes. Guillermo walked along the corral perimeter and approached El Loco from the right. Again he extended his hand with the panoche, coaxing the horse with a clucking sound. "C'mon, boy. It's okay."

The horse's nostrils flared as he pawed the ground while keeping an eye on the treat. Guillermo took one cautious step forward. The horse whinnied and retreated, bumping the railing for a second time. Guillermo turned around, walked to the center of the corral, and stopped. He was facing Alfredo and Marco, who were poised on the railing, watching El Loco behind him. Alfredo's broadening smile told him the horse's curiosity was overriding his fear, but Marco's face was a mask. Guillermo heard a neigh and then the clopping of hooves in his direction. He took another step forward and heard El Loco follow. If the horse wanted to, he could have struck Guillermo with his hoof, but instead he followed as Guillermo slowly walked. When Guillermo stopped, so did El Loco. They circled the corral two times.

Guillermo turned to look at the horse and offered the panoche again. The Appaloosa studied him, took a tentative step forward, and sniffed the extended hand. Stretching his neck, he took the treat with his lips and tongue. Guillermo murmured encouragement and rubbed his forehead while the horse chewed. The rope was inches from his fingers, but he resisted the urge to reach for it, turned, and walked several steps away. El Loco followed and nickered. When Guillermo ignored him, El Loco bumped his shoulder with the bridge of his nose, sending Guillermo a couple stuttering steps forward.

Guillermo turned and said, "Oh, so now you want to be amigos. Good. Let's see if I have any more." He rooted through his pockets, found a morsel, and offered it to the horse. El Loco sniffed and gobbled it up. This time, he allowed Guillermo to rub his shoulder as well as his forehead. In one smooth motion, Guillermo slipped the rope from his neck with his left hand while petting him with his right. "He's got scars on his legs. Probably got them from running through the chaparral. Somehow he injured his left eye. Not sure if he can see out of it."

When he turned back toward the boys, he saw Alfredo's eyes shining with admiration, but Marco had turned away, gesturing across the way. Alfredo put his fingers to his lips and whistled. "Hey, Fuentes. Come see this!"

"What are you doing?" Guillermo hissed.

"Relax. You need a saddle and blanket, don't you? You can use his."

Normally Guillermo would have waited longer before attempting to saddle a horse so early in the process of winning its trust, but Marco was intent on forcing the issue. When Guillermo returned his attention to El Loco, the horse had stiffened and retreated two steps.

Again Guillermo rooted through his pockets and whispered, "It's okay, boy, you're fine, no one's going to hurt you." When he found another piece of panoche, he offered it with an extended hand. The whip lay in the dirt where it had been abandoned a dozen paces away. He heard from behind, "What do we have here? Señor Foxen has him eating out of his hand? Suppose he's planning on saddling him, no?"

Guillermo turned to see Fuentes watching from atop a handsome black gelding.

"Too soon for that. He's just getting used to being touched."

Fuentes scoffed. "It's not like it's the first time he's been broken. It'll all come back to him soon enough."

Guillermo knew he was being baited.

"Well, if you won't try it," said Marco, "let someone else do it. How about it, Alfredo? Guillermo will stay in the corral and help you."

Guillermo heard high-pitched giggles behind him.

"Why would I do that? If anyone's going to saddle him, it's Guillermo. The horse trusts him, not me. Back off, Marco."

Guillermo wished the bickering would stop. The tension in the air wasn't helping the situation.

"Hurry up, Guillermo. If you don't put a saddle on him, I will," said Marco. "Your choice."

"Thatta boy, Marco. I'll help you," said Fuentes. In no mood to wait, he swung off his horse and undid his saddle. He hoisted it onto the fence rail and removed the two layers of blankets, pulled the reins over his horse's head and removed the bit from his mouth. El Loco watched with wary interest.

Marco called out, "Last chance, Guillermo. If you're not going to ride him," he stuck out his arm, "hand him over!"

Guillermo knew if he thwarted Marco's plan to tame the Appaloosa, he could forget trying to repair the hard feelings from their last encounter, but he wasn't about to relinquish El Loco to their brutish ways. It was obvious the horse had experienced trauma in the wild these past months. What had been out of the question minutes before was looking like the best chance El Loco had of being rehabilitated. Rubbing the horse's nose, he said, "What do you think, amigo? Willing to give it a try?"

El Loco looked at him with a big, liquid eye, nudging his chest and sniffing for a treat.

"You can have more if you let me put a blanket on you."

The horse followed him to the fence where Guillermo retrieved the blanket.

Fuentes climbed up on the fence next to Marco, jabbed him in the ribs, and winked. In a loud whisper, he said,

"Knew he'd take the bait. Can't help himself." He chuckled and sneered at Guillermo. "Show us how it's done, Señor Bron-co Buster." He jerked his head to his cohorts, saying, "This oughtta be good," which elicited a round of snickers.

How had circumstances spiraled out of control so fast? Guillermo's intention had been to keep a low profile and reunite with his friends. Now he was in a showdown with the person who threatened his family and may have had a hand in killing their livestock! Ay, yi, yi! He needed to clear his mind of the chatter and focus on keeping El Loco's trust.

Guillermo carried the blanket back to the middle of the corral, running his hand along the underside of it, checking for burrs. Sure enough, he found a couple and furtively picked them off. He hid them in his hand so Fuentes wouldn't know he'd found them.

An audience had gathered. The expectant faces of his sisters, Alfredo's sisters, and Maria squeezed in on the corral fence. O Dios mio! As if there wasn't enough pressure!

El Loco followed, eyeing the folded gray wool. "Remember this?" Guillermo let the Appaloosa sniff it. "I'm going to lay it on your back, but you have to hold still. Comprende?" He ran his hand along the horse's back, getting him used to being touched, lifted the blanket, and laid it gently on his back. El Loco moved to the side, looking back at Guillermo in curiosity. As Guillermo smoothed out the blanket, the Appaloosa whinnied and swished his white tail, but it was all for show. In a few minutes Guillermo had him outfitted and ready to ride.

Several more vaqueros gathered around the corral, and Juan Carlos from La Laguna said, "Want me to hold him for you?"

As much as Guillermo would have preferred to have him help, he knew Marco was chafing to show off in front of the audience. It was a risk trusting him, but it might ease the tension between them if he got to share the limelight. "No thanks. Marco can do it."

"Sure!" said Marco as he jumped into the corral.

"Make sure you approach from his right side," said Guillermo. "He's got a bad left eye. Think that's been part of his problem."

Marco swaggered over to the horse's right, greeting him with a steady voice. "Hey boy, you're doing great."

Guillermo sensed from Marco's tone that he genuinely wanted the horse to overcome his fear. If they succeeded, Fuentes' plan would backfire. Guillermo handed the reins to Marco and stroked the horse's shoulders. He whispered in the horse's ear, "I'm going to climb on your back, and you're going to be fine."

"Want a boost?" asked Marco.

"Let's walk him over to the fence, and I'll mount him from the railing."

They led El Loco to the fence, away from onlookers. Guillermo climbed onto the first horizontal rail. As Marco was getting El Loco in position, a cheer went out from the crowd across the way. Alfredo shushed the onlookers. "Quiet!"

As Guillermo swung his leg over El Loco's back, Fuentes yelled, "Bra-vo!"

Startled, El Loco reared back, whinnied shrilly, and pawed the air. Marco scrambled out of the way, narrowly missing being struck by a hoof. Guillermo grabbed the saddle horn with both hands as his head was tossed back and forth. He struggled to get a toehold in one of the stirrups, but the violent motion kept him off balance. The horse whinnied and kicked, doing his best to buck his rider off. Guillermo managed to hold onto the saddle horn with one hand and swing his other arm out to the side for balance. He relaxed his body enough to fall into El Loco's rhythmic gyrations.

Girlish voices cheered him on. "You can do it, Guillermo!" and "Stay on him!"

After a long minute of intermittent bucking, El Loco's frenzy subsided. The fight had gone out of him, and he circled the corral in a high-stepping cantor.

Guillermo leaned forward and stroked the Appaloosa's neck. "Thatta boy. See, it's not so bad. You're doing great."

"You did it! Muy bien!" Alfredo called out. "Want us to open the gate so you can ride around the grounds?"

Guillermo patted the horse's neck. "Think you can do this, amigo?" El Loco nickered. "Go ahead and open the gate!"

While Guillermo trotted El Loco around the corral two more times, Alfredo called out, "He's looking good! He should do fine!"

Guillermo leaned down and patted the horse, whispering, "He's right. You'll do fine. Let's show everyone what you can do." He reined El Loco out through the open gate. As they headed across the wide yard of the mission grounds, he felt the horse's taut muscles relax beneath him.

One of the vaqueros from the playing field cried out, "Hey, look at that! El Loco's been tamed! Who's the rider?"

"Guillermo Foxen!" cried another vaquero, his teeth flashing behind his handlebar mustache.

Ramona lifted her skirt and hurried across the mission grounds to the courtyard to announce the news. A short time later, Padre Sanchez and a group of people streamed out into the corridor to see for themselves, Guillermo's father and grandfather among them. Pedro Ortega and two compadres stood in the rear of the crowd, sipping drinks and nodding.

Guillermo chuckled and whispered, "Gracias, El Loco. There's no better way to win a caballero's respect than to handle a difficult horse. This is shaping up to be my lucky day!"

Padre Sanchez called out, "Well, congratulations, Guillermo! You managed to saddle and ride El Loco! He's yours to keep if you want him!"

Guillermo smiled, took off his hat, and bowed to the onlookers. "Gracias! He's a fine mount. From now on, I'm calling him El Rey. He carries himself like a king!" He trotted around the mission grounds before returning the Appaloosa to the corral.

Marco ran up to meet him at the gate. "Bravo! You did it!"

Alfredo said, "Well done! You had me worried there for a while! Thought for sure you were going to be bucked off!"

"I'm as surprised as you are. I thought for sure I'd wind up flying through the air." Guillermo turned to Marco. "Want to show Padre Sanchez you can ride him as well?"

"Really?"

"Absolutely!" Guillermo dismounted and handed Marco the reins. "Let me give you boost."

As Guillermo watched Marco trot El Rey around the mission grounds and wave his hat at the onlookers, he marveled at the turn of events. If his luck held out, maybe he'd squeeze in a dance with Maria. That would be the perfect ending to the day—as long as her father didn't notice.

CHAPTER 29

As the sun sank behind the oak-studded hills, guitars and violins began warming up for the evening's festivities. The lilting melody of "El Jarabe," the Mexican hat dance, called the revelers to the courtyard. Chairs were assembled along the wall in the corridor for the older folks. A merry José Covarrubias started things off by escorting his wife to the dance floor and showing off their impressive footwork. One by one, couples joined them while onlookers clapped in rhythm with the beat. Laughter echoed in the quadrangle as the fandango got underway. Girls whispered behind their fans, furtively glancing across the way at the young men who leaned against the opposite wall. The Cabrera brothers were the first to cross the courtyard and ask Chatta and Arcadia to dance. That prompted Marco and Alfredo to ask Maria Estefana and Martina, which emboldened Guillermo to ask Carmelita Cota. Soon, five young couples were stamping their feet to the lively beat.

Every time Guillermo glanced Maria's way, she flashed him a coy smile and fluttered her velvety lashes. She moved nimbly across the dance floor, holding her ruffled skirt in one hand and twirling it this way and that with Marco by her side.

When the song ended, they remained on the dance floor, catching their breath and chatting. Judging by the silly grin on Alfredo's face, he was smitten with Martina. Though more reserved than Carmelita and Maria, her shining eyes revealed that she enjoyed herself.

Guillermo kept an eye on Pedro Ortega, who sat on a bench across the way, smoking and chatting with some other dons. Occasionally, he glanced in his daughter's direction and then returned his attention to his companions.

When the music resumed, the couples remained with their partners for two more dances. The girls announced they were thirsty, and they headed for the refreshment table.

Guillermo whispered in Marco's ear, "How about we switch partners?"

"Aren't you worried about her father?"

"He left a while ago, and I want to squeeze in a dance before he returns. Please." Guillermo flashed a dimpled smile. "Just one. You ask Carmelita, and I'll ask Maria."

The music started again, but before he had a chance to ask Maria, Guillermo felt a tap on his shoulder. When he turned around, Sarita Covarrubias' hopeful face peered up at him. "Would you like to dance, Guillermo?"

He did his best to hide his disappointment. "Sí, of course."

She was light on her feet despite her plump figure. Like her convivial father, she had an infectious laugh. Guillermo spotted Ramona dancing with eleven-year-old Lino Ruiz. She flashed a grin in his direction, delighted to see him dancing with her friend. Leave it to Ramona to intervene just as he was prepared to make his big move.

When the dance ended, Marco took off his hat and placed it on Maria's head. She laughed and tossed it on the ground, meaning she had no intention of being his partner for the evening. When he turned his attention to Martina,

Guillermo saw his chance. He excused himself from Sarita and made a beeline for Maria Estefana, praying Alfredo would not get to her first. He snuck up behind her, plopped his hat on her head and followed her as she glided around the floor, with hands on her swaying hips. He stamped his foot in time with the music, uncertain if she knew he was the owner of the hat.

She turned to face him and giggled with delight. "Finally!" She winked. "I was beginning to think I would have to ask you. Come!" She grasped his hand and dragged him to the center of the dance floor.

Guillermo scanned the crowd for her father but did not see him—if he returned and saw them dancing, would he cause a scene? After two dances, Guillermo was willing to face the consequence of his rash act. This was the first fandango where he danced more than watched. It was great fun, and he did not want the evening to end. He stared down into Maria Estefana's sparkling brown eyes and asked, "Will your father be upset that you're dancing with me?"

"Because you helped Fremont?"

"Sí. I've seen him giving me hard looks."

She threw back her head and laughed. "He does that with all the young men! Ask my sisters. It's his habit to put on a stern face to discourage them."

"Maybe he holds a personal grudge against me. I would understand if he did. I don't want to make any trouble for you."

"Well, if he does hold a grudge, he's wrong to do so. You're as nice as you are handsome." She fluttered her eye-lashes. "Forgive me if I'm being too forward."

Tongue-tied, Guillermo said, "Oh no…you're not. Uh, gracias!" He regained his composure and bowed slightly. "I'm honored to dance with the prettiest girl here."

She beamed up at him with glowing cheeks. "Muchas gracias! It's very kind of you to say, but...Guillermo, what is it? You look like you've seen a ghost."

He stood frozen, unable to speak.

Maria turned in the direction he was staring. "What's going on?" She stood on tiptoe to see over the heads of the people milling about the courtyard like sheep.

"It's Gustavo Davila and he looks upset." Rios and Fuentes were his vaqueros, and it was assumed the former rebelista was angry at Don Julian for helping Fremont. Guillermo's blood ran cold when he glimpsed Davila's face contorted in anger as he worked his way through the crowd toward his father. Judging from Davila's purposeful gait, he was primed for a showdown. When he reached Don Julian, he shook his finger in his face, yelling, "You've got a lotta nerve showing up here, Foxen!"

The words became indistinct as onlookers closed ranks around them. Guillermo could barely make out his father, who gazed down on Don Gustavo while calmly sucking on his pipe.

Alfredo and Carmelita rushed over. "What's happening?"

"It's my father and Gustavo Davila. Ever since we helped Fremont, we've been threatened by his crew and had our livestock stolen and killed."

"Ay, caramba...why does he have to make a scene now?" asked Alfredo.

"Exactly. Why now?" Guillermo moaned. He looked around for Martina and Marco and saw them returning from the refreshment table with furrowed brows. Upon learning about the confrontation, Martina rushed off to search for Ramona and Panchita and hustle them away.

Guillermo and Alfredo excused themselves from Maria

and Sarita and wove their way through the crowd. The music died away as everyone became aware of Davila's raised voice. Padre Jimeño and Augustin Janssens encouraged Davila to accompany them indoors, but he was having none of it.

"Anything we need to say to each other can be said right here! I don't understand why this traitor is welcome here!" Davila's fiery eyes bulged, and a corded vein in his neck pulsed.

Señores Francisco Cota, Joaquin Carrillo, and José Covarrubias rose from their chairs. The womenfolk retreated a distance away, where they whispered behind their fans. Guillermo was grateful that his mother had stayed at their campsite and would be spared the indignity of witnessing her husband being called a traitor in front of her paisanos.

"Gustavo, let's take this matter inside," Janssens said. As newly appointed justice of the peace, he held the highest civilian post in the valley and had the authority to arrest Davila if he deemed it a matter of public safety.

Davila glanced around at the collection of rancheros surrounding him and ranted. "I don't understand you! This man doesn't deserve your civility! Nor should he be allowed to keep his land grant! He took an oath vowing he'd defend the province against foreign invaders! Instead, he helped the infidels steal our horses, and you all," he waved his hand at the men, "treat him as if he's done no wrong!"

Marco's father, Joaquin Carrillo, stepped forward and spoke up. "Now listen, Gustavo, you're not the only one who was offended by his actions. But this is not the time or place for a showdown. Let's handle this like gentlemen. Have you forgotten it's a holy day? There are women and children present."

"That's easy for you to say, Señor Super-in-ten-dent of the mission! Look at you! Your connections with the former governor have provided you and your brother-in-law," his arm made a sweeping motion, "with all this! What do I have?" He held up a finger. "A rancho whose creeks run dry by early summer," a second finger popped up, "and a traitor on the other side of me who plays host to every Yankee scoundrel who passes through the area! My man Fuentes claims they're stealing our livestock!"

"That's nonsense! No one's stealing your livestock. If anyone's stealing, it's your crew!" said Don Julian.

"That's ridiculous!" said Davila. "You talking about that horse raid? That was Tulares. They can't stand traitors either!"

"We had a bull shot. No Tulare did that," Don Julian said.

Padre Jimeño gently tugged on Davila's arm. "Come along, Gustavo. Let's go inside where we can discuss this in private."

Davila started to object, but Covarrubias, one of his former trail mates from the Hijar-Padres Expedition in 1834, coaxed him away in the direction of Padre Jimeño's office. As the crowd dispersed, Guillermo overheard Joaquin Carrillo say to Francisco Cota, "Not surprising there was trouble. Foxen took a big risk coming here."

"I agree," Carrillo said. "There was bound to be a scene."

"Wouldn't surprise me if Fuentes and his sidekick are harassing Foxen," said Cota. "With or without their boss' knowledge. Don't you remember Fuentes was fired from Rancho Jonata for stealing?"

"I do. Why Davila keeps him around is a mystery to me." Carrillo shrugged. "That hombre is trouble. Foxen better be careful." They ambled away toward the refreshment table.

Alfredo said, "You've had a bull shot?"

"I didn't want to say anything in front of Marco. For whatever reason, he likes Fuentes. Besides, the last thing my family wanted was to stir up trouble," said Guillermo.

The music resumed, and the crowd of onlookers slowly dispersed.

"Hope you never suspected our crew of killing your bull. We've always considered your family and crew amigos, not just our neighbors," said Alfredo.

"No, never. We feel the same way. Let's hope Padre Jimeño and Covarrubias can calm Davila down." Guillermo craned his neck, trying to spot Maria. "C'mon, let's see if we can find the girls and continue the fun."

Maria Estefana was nowhere to be found, but Guillermo caught Sarita approaching him out of the corner of his eye, so he bid buenas noches to Alfredo and made his way back to camp. Although the evening ended on a sour note, the fandango had been great fun. The music and laughter had worked their magic to heal the sense of alienation that had plagued him for months. Having his family's social ties restored with most of their paisanos filled his heart with gladness. It was good to know there were still people who cared.

The following morning, the Foxens bade farewell to family and friends. Guillermo and Maria exchanged surreptitious waves as he saddled up to leave, and Alfredo and Marco made a special point of saying goodbye before morning classes. They expressed their anticipation to meet with Guillermo at the spring roundups.

As the caravan of horses and Sadie headed out, Covarrubias and Padre Moreno met Guillermo and his father at the corral. Covarrubias formally presented Guillermo with the Appaloosa, leaving it to Guillermo to slip a rope around his neck. "There's no one I trust more to care for him than you. It's going to take time, but eventually he'll settle down."

"Muchas gracias! I promise to take good care of him. I've decided to rename him El Rey" Guillermo said as he stroked the horse's forehead.

"Good choice. I'm sure you'll bring out the best in him by the time I see you again. Likewise, it may take time for all this business about retribution to die down. Davila seems to be alone in his campaign to exact some kind of punishment on your family. Be patient. I was born a Frenchman, immigrated to Mexico and became a naturalized citizen, and now I'm an American. Like your father and Padre Moreno, we Europeans yearn for progress. Right?" Both men nodded, and Covarrubias tapped the side of his head. "We're more pragmatic than the provincials. Loyalty for the paisanos comes from their hearts, and that can take longer to change, but they'll come around in time. Mark my word." He continued. "I had a talk with the padres last night. We've come up with a way for you to attend school here in the fall. Would you like that?"

Wide-eyed, Guillermo swiveled to see his father's amused reaction. "Of course, but how?"

It was Padre Moreno's turn. "Our Chumash population has dwindled to the point where we don't have the labor to adequately care for the livestock, and we need help with the horses. If your father can pay half of your tuition, you can work off the other half. Sound like a deal?"

Don Julian said, "He's grown up a lot this year. I'll miss him on the rancho, but it's time for him to have some formal learning. It's a deal, Padre. José, thank you very much."

Guillermo's head spun at the news. But alas, his high spirits lasted only as long as the journey home. Upon returning to the hacienda, his family discovered that vandals had set their roof on fire.

CHAPTER 30

Seeing the gaping hole in the roof and the pile of burned debris beside the house, Doña Eduarda clasped her hands to her mouth and stared in disbelief as her daughters clung to her. "Oh my goodness, how did this happen?"

Guillermo knew this was no accident. It was payback for helping Fremont or taming the Appaloosa. He suspected Fuentes and Rios left the mission early to carry out their evil deed before the family returned home.

Don Julian put a brawny arm around his wife and promised their home would be in ship shape before the week's end. "We needed to make repairs on the roof anyway. At least this way we'll be ready for the fall rains." He unpacked the canvas sails from his horse and, with Juan's help, stretched them over the holes in the roof to provide temporary protection from the elements. He made good on his promise by deferring work on the stable and enlisting Juan and Manuel to help him with the roof.

However much his parents tried to minimize the incident, it struck fear in Guillermo. The trip to the mission was overshadowed by this latest act of violence. The lighthearted interlude with friends should have sustained him through the summer and fall, but sadly, those fond memories were overshadowed by the burned roof. His family was back to living under a cloud of dread as they had before they left home. It was as if the refuge of the mission was farther than the six leagues they had traveled. It may as well have been in another world.

The one bright spot to the homecoming was that one of the dogs had given birth to a litter of six puppies while the family was gone. They were nestled in a blanket under the veranda. The girls delighted in watching the rodent-like creatures crawl over each other to suckle. Their mother lay on her side, looking at the girls with weary eyes.

Ramona said, "Shadow, you're such a good mama, and to think the house was set on fire the same day your pups were born! I'm naming the gray puppy Smokey."

The weeks following the trip to the mission were busy. After the roof was repaired, roundups and matanzas were rotated between Ranchos Tinaquaic, Tepusquet, Zaca, and La Laguna. Normally Corral de Cuati would have been included. Not this year.

When Don Julian informed his wife about the padre's offer to reduce the tuition by half so Guillermo could attend seminary school in the fall, she said, "That's generous, but how can we afford half?"

"From profits of the barley crop. Tomás heard that the army regiment assigned to Santa Barbara is willing to pay three dollars a bushel for barley, so I'm hoping my crop will bring a tidy sum."

"Well then, let's pray for a bumper crop! Imagine, our son studying at the mission school!" She clasped her delicate hands to her breast. "I look up at him and can't believe he's the same baby I held in my arms. He's growing into manhood before our eyes, and so handsome, like his tio. If it's God's will that he attend school, the money will come."

The hope of attending school in the fall competed with Guillermo's worry for his family's safety. Had he not been motivated to improve his writing from observing Lieutenant Bryant, he would not have been open to the idea of being confined indoors for days on end, but his competitive nature would not allow him to fall behind his friends. With the Yankee takeover, life was bound to change, even on an isolated rancho. The American settlers would have an advantage over the native sons in understanding the ways of government and commerce. He would need to sharpen his skills in both Spanish and English. Until he obtained something better, like an American newspaper from Ike's store, he would pore over his father's ship logs and almanac in the evenings.

Don Julian made sure the long summer days were put to good use, and work on the stable progressed steadily. Manuel and Juan spent one day a week making adobe for the bricks by mixing clay, straw, and lime water and pouring the thick mixture into wood molds. It took the bricks a week to ten days to cure in the summer heat. The east wall formed an L with the south wall, which was two-thirds complete. By the end of summer and another five hundred bricks, the stable would be complete. Fernando hewed planks of oak for the roof from the massive tree that fell in the winter storm. A door would be built, enabling them to securely lock their most valuable cow ponies in at night. That would go a long way in protecting their remuda. However, the cattle were always vulnerable to being stolen or killed.

When Manuel and Juan were not making bricks, they tended Don Julian's fields of barley, wheat, and corn. All three had sprouted. The barley was a foot tall, the wheat double that, and the corn even higher. The Foxen girls had made scarecrows to ward off the flocks of birds. Water had to be hauled from the creek in buckets suspended from a long pole; this and weeding consumed a good part of the laborers' days.

The hides staked out in the matanza field were dried stiff and ready to transport to the pueblo of Santa Barbara five weeks later in mid-June. The fat had been rendered in large vats and the tallow stored in twenty-pound arrobas. Besides the regular supplies that needed to be traded in Santa Barbara, Don Julian intended to stock up on lead for ammunition. A portion of it would be repaid to Rancho Tepusquet for what had been borrowed. He hoped the remainder would be sufficient to protect them in the coming months.

CHAPTER 31

D on Julian and the Indian servants set out for Santa Barbara shortly after daybreak one morning in late June.
The ox-cart was piled high with stiff, black cowhides
folded lengthwise. Sadie followed behind with containers
of tallow strapped to her sides.

Each vaquero took on extra duties to make up for the
absence of the three travelers. Guard duty of the horse corral
was rotated so that each man had one night on and two off.

Shadow stayed at her post on the corner of the veranda
with her rambunctious pups, while the other rancho dogs
roamed about the yard, patrolling.

The Foxen girls also took on extra chores. In addition
to tending her flock of geese, Ramona fed and watered the
corralled livestock. Supervised by Martina, Panchita and
Juanita were assigned the duty of hauling buckets of water
from the creek and keeping the ollas filled. Each room in
the adobe casa had a clay pot hanging on the wall in addition to the ones outdoors that Concha used for soaking and
cooking beans. The girls tended their mother's rose garden
and weeded the vegetable patch. When the chores were
done, Martina helped her mother teach the younger girls
their catechism and memorize prayers in Latin.

In addition to running the well-organized household,
Petra helped Doña Eduarda care for Alejandro. She made

sure each room was tidy and the hard-packed dirt floor was swept twice daily. Rosita, in addition to her regular duties of helping her mother cook, washed clothes, stoked the ovens, and ground corn for tortillas. Everyone except Alejandro contributed in some way toward running the household.

After the initial adjustment to Don Julian's absence, the sixteen remaining residents of Rancho Tinaquaic settled into a routine. Each night after prayers, Martina made sure candles were lit for the safe return of her father, Juan, and Manuel. Guillermo and the Gonzalez men spent their days looking for strays. As grass became scarce, the herd wandered farther into the backcountry to graze. Each afternoon, one of the crew rode in from the range to pick up a kerchief full of warm tortillas and carne seca to deliver to the other vaqueros.

On day five, it was Guillermo's turn to retrieve the food. He looked forward to taking a break and sipping a cool drink in the shade of the ramada before returning to the range. As he galloped over the low hill and the adobe came into sight, he noticed that the front windows were shuttered. He figured Petra had shut them to keep the house cool. Shadow rose from her station at the corner of the veranda and trotted out to meet him, her puppies scampering behind. El Rey and the other horses in the corral whinnied to Benito as he trotted by the sprouted willow pole enclosure. Horses, as social creatures, greeted each other with neighs when they returned from the range. Across the yard, a thin white plume of smoke wafted from the unattended firepit. He caught the distinct whiff of gamy meat coming from it, and his eyes fell to the gray feathers that littered the ground nearby. They tumbled and fluttered in the light breeze, dangling from the grape arbor. Goose feathers. His stomach knotted as he unholstered his rifle, dismounted, and tied Benito to the hitching post.

Guillermo made his way across the yard, his eyes darting about for things that were not as they should be. His footfalls echoed on the hollow floor of the raised veranda, announcing his arrival. When he pulled on the door handle, it was bolted from the inside.

"Hola! It's me, Guillermo! Let me in!"

Something was wrong for the door to be bolted during the day. The muffled sound of female voices could be heard in the background while someone unlatched the door.

"Oh, Guillermo!" Martina gasped, her face flooded with relief. "Come in! Come in! So glad to see you!"

Before his eyes had time to adjust to the darkened sala, Guillermo was engulfed by arms wrapped around his chest and waist.

Panchita blurted, "The Tulares came and stole one of the horses and…"

"Hush, Panchita," said Doña Eduarda. "Give your brother a chance to sit down." She pulled him by the hand to his father's cowhide chair where he rested his rifle against the wall and took a seat. He caught a whiff of gunpowder. Had the old carbine been fired? "Sit down, mijo. As you can see, we're all fine. God watched over us." She held his hand, kissing it tenderly and bringing it to her cheek. Tears glistened in her soft, brown eyes. A few feet away, Concha dispatched Rosita to get him some water.

His head was spinning with the news. Híjole! An Indian raid in broad daylight? The Tulares were getting bolder! Even though the crisis had passed and his family had escaped unharmed, his first reaction was guilt. This should not have happened, especially with his father gone.

He heard the collective relief in the females' voices now that he was home. As he made out details in the darkened room, Ramona's hunched form took shape. She sat on the settee with her face buried in her apron, sobbing. When she lifted her tear-stained face, she hiccupped, "Gui-ller-mo, they killed M-mar-guer-ite."

Martina sat down and pulled her sister toward her.

Looking down at Ramona, Guillermo knew she would be suffering. Marguerite had been the children's favorite goose because of her pleasant disposition. He reached down and patted her shoulder. "I'm so sorry. I'd have been here sooner, but I came across a heifer in labor. I stayed to make sure she and her calf were okay."

"It's not your fault." Ramona sniffed. "If Papá had been home, none of this would have happened. Why did he have to go?" Her lower lip trembled, and big tears spilled down her cheeks.

Guillermo rubbed her heaving shoulders.

Doña Eduarda knelt beside Ramona and caressed her head, tucking a stray lock of hair behind her ear. "I know it seems like a terrible loss, my dear, but think of it this way. The Tulares were hungry and needed to eat after a long, hard march over the mountains." She looked at her other three daughters, huddled together solemnly on the settee. "You handled yourselves like brave girls today. I'm proud of you, as your father will be when he returns home. Sometimes we have to make sacrifices to protect ourselves. You must always give the Tulares what they want so they'll go on their way. You never want to make them angry." She spread her arms. "Here we are, safe and sound. That's all that matters."

"How long ago did they leave?"

She stood and smoothed her apron, "About an hour ago, but promise me you won't go after them, mijo. Please? We've had enough trouble for one day."

"Did you notice which horse they took?"

"They took the pinto with the light-colored mane and tail."

"That was the mustang Chico's been training to be a cutter." Guillermo winced and shook his head. "He spent hours working with her. She showed so much promise."

"Hmph!" Concha said. "She was the only one they could catch. They were already skittish before the Tulares entered the corral! The horses panicked and kept rearing and pawing the air! Mercy! You should have seen the long knives hanging from their waists! I was afraid they'd start stabbing the horses in a frenzy or take out their anger on us, but your mother…" She made the sign of the cross and kissed the crucifix on her chain of rosary beads. "O Dios mio! I've always thought she was a saint, and today I saw proof. God's grace shone down on her. She showed no fear."

Guillermo glanced at his mother, who had settled into her rocker. Removing a lace handkerchief from an apron pocket, she dabbed at the beads of perspiration on her forehead and neck. He marveled that despite her petite stature, she projected an inner strength that the Tulares must have sensed. She carried herself with the grace and dignity of one who was raised in privilege, yet she also possessed a hardiness, much like her Castile roses, that flourished far from their native Spain. This outwardly delicate-looking woman had adapted remarkably well to being transplanted to the wilderness.

She dismissed the praise with a wave, "Oh my goodness! I was so startled when they appeared in the patio. When I looked up into the eyes of the one who was leaning over me, I was terrified. I'd never seen such black eyes in my life, yet it was the strangest thing. They lit up like a child's at seeing the red satin. Out of the corner of my eye, I saw Alejandro's mouth hang open in shock and his little nose scrunch up at their smell! I didn't want him to be frightened, so I kept smiling. He watched them, bewildered, and then giggled when they pranced around, waving their cloth streamers in the air. He must have thought they were playing a game." Turning to Martina, she said, "You did such a good job of not showing fear and keeping him calm. He even dozed off and took a nap." She gazed down at her twisted handkerchief and murmured as if in a dream. "I kept telling myself if I stay calm, they'll eventually go, and they did. Thank goodness for the red satin. It was a gift from God."

"You should have seen your mother," said Concha, her round face framed by unruly strands of graying hair, "sitting there all prim and proper." She straightened her back, lifted her double chins in a queenly fashion, and pretended to pass out strips of cloth. "She acted like it was nothing out of the ordinary to be ripping up her beautiful petticoat she had been working on for weeks and handing the pieces to the savages. You'd think she'd sewn it just for them!"

Rosita reentered the room and offered Guillermo a cup of water with a shaking hand. "Here, Guillermo. It's so good to have you home." Her wan expression told him she was wrung out like the others but putting on a brave face.

"Gracias," he said. "Just wish I'd been here sooner." He took a long gulp and wiped his mouth on his poncho.

"Señora," Concha said, "how about I make some lemonade? I think that would help calm our nerves, no?"

"That sounds lovely. Gracias," said Doña Eduarda. She sank back into her chair wearily and turned to Guillermo. "Please don't leave. Stay and have a drink with us."

"Don't worry. I won't leave you, but I do need to go check on the horses. Since the rest of the crew is expecting me to return with lunch, I'll fire a couple shots to let them know there's a problem. Someone from the crew will come to investigate. From now on, one of us will stay behind to keep an eye on things." He shook his head in confusion. "For the Tulares to make a raid during the day, they were confident that no men were around or so desperate that they were willing to risk encountering one of us. They didn't show interest in coming inside?"

"At one point, I feared they might, but…" Doña Eduarda hesitated, glancing at her solemn-faced daughters. "They were distracted by…other things." She shook off the thought with a shudder, reached for her fan, flicked it open, and cooled herself in the stuffy room.

"Mamá, how about I accompany Guillermo to check on the horses?" said Martina. "Then he can shoot the warning shots."

"I'll go with you," said Panchita.

"No dear, you've spent enough time outside for the day," Doña Eduarda said. "Besides, Concha's making lemonade."

Panchita's shoulders slumped in disappointment.

Martina disengaged herself from Ramona and led the way out of the room. Guillermo grabbed his rifle and followed her through the dining room and out through the storage room. He grabbed a couple of dried apples from a barrel as he headed out onto the patio. They were met by a gust of wind that kicked up dirt from the yard and sent feathery willow seeds floating in the air. The sky was hazy with dust. "Wonder where Papa is," said Martina. "Hope he's in a sheltered canyon somewhere and not blinded by the dust."

Rosita raked the area around the fire pit while Concha squeezed lemons into a pitcher. "Rosita, please remove the bones from the ashes," said Martina.

"Sí. I'll gather them up and hide them so Ramona won't be reminded."

"Gracias," said Martina.

Guillermo paused and fired off three warning shots. "Come, let's go check on the horses," said Guillermo. "I'm anxious to hear exactly what happened." It seemed the rancor against the Foxens was rising.

CHAPTER 32

Martina hurried to keep up with her brother's long strides. The top of her bobbing head barely reached his shoulders. It was clear from Guillermo's determined gait that his concern had shifted from family to the welfare of the horses.

When they reached the corral gate, he untied the rawhide thong and entered the sprouted willow pen. He spoke to the five remaining horses softly, holding out his hand for them to sniff. One by one, they approached him, curious about what he was offering and surrounding him for a nibble of apple. He rubbed the neck of the Appaloosa who had yet to be completely gentled but acted like they were long-lost friends.

"Now we're amigos, eh?" Guillermo chuckled. He ran his hand along the horse's flanks and legs, satisfied he had not been injured. "Turned out that mean streak of yours saved your life today."

He examined the others, soothing them with pats and reassurances. The horses huddled around him as he filled their water troughs and hand-fed them apple pieces. He turned to Martina, who watched him from her perch on a horizontal pole. "I'm surprised none of them ran off when the gate opened. Guess they know they have it good here."

El Rey nudged his shoulder for more apple.

"He's coming around, isn't he?" she said.

"Sí. He's becoming more trusting day by day. Not so standoffish anymore."

"I was afraid they were going to stab him, but he fought them off. He kept rearing up and trying to strike them with his hooves. If they'd had a gun, they would have shot him. They were angry. At least they took only the pinto. Rosita ran over and closed the corral gate as soon as the Tulares left, and the remaining horses bunched together in the corner, knowing it wasn't safe to leave the corral."

Guillermo scanned the hillside and the willows that followed the creek. "They must have been watching the adobe from there and knew all the men were away. Why else would they take that chance?"

"I agree. They looked like they hadn't eaten in a while. Their chests and bellies were sunken. Oh, Guillermo." She took another deep breath and sighed. "What made it so scary was we didn't know what they'd do next. One minute they were dancing and yelling, waving Mamá's red cloth streamers, and the next, they were killing Marguerite. It all seems like a bad dream now." She stared off into the distance. "I don't know if I'll ever feel safe like I used to. I hated the feeling of being defenseless." Turning back to him, she asked, "Would you teach me to shoot?"

"I agree, you need to learn. We can start tomorrow."

"All right then," she said with resolve. She hopped off the fence and brushed the leaves from her skirt. "Tomorrow I'm going to learn to shoot. Maybe Mamá will let Ramona join us. She'd be thrilled, and it will help take her mind off Marguerite."

They turned at the clomping of approaching hooves and saw Chico and Sal gallop into the yard. Reinforcements had arrived.

CHAPTER 33

The following morning, Doña Eduarda suspended the usual schedule of chores for the household. She announced the day was to be devoted to sewing each girl a new rag doll complete with a dress. She took folded remnants of cloth from a special camphor trunk and fanned them on the dining room table—leftover pieces from the dozens of dresses she had sewn for herself and the girls over the years. There were blues, yellows, reds, greens, blacks, and ivories in muslins, cottons, linens, and broadcloths as well as elegant silks, satins, brocades, taffetas, and laces. The scraps were from dresses and gowns sewn for weddings, christenings, and fiestas, and the palette of colors was a reminder of happier times and strong social ties. This was not the usual stash of remnants reserved for rag dolls but included her choicest fabrics imported from the Orient by Yankee trading ships.

Despite the Foxens' isolation, there were friends and family concerned about their well-being who would be shocked to learn of their ordeal. There was comfort in that.

Guillermo and Fernando busied themselves around the hacienda, tending to the livestock and doing chores. The other members of the crew rode to the top of the hill and scanned the countryside for signs of trouble. There had been no sign of the Tulares except for the tracks that led south.

As promised, Guillermo set aside some time to give Martina and Ramona a shooting lesson. It confirmed they would be hard-pressed to defend themselves or livestock if it came to it, but if learning how to load and shoot a gun gave them some measure of comfort, Guillermo didn't want to deny them that. Despite padding her shoulder with a folded shawl, Martina flinched so much from the kick of the rifle's butt that her shots went wildly astray. With each successive shot, she anticipated the recoil by squeezing her eyes shut a moment sooner. He allowed four shots apiece, enough to give them a feel for his rifle.

Ramona's flock of geese grazed nearby, searching for bugs. Every time a shot was fired, they honked and fluttered their wings. She kept an eye out for Señor Gruñón, guarding Martina and Guillermo from his sneaky nips at the heel. Shadow did her part, pacing to keep the gander at bay.

Ramona's first shot nearly knocked her down and went high and wide, so Guillermo had her spread her feet farther apart and plant them in the ground. He crouched behind her and reached around her to hold up the long barrel while she took aim. He whispered, "Center the sight on that tree down there, and lower the barrel slightly to compensate for the kick. When you have it, pull the trigger." He slowly removed his hand from the barrel and backed away.

Crack! Leaves sprayed in the crown of the tree. She turned to check his reaction.

"Not bad for a beginner," he said.

Ramona beamed with pride and refrained from complaining about the pain in her shoulder. Martina helped her reload, gingerly shaking a trickle of powder into the barrel, and Guillermo showed her how to tap in more.

"Híjole! At this rate, your target could come up and grab the gun out of your hands. Don't be afraid to waste some powder if you need to."

"Do you think the Tulares are coming back?" Ramona asked, peering up at him with anxious eyes. "You keep glancing around like you're on guard."

"Ay, caramba! Nothing gets by you! I suppose I look around out of habit now. Neely warned me to always be aware of what's going on around me. He was right. We can't afford to let our guard down, even though I think the Tulares are gone—for now." When his words failed to relax her knitted brow, he spread his arms in supplication. "I was kidding about a person grabbing the gun out of your hand. Around here, we're more likely to encounter a rattler or a bear. I'm sorry, I didn't mean to scare you."

Martina, who stood four inches taller than her sister, faced Ramona, put her hands on her shoulders, and bent her knees so they were eye to eye. "I asked Guillermo to give me a lesson so I wouldn't feel so helpless. Even though none of us were hurt except for Marguerite, we need to learn from that experience. Just because we're girls doesn't mean we can't learn to defend ourselves."

"I know, but I don't understand. Why did God let that happen? Marguerite was innocent! What if they come back?" Ramona's shoulders heaved, and her face crumbled as tears streamed down.

Martina handed the rifle to Guillermo and took her younger sister in her arms, letting Ramona bury her face in her chest. She patted her head. "I know, I know…"

Guillermo knelt beside her and rubbed her back. "Ramona, after the march over the San Marcos Trail, my world was rocked too. I couldn't understand why so many horses and mules had to fall to their deaths in the storm. I thought I'd never get their screams out of my head, but as the days passed, the sounds faded. I kept reminding myself that every man survived. As Mamá says, people are more important than animals or property. No one got hurt yesterday because you stayed calm and were brave. It's no small thing. Papá's going to be very proud of you, just as I am."

Martina dried Ramona's tears with a corner of her apron. "Just like Guillermo's, your bad memories will fade in time, but in the meantime, we need to take steps to protect ourselves. We were caught off guard and need to be better prepared. It will make me feel better to know I can load a gun if I need to. If we work together, we can load it faster."

"I'm not sure," said Ramona, "and I hope I never have to find out, but maybe just aiming a rifle could scare someone off. In either case, I want to be prepared."

"Neely said all the women in his family learned to shoot as girls, and they were decent shots," said Guillermo.

The mention of Neely's name for the second time put a wan smile on Ramona's face. She nodded. "I miss him. Wonder what he's doing now?"

"Probably helping his father and brother. If he were here he'd tell you, 'Chin up, don't let circumstances get you down.'" He lifted her chin. "You better do what he says, or next time I see him, I'll tell him you're slacking off."

A smile brightened her face. "In that case, I better make these last two shots count." Ramona brushed back a loose strand of blond hair and took back the rifle.

Guillermo scanned the area for cattle and, finding it clear, gave her the go ahead to shoot. Martina helped her load the barrel.

Ramona took her stance. This time, her right arm was high, not sagging under its weight. She squinted, aimed at the tree again, and squeezed the trigger. *Crack!* Leaves sprayed out again, but this time, a flock of crows flew out of its branches and scattered angrily in all directions. On her final shot, she took aim at the trunk, paused just before pulling the trigger, and swiveled the barrel to the right and downward. The ground exploded within a foot of a squirrel's hole. "Did you see that? I almost got a squirrel! He peeked his head out of his hole just as I was ready to shoot!" she said, flushed with excitement.

Martina and Guillermo stared at her in amazement. He exclaimed, "Good eye! Sure you didn't get private lessons from Neely on the side?"

Ramona beamed with pride as she shook her head. Martina said, "Sewing and shooting. What a curious combination. Thank you for the lesson, Guillermo."

They followed Shadow back down the hill as she herded the flock of geese to their night enclosure. Señor Gruñon honked his displeasure at being rushed along.

As they rode home, Guillermo wondered how the family would fare without him when he went to school. Would he be able to concentrate on his studies, worrying about their safety? Ay, yi, yi…the last thing he wanted to do was to waste his father's money. Maybe it wasn't in the cards for him to attend school in the fall. Time was slipping away. Alfredo and Marco had years on him, but at nearly six feet tall, he would stand head and shoulders above his classmates. He wondered what it would be like not to be weighed down with worry about his family. A part of him envied the other boys' ability to focus on their studies. In the past weeks, he had forged a special bond with Martina and would miss her.

"Oh, look at that beautiful sunset!" Martina exclaimed. The western sky was ablaze in hues of magenta. "What is it Papá says? Red sky at night?"

"Sailors' delight. Red sky in the morning, sailors take warning," he said.

"Sounds like a good omen to me," she said. "Somewhere, hopefully not far off, Papá is seeing it and thinking the same thing. Let's pray he'll be home by this time tomorrow."

Guillermo hoped so as well.

CHAPTER 34

Martina's prayer was answered. When Guillermo rode up the hill overlooking the hacienda the following day, he spotted his father's horse and Sadie in the corral.

The late-afternoon sun lit the adobe and its yard in a golden glow. He heard laughter coming from the patio as a merry group gathered under the grape arbor. Concha and Rosita bustled nearby in the outdoor kitchen, stoking the fire in the hornito and cooking frijoles over the open fire. From the looks of it, the travelers had arrived home within the hour. Manuel and Juan were unloading much-needed supplies into the storeroom.

He hoped his mother had told his father about the Tulare raid and he'd had a chance to absorb the shocking news. She had promised Guillermo she would make it clear to his father that he had been faithful about checking in on the family throughout the day.

Guillermo found his father stretched out in a chair, smoking and bouncing Alejandro on one knee. Panchita leaned over his shoulder, grinning broadly at her younger brother.

"Guillermo!" Don Julian bellowed. "Good to see you, mijo! Sounds like you had your hands full while I was gone!" His pale eyes were accented by the white crow's feet on his sunburned face, but these were mellowed from the brandy he had been sipping. It was a relief to find him in a jovial mood.

"Sí, Mamá did a great job keeping the Tulares calm. She was brave. I just wish I'd been here. Did she tell you I was delayed when I came across a cow delivering a calf? Coyotes were circling, and I couldn't leave her." He couldn't hide the defensiveness in his voice.

"Well, all in all, I'd say we were mighty fortunate." Don Julian looked toward Panchita, meaning they couldn't talk candidly in front of the girls.

Guillermo ladled a drink of water from the clay olla hanging from the upright beam that supported the ramada and sat across from his father on a bench. He watched with envy as his father bounced a giggling Alejandro. Why was it that no matter how hard he tried to please his father, he always seemed to fall short, yet Alejandro's innocent baby laugh could magically lighten his mood even after the news of an Indian raid? "How was your trip?"

"Here, Panchita. Take him, por favor, so I can talk to Guillermo." Don Julian passed off the youngest Foxen, took a long draw on his pipe, and exhaled. In a cloud of white smoke, he said, "Long, but productive. It didn't start off well. Remember how I told you we planned to cut through Cat Canyon and head south to avoid crossing Corral de Cuati? Well, who rides over a hill as we're entering Alamo Pintado? Gustavo Davila! He was on his way back from the mission and fuming at the news Padre Jimeño was using Indian labor to paint the inside of the sanctuary. He was insulted that his offer to paint it had been turned down."

"Ay, caramba. Did he ask you about our matanza?"

"No, I guess he figured out that we went ahead and held it without asking for his crew's help, but he was curious

197

about Sadie and where I got her. When I told him, he made a snide comment about it being a Yankee mule and rode off. I hated the thought of Fuentes finding out I was going to be gone for a while. I considered turning around and heading for home, but I had no choice. I needed to get the hides to port. I feared I'd return home to news of more harassment. Didn't expect a Tulare raid."

Don Julian glanced over at the girls playing nearby with Alejandro and whispered confidentially, "Never in the seven years we've lived here have the Tulares been so bold as to come in broad daylight." He shook his head and rubbed a hand over his bristled chin. "Just when I dared to hope things were settling down, the threats keep coming. My goal is to get the stable done in the month before you leave for school."

Guillermo was feeling increasingly uneasy about the prospect of leaving his family after the string of hostile incidents, but he kept his thoughts to himself.

"It's troubling that the Tulares felt comfortable staying here as long as they did," said Don Julian. "Your mother said they were here a little over an hour. That was a big risk on their part. How late were you in checking on things here?"

"About an hour. I was on my way home around noon when I came upon the heifer. I stayed with her for nearly an hour. Shot a pair of coyotes who were waiting for me to leave. Took another twenty minutes to ride home, so it was a little after one when I arrived home. The Tulares were lucky, that's all I can figure."

Don Julian swirled his glass of amber liquid. "Something about this is off." He lifted his glass, polished off the liquid in one gulp, and swiped his mouth with the back of his hand. "Can't put my finger on it, but my gut tells me there's more to this."

Later, Guillermo mulled over his father's comment as he brushed down Benito. The question was whether Fuentes and Rios had a hand in this latest Indian raid. They would have learned from Davila that Papá would be gone for at least ten days. That meant they knew Tinaquaic's crew would be spread thin and there'd be less protection. Was it possible they had kept watch of the comings and goings at the hacienda and recruited the Tulares? That would account for the Indians' boldness. Then again, it could have been a coincidence the raid occurred when it did. Either way, it had succeeded in increasing the Foxens' anxiety. It seemed that no matter where the Foxens turned, danger was at their doorstep.

CHAPTER 35

The following week, Guillermo arrived home for the midday meal to discover Padre Jimeño on the settee in the sala. His round face was ashen. He and his Indian helper, Mateo, had come from Antonio Paljalchet's rancho, south of the Foxen's, and made the grisly discovery. The family had been massacred. All nine of them!

Stunned by the news, Guillermo flashed back to seeing them standing in the back of the church at Easter Mass a couple months earlier. Antonio's wife, Juanita, was holding their baby, a wide-eyed infant wrapped in a blanket. Híjole! His legs went weak, and he lowered himself into his mother's rocker.

The teacup in Padre Jimeño's hand clattered against the saucer.

Don Julian called, "Rosita! Bring the padre some brandy, por favor!"

She scurried in with a crystal decanter and handed it to Don Julian, and he poured some of the amber liquid into the friar's teacup. "Here, Padre. This should help settle your nerves."

Childlike, the shaken man held the cup with both hands. He shook his balding head and stared into it. "Who could commit such an evil act and to innocent children?"

"Could you tell how they died?" asked Don Julian gently.

Doña Eduarda had taken the girls outside so they wouldn't overhear details of the story.

"Alas, Julian." He shuddered. "It was ghastly. At first, I wasn't sure what I was seeing. Of course, the vultures told us right away that something had died, but we had no idea..." He took a sip. "Bear in mind this must have happened some days ago, because...of the condition of their bodies." He grimaced, waved a hand to indicate the memory was gruesome. "We couldn't tell how they were killed, but it was violent, I can tell you that. There was lots of blood, so maybe they were killed with knives. Could have been guns, but that would mean it wasn't Tulares. If not them, who?"

Guillermo and his father exchanged glances. Don Julian said, "Father, last week while I was returning from Santa Barbara and the crew was out on the range, three Tulares came in broad daylight. They were armed with long knives and stayed for over an hour, eating whatever they could get their hands on. Thank God they didn't harm Eduarda or the children, but they frightened them. What troubles me is their boldness to come during the day and stay as long as they did. They killed Ramona's favorite goose and stole one of our horses, and you can imagine how traumatic that was for the girls. Thankfully Concha and Rosita were able to lock up Shadow and her puppies in the shed. No telling what would have happened."

"Poor Eduarda and the girls!" Padre Jimeño gasped. "You say that happened last week? Good Lord. Do you think these events could be related? That after the Tulares left here they went on to Zaca Rancho?"

"Seems too much of a coincidence," said Don Julian.

They sat in silence, listening to the ticking of the mantel clock as the sobering implication sunk in.

Padre Jimeño lifted his glass and gulped the remainder of his drink. He sat dazed, bewildered at the notion that the tragedy he witnessed at the Paljalchets' could just as well occurred here at the Foxens' hacienda. The room they were sitting in could have been reduced to a pile of ash if the savages had unleashed their bloodbath a day or two earlier. "Antonio and his family were Indian. Why would they kill their own kind?"

Don Julian shrugged. "Maybe the Tulares didn't see it that way. Didn't you say Antonio originally came from Buenaventura with Padre Uria and served as his handyman, living in the servants' quarters instead of the rancheria? He could have been viewed as more Mexican than Chumash. Who knows?"

"When Padre Uria wrote to the governor requesting Antonio be granted the parcel of land, none of us thought it could lead to this. We knew there would be those who resented a Chumash acquiring land, but we figured who else would want land partway up a mountain? Besides, the area was sacred to the Chumash."

"As more settlers stream into the territory, land considered less desirable will be coveted," said Don Julian. "In time, the Tulares will be driven farther inland, and we'll have squatters to contend with. Antonio's days on his rancho were probably numbered, one way or another. Don't get me wrong, I'm not saying it's right, but unfortunately, unstable times like these can bring with them violence."

Guillermo shuddered to think of the horror the poor Paljalchet family must have endured. He gazed around the familiar room. Despite its thick walls and stout door, its security was an illusion. All someone had to do was toss a burning stick onto the tule roof. That would force whoever was inside to flee into the open, making them sitting ducks for attack.

Padre Jimeño continued. "I don't know when you were up there last, but Antonio had planted an orchard and built two outbuildings. I was impressed by how much he had improved his land. That could have contributed to his demise." He hung his head in despair. "We're going to need to send a party of men up there to attend to the bodies and make sure they have a proper burial."

Don Julian leaned forward, rising out of his cowhide chair, and put a meaty hand on the friar's knee. "I'll send some of my crew to help you bury the bodies."

That night, Old Fernando stayed up late hewing nine crosses out of oak logs to mark the graves of his friend's family. The following morning, he joined Don Julian, Padre Jimeño, Mateo, Juan, and Manuel as they journeyed up Zaca Mountain to bury the bodies. The crosses were tied to Sadie's sides. Guillermo stayed behind with the Gonzalezes to guard the rancho.

Two days later, the Rancho Tinaquaic contingent returned from their somber duty. The Palchaljets' horses were missing, presumably stolen. Some sheep and chickens were brought back. It was calculated there were a couple hundred head of cattle roaming the hills with the Zaca brand. Padre Jimeño said he would contact Augustin Janssens, the local justice of the peace, and notify the Americano officials in Santa Barbara.

Efforts to finish the stable were doubled. The sooner it was finished, the safer the livestock would be, but the rest of them? It remained to be seen.

CHAPTER 36

As word spread throughout the Santa Inés Valley of the massacre, so did the rumors as to who attacked the Paljalchets. Most blamed the Tulares, but some wondered if it could have been squatters. If anyone settled on the mountain in the next few months, they would be suspect.

Augustin Janssens visited the Foxens two days later to hear Doña Eduarda's account of the Indian raid. After being served tea, he asked her to describe the incident. When she told him about ripping her petticoat into strips for the Tulares to dance around with, Janssens reached into the breast pocket of his jacket and pulled out a handkerchief. A crumpled strip of faded red cloth was inside.

"Where did you find this?" she asked.

"It was found at the Paljalchet's, snagged on a willow post in the corral."

"O Dios mio!" She gasped. "So the same Tulares who came here went on to the Paljalchet's!" The color drained from her face as she clutched a handkerchief to her mouth.

Don Julian and Guillermo escorted Janssens to his horse. "Augustin, what's going to happen with Antonio's land?"

"Since he had no surviving relatives, it'll be available for purchase," said Janssens.

"I wouldn't be surprised if Davila tries to acquire some of the land along the creek since the two ranchos are adjacent.

He complained that Antonio diverted some of the water from the creek for his orchard. It'll be interesting to see if he takes steps to annex it to his land. That would be telling."

"I remember him complaining about that when he made his scene at the mission."

Don Julian said, "What you don't know is that I found out from my Indian friends in the Tulare Valley that some vaqueros from around here recruited Tulares to steal horses. They wanted to punish a gringo ranchero, me, for helping the Americano army. I'm convinced those vaqueros were Fuentes and Rios, Davila's men. I say that because in January, shortly after the treaty was announced, we had a night raid. We managed to recapture all our horses except for one. Members of my crew came across Fuentes and Rios with Guillermo's horse the next day. They claimed they found him wandering on Rancho Corral de Cuati land and were on their way here to return him. Fuentes informed my men that we should expect retribution for helping Fremont's army, and since then, we had a bull shot and our roof set on fire. I happened to cross paths with Davila as I was heading to Santa Barbara a few weeks ago. He knew I'd be gone when the Indian raid occurred. I'm not accusing him outright, but I wouldn't put it past Fuentes and Rios to recruit Indians to harass the Palchaljets and us. In the seven years we've lived here, we've never had a raid like that during the day. It was as if they knew our crew was spread thin. Mighty suspicious, if you ask me."

"I agree." Janssens put his hands on his hips, revealing a pistola strapped to his waist. "We'll probably never know what really happened. Without proof, there's nothing I can do."

"You've known Davila longer than I," said Don Julian. "He's intense, that much I know. Do you think he'd condone violence and look the other way while others did his dirty work?"

Janssens thought for a few moments. "Not the Gustavo I knew fifteen years ago who traveled with us in the Hijar-Padres Expedition. Back then, he was idealistic and zealous about establishing a settlement that would become the leading cultural and commercial center in the province. He took it hard when Commandante Mariano Vallejo and his men viewed us with suspicion and didn't receive permission to settle, so he turned his attention to renovating the mission sanctuaries. He was appalled, as we all were, at how they'd been allowed to deteriorate. He's talented artistically and hoped that after repainting the inside of Santa Clara's church, he'd be commissioned to do the same with others, but when the padres weren't able to pay him for his labor, he took it hard. I think he expected his talent would be more appreciated than it was. Artists are passionate people."

"And in his case, hot tempered."

"Yes, he's that, all right. I think the Yankee takeover has been a bitter pill for him to swallow. It's not a good sign that he keeps a thug like Fuentes around. Rios isn't much better. Seeing the wild look in his eye at the mission last Easter was unnerving. He's convinced your land should be confiscated. Who knows, maybe because he didn't get the support he wanted from the paisanos, he decided to take matters into his own hands, but since he or his henchmen wouldn't have wanted suspicion directed toward them, they could have recruited the Tulares." He cast a solemn look to Don Julian and then Guillermo. "You need to be careful."

"Don't worry. We're always on alert. Hopefully things will settle down in time."

Janssens nodded and looked around the yard and out-buildings in admiration. "Have to hand it to you, Julian. You built up quite a spread here. Fine-looking stable over there, and didn't I see barley when I came riding in?"

"Aye, and it'll be ready for harvest in a couple weeks. Got a field of corn out back by the creek too. Six feet tall now. This heat's been good for it. Should have a decent yield." Don Julian's chest swelled with pride as he surveyed his grounds.

"Well, I best be getting along. Please tell Eduarda I regret she had to recount the incident. It's a miracle she's here to tell about it. Her courage and poise saved her and the children. If there's any more trouble, send a rider to inform me."

"Will do. Thank you, Augustin. Take care."

Janssens tipped his hat. "Good day, gentlemen."

Guillermo and his father watched as Janssens rode off on his black mare. Don Julian said, "He's a good man and a practical one. Hard to believe we were on opposite sides of the war just months ago. He accepts the inevitable and adapts, like José Covarrubias. It pays to be flexible, mijo. One needs to bend with the winds of change."

"Papá, are you sure this is the right time for me to go off to school with the Tulare raid and what happened at Zaca? Maybe I should wait another year. Besides, how can I learn if I'm worried about you all?"

"I appreciate your concern, mijo, but I don't want to be short-sighted and have you lose a year of schooling out of fear of what might happen. There'll still be six of us who can protect the family. I'm depending on you to get an education. We've got seven weeks before you leave and lots to do. We need to finish the stable, build up our arsenal, and harvest the crops." He slapped Guillermo's shoulder. "Come on, let's see how much progress Fernando and Manuel made today."

As they walked toward the stable, Guillermo allowed himself a sense of relief. The massacre put a damper on his excitement about attending school in the fall, but maybe his father was right and there was reason to hold out hope. A family of finches was merrily chirping in the oaks, and he envied their simple lives.

Seeing the remnant of his mother's petticoat was stark proof of how close his family's brush with violence had been. Living with the constant threat of danger was taking a toll. He feared letting his guard down for even a moment, and the knot in his stomach was becoming his constant companion.

CHAPTER 37

The massacre had everyone in the vicinity on edge. The vaqueros from the different ranchos began riding the range with loaded weapons, on the lookout for Tulares. The final touches to the stable were completed by mid-August. After the beams for the sloping roof were laid from wall to wall and covered with tar and tules, the door was hung. Fernando and Don Julian attached it with hinges and installed a sturdy latch with a bell. Seven individual stalls were built inside, and one corner was devoted to tack and feed. On the day it was finished, the family and crew gathered around to admire the addition to the rancho. Such a fine one it was. Fernando showed off the loft with two narrow windows that could be used as a lookout post—it had a clear view of the southern entrance of the canyon, the barley field, and the creek beyond.

Guillermo spent the first night in the stable with the animals, partly to help them adjust to their new quarters and partly to see what the conditions were like for himself. A heat wave had descended earlier in the week. The narrow canyon was stifling during the day. Nighttime brought some relief from the heat, though he suspected the animals would view it as punishment to be confined in the stuffy enclosure. He hoped his presence would have a calming effect on them. He dragged a pallet in from the storeroom and covered it with hay and a blanket.

The stable was nine feet high, twenty feet long, and fifteen feet wide. It smelled of drying adobe, dried grass, and manure, but it was a grand feeling to finally have the animals secure, though he could tell they were confused by their new accommodations. They kept testing their stalls to see if they could escape and join the others outside. They neighed to each other, and Guillermo murmured his reassurances in the dark. El Rey draped his neck over the railing, his nostrils flaring to pick up Guillermo's scent. The moonlight shone through the window and was reflected in his big eyes. Guillermo soothed him. "It's all right, boy. I know this is strange, but come winter, and you're going to be glad you have shelter. Now go to sleep."

Sometime after midnight, Guillermo awoke to the wind rustling the branches of the oaks nearby. The lonely cry of a coyote was met by howls from the rancho dogs. The animals in the corral outside became restless, and their whinnies agitated the horses inside. Guillermo shifted his body on the pallet and strained to listen for the cause of their unrest. He thought he heard the distant whinnying of horses, but the wind could do strange things with sounds. The rancho dogs were barking in earnest now, and he heard Shadow giving her alert bark.

"What in tarnation?" he grumbled. Of late he had taken to adopting some of his father's favorite expressions. Rising from the pallet, he fumbled in the dark for the ladder. He found it leaning against the tack room wall, dragged it a few feet, and hooked it to the edge of the loft. He ascended the rungs and dragged himself onto the oak beams, crawling on his stomach to the window.

Hot winds were blowing in from the desert across the mountains. The moon had partially sunk behind the hills, but rays of iridescent light shone through the rustling oaks.

Guillermo squinted to catch any movement that didn't belong. He could make out Shadow and Smokey racing across the barley field, jumping through the three-foot-high grain—it could have been a bear they were after. He heard horses whinnying down by the creek, scanned the tree line, and thought he caught movement, but the whipping branches obscured it. The dogs disappeared into the shrouded darkness of the willows.

A faint glow caught his attention. Was he seeing things? The light grew and erupted into orange flames. The barley field was on fire! He barely made out the dark shapes of two horsemen with torches racing across the field.

"Fire! Fire!" he screamed through the window, hoping the Gonzalezes would hear him.

Guillermo scrambled down the ladder and grabbed his rifle leaning against the wall of the stable as he threw open the latch to the door. Racing into the yard, he yelled again, "Fire! Fire!" He halted to load his rifle and fired off a shot as the vandals disappeared down the trail toward La Laguna with the dogs in pursuit. Several patches of fire glowed in the barley field.

Chico, Sal, and Angel were the first on the scene, wearing only long underwear. "What's going on?" gasped Sal.

Guillermo pointed to the field and yelled over the wind, "I heard noises and saw two riders setting the barley on fire! They took off across the field when I fired at 'em. No point in trying to chase 'em, they've got too much of a head start!"

Sal gazed at the spreading flames fifty yards away and yelled, "The wind's kicking up embers and sending them flying everywhere! We gotta get someone on the roofs to keep the embers from catching the tule on fire! Good, here comes Fernando with some gunnysacks."

211

"I'll take the stable, and you take the adobe, Guillermo," called Chico.

Guillermo nodded, and Chico dashed into the stable to retrieve the ladder. Don Julian emerged from the adobe, shrugging into his suspenders, an expression of vexation on his face.

Sal shook his head and sighed heavily. "I fear he's going to take this hard!"

Guillermo steadied the ladder for Chico as he scrambled up to the stable's roof, tossed a wet gunnysack up to him, and called to Manuel to get the horses out of the stable and picket them near the hitching post. As soon as Chico hefted himself onto the roof, Guillermo raced across the yard, headed for the adobe. He was intercepted by his father, who was trotting stiffly toward him.

"I heard the shots! Was that you, mijo?" said Don Julian.

"Sí. I spotted two riders from the stable loft. Gone now."

Sal and Fernando joined them, and Sal said, "We're headed out to the field, el jefe. Guillermo and Chico will take care of the roofs."

Don Julian took off running toward the burning field with the Gonzalezes and was joined by Manuel and Juan.

Guillermo passed his mother as he lumbered across the yard with the ladder under one arm and a dripping sack in the other. She pulled her shawl over the shoulders of her nightgown and glanced around in confusion. "What's going on?" She gazed out into the darkness, and her hands flew to her mouth. "O Dios mio!"

"It'll be all right, Mamá. We were lucky I spotted them when I did."

He turned his back on her and leaned the ladder against the adobe wall. Petra stood in the yard alongside Doña

Eduarda, holding Alejandro in her arms. Both stared at the spreading fire. They were joined by the girls, who huddled together in disbelief.

Glowing embers fell on the dried tule and tar roof. Guillermo scampered up the ladder to the roof and spied several narrow plumes of smoke! He hoisted himself onto the roof and dashed about, stamping out the hotspots with his botas. From his vantage point, he caught a glimpse of the men running through the barley field, trying to extinguish the flames with gunny sacks of their own. As fast as they stomped out flames, wind gusts sent swirling clouds of embers into the night sky. Most died out before they landed, but some ignited the dried brush and leaves on the oak trees.

He yelled down to Angel, "Need another wet sack!"

Angel disappeared for a few minutes and returned empty handed. "There aren't any more! Throw down the one you have, and I'll soak it again!"

Guillermo tossed down the blackened sack and frantically stamped out embers. Angel returned with the dripping gunny sack, climbed halfway up the ladder, and lobbed it onto the roof. Guillermo snatched it up and returned to slapping down flames. The tule would have to be replaced, but so far, the wood beams were only scorched.

Down below, Ramona and Martina rushed down to the creek with Concha and Rosita, carrying buckets to haul back water. Old Fernando and Felipe were scrambling to stomp out embers in the dried grass that skirted the yard.

After an hour, the gusts subsided and the last of the flames were extinguished. Finally it was safe for the women and children to return indoors. The menfolk rested in the patio, drinking tea that Concha had brewed for them but keeping an eye out for flare-ups. It was the first opportunity they had to discuss how the incident unfolded. Guillermo explained how he awoke to the dogs barking and the agitated horses. When he climbed up to the loft, he spotted movement in the far corner of the field and the faint glow of flames. The loft had proven to be of strategic value on its first night of service.

"I know it was dark and they were across the way, but could you make out anything about the horses or riders?" asked Don Julian.

"No, I only saw dark figures moving about. They took off down the south trail, which is no surprise."

"Back in the direction of Corral de Cuati." Chico sniffed.

"At daybreak in a few hours, we'll look for tracks, see if there's any distinctive hoofprints," said Don Julian. "This confirms there's an undeclared war being waged against us. No two ways around it."

"I agree." Sal nodded. "If it hadn't been for Guillermo alerting us so soon, things could have been disastrous. We're mighty lucky he and Chico were able to snuff out the embers on the roofs, or both buildings could have been lost, not to mention loss of life. Mighty rare to have a dry night with no dew. The hot winds and dry brush made for ideal conditions for a fire to spread under the cover of darkness. These hombres jumped at a rare opportunity to strike."

Guillermo stared numbly into the campfire and saw his dream of attending school go up in smoke. There was no way he could leave home when war continued to be waged against his family. The only question was when the next attack would come.

CHAPTER 38

With more than half of the barley crop destroyed, there wasn't enough to sell to the regiment in Santa Barbara. There would be no money to pay for Guillermo's tuition, but that was the least of his concerns. Fear and worry for his family's safety outweighed his disappointment, and the horror of the Paljalchet massacre haunted his dreams. What was to prevent his family from being next? A fire at night had the potential to be tragic for a sleeping family. Thank God he had discovered it when he did, but the harassment was escalating. How long would their luck hold out?

As his mother pointed out, he could enroll in school the following year. A lot could change in the intervening months, and hopefully the harassment would end. She informed him that he would be getting a new baby brother or sister in the spring, all the more reason that his place was there on the rancho, not six leagues miles away at school.

A month later on a chilly September day, Guillermo rode with Sal to the barley field where Don Julian was supervising the harvest. Manuel and Juan were swinging scythes through the golden stalks that had survived the fire, and they were covered in ash from tramping in the sooty field. Upon seeing Sal and Guillermo approach, Don Julian straightened and called out, "Have you come to watch some real work?"

There had been an ongoing debate between Sal and his boss about which was a worthier endeavor: herding cattle or farming. "You know my opinion about that." Sal chuckled. "I'm here to find out when I can tell the Oliveras to come for the fall roundup. We can't put it off much longer. Makes it easier for calves to be stolen the longer they go unbranded. I say we schedule it pronto."

"I hear what you're saying, Sal, but I can't spare Manuel and Juan until the barley's threshed. Figure that'll take another week," said Don Julian.

"Jefe," Sal sighed, "we risk losing cattle every day we postpone. We can't afford to lose any more. This is," he gazed at the blackened field with a cattleman's disdain for farming, "secondary to the cattle."

Guillermo's mouth twisted as he stifled a grin.

Don Julian's head bolted back. "Whaddya mean, secondary? This here's going to benefit the horses and Sadie. You'll be singing my praises when you see how much they enjoy the barley. The drought's affecting them too. They're the real workers and deserve nutritious grain. The cattle aren't work animals."

Sal stared at his boss, dumbfounded. "They provide us hides and tallow, not to mention calves. If that's not working, I don't know what is. They're what keep this place going. I need to know…can I tell Ramon Olivera to come with his crew on Tuesday?"

Don Julian removed his hat and scratched his head. "Go ahead." He gave a dismissive wave like he was swatting a fly. "How many calves do you think there are?"

Sal rubbed his chin. "Should be at least sixty, but I'm afraid the number will be far less. It's important to keep track of our losses."

When Sal and Guillermo rode away, Sal muttered, "That father of yours is one obstinate hombre. Once he gets a notion in his head, it's a struggle to get him to change course."

"Like when he insisted on getting those whaling vats here to the rancho," said Guillermo.

Sal shook his head and sighed. "Don't remind me! I thought he was out of his mind!"

Five years before, two huge vats from a whaling ship had been left in the port of Santa Barbara. When Don Julian heard about them, he was determined to acquire them for making soap, but how would he get the six-foot-wide iron pots to the rancho when they were too bulky to carry by ox-cart? His solution was to send Manuel and Juan to roll the awkward vats over sixty miles of rugged terrain! It took them four months to complete the arduous task. When word spread of Don Julian's audacious endeavor, he gained the reputation of being the bull-headed Englishman who refused to take no for an answer.

Sal pulled up on the reins and halted under a shady oak to take a swig of water from his leather pouch. Wiping his mouth on his sleeve, he said, "I know you were hoping to go to school. Sorry it didn't work out. Maybe next year. Can tell your father's mighty disappointed."

"This is where I need to be for now," said Guillermo.

"I agree, but your father wants you to be prepared for the changes coming and feels he's let you down."

"Well, he has. Why did he have to risk everything for a stranger? Fremont's long gone, and we're left to deal with the consequences of betraying our own people to help him. I'm worried some paisanos will never forgive us."

"Your father's not one to give a hoot about what others

think. He's a man of action who cares more about getting things done. In time, people will forgive him."

"It seems he puts his wants above our well-being. Who besides him makes the dangerous trip to the Tulare Valley for matorral weed so his Castile soap will be better than anyone else's? No one. Then he spends three additional days mining for lead ore! We both know he could have traded some from Ike Sparks and gotten a good deal, but he has to get it for free even though he knows we're stretched thin trying to cover the responsibilities around here. Only six weeks later, he leaves us alone again when he goes to Santa Barbara, and during the couple days he lingers in the pueblo, visiting with friends, we're attacked by Tulares. The females and Alejandro could have been massacred like Antonio's family, and you could have lost Concha and Rosita. Then his barley field is set on fire. If I hadn't discovered it when I did, the adobe would have burned down from the flying embers landing on the roof. The horses could have perished in the stable, all because we were trying to protect them from being stolen. If it's not one thing, it's another! Things are out of control. Who knows what's going to happen next? It's crazy!" Guillermo slumped in the saddle, deflated from his release of frustration.

Sal's mouth compressed in a straight line. "Guillermo, you're more right than you know. Your grandfather, Don Tomás, sent me out here to teach your father how to ranch, but frankly, I feel I've had more success with you. You're a natural horseman. It's in your blood. Your father is cut from a different cloth. He's a jack of all trades, and ranching is just one of his interests. Being an ex-seaman and an Anglo, his mind is always working to find a better way of getting a job done. My boys and I have learned a lot from him, but

218

he's different from us." He took another swig. "The problem is his stubbornness can cloud his thinking. I'm afraid the time may come when the risks become too great to stay here. Your grandparents came to that conclusion after Ausencio died. I'm concerned your father may wait too long."

"What do you mean?"

"It's his tendency to take chances. As you've heard, when you were a baby, he was quite the gambler. Your mother found out about his poker games and made him promise to quit. She wouldn't tolerate him playing the devil's game. He kept his promise to her, but I see him rolling the dice with all manner of things, like his insistence on harvesting the barley before holding the roundup. He's gambling that calves won't be stolen. I think life on a rancho is monotonous for him, so he ups the ante by trying to beat the odds."

Guillermo looked at Sal in wonder. "You're right. That's exactly what he does. I keep wondering how far Davila, Fuentes, and Rios are willing to go. Will Papá call it quits before it's too late? Since the massacre at Zaca, I'm afraid we're going to be next."

"I say if we have another night raid, that's it. It's just a matter of time before more people will die," said Sal.

"I agree. Can't believe I'm saying this." Guillermo sighed heavily and scanned the surrounding hills. "Leaving is the last thing I want to do, but there comes a point…" His voice cracked.

Sal nodded soberly. "Least we're in agreement. It may take the two of us to convince your father it's time for the women and children to go somewhere safer. C'mon, let's go talk to Ramon about the roundup and fill him in on what's been going on."

CHAPTER 39

Sal's suspicions were confirmed when at least a dozen calves were unaccounted for along with several heifers. Someone was stealing them! There had been no more raids, but it seemed there was always a new worry to replace an old one. The rains were late in coming, and the livestock had nibbled the dried grass down to the parched ground.

While herding the cattle one blustery morning in mid-November, Guillermo gazed at the darkening clouds scudding across the sky and asked, "Think these clouds will bring rain, Sal?"

Sal rubbed a knee. "Judging by the way my old bones are aching, I think a storm is moving in."

He was right. The first storm of the season rolled in off the Pacific within hours. By late afternoon, the skies had turned inky while the wind whipped the sturdy branches of the oaks. The willows that lined the creek swayed violently and fluttered their two-toned leaves.

The horses that weren't kept in the stable huddled in the corral, turning their rumps to the wind. Their barley was stored in barrels, safe from a leaky roof and mice. As Don Julian had predicted, the horses had been happy with their change in diet, especially since there was precious little forage left on the hills. The cattle had been forced to feed on leaves from low-hanging oak branches. The tree foliage was evenly trimmed as high as the cattle could reach. With the accessible leaves consumed, the crew had been forced to cut limbs from big trees and chop down smaller ones. Within days, the hills would be dusted with green, and scarcity would give way to life-giving abundance. California's arid climate made cattle ranching a high-risk game of chance. In a typical seven-year cycle, two would be marked by insufficient rain, three would provide adequate rain to feed the livestock, and two would be wet, marked by lush grass and sporadic flooding in the creeks.

By La Nochebuena, two more storms had dumped several inches of rain. The hills and valleys had sprouted tender blades of grass four inches high. By all accounts, 1848 was shaping up to be a wet year, despite its late start.

No sooner had the rainfall problem been resolved than others cropped up. Like Egypt in biblical times, Rancho Tinaquaic was beset by one vexation after another. It started with an ague that spread through the Foxen household and then the Gonzalezes'. Its onset was marked by sudden chills and fever, a cough, and debilitating fatigue. From start to finish, it lasted ten days. On some days, only two vaqueros were available to herd the cattle. This meant that cows strayed into the backcountry and were easy prey to bands of coyotes and prowling bears. The temperatures were mild, and the bears were slow to retreat to the higher elevations to hibernate. The losses of heifers and calves exceeded previous years. By late January, thirty head had been lost.

Moisture seeped into one of the barley barrels that had been left slightly ajar. Before anyone realized, it had gone moldy and, worse, inadvertently fed to the horses. Their bellies bloated up with gas, causing them to suffer a bout of colic. Benito laid on his side, unable to get to his feet for nearly six hours. He'd die if he couldn't stand. Guillermo and Juan were able to coax him to a kneeling position, which lessened the strain on his heart. Eventually, he mustered the strength to stand upright on wobbly legs, and he recovered. The belle mare's yearling was not as fortunate. He was found dead one morning in the stable, his mother licking his cold ears.

By early February, the crew of Rancho Tinaquaic had recuperated from the sickness. They discovered that a portion of the cattle herd that had been pastured to the east had drowned in the Sisquoc River. During the storms of the preceding month, the river had swollen and cut a new channel into the silty riverbed. A dozen head became mired in the quicksand and drowned, and Sal suspected they had been driven into the river by Fuentes and his men. In all his years of herding cattle, he had never seen such a large number be caught off guard like that. Cattle weren't known for being intelligent animals, but they knew to be wary of flowing water. Besides, there was feed on the hills, and there was no need for them to wander all the way to the river. The harassment appeared to be continuing.

As if to belie the specter of evil that seemed to hang over Rancho Tinaquaic, the hills were green from the late rains, and wildflowers grew in abundance. Doña Eduarda was heavy with her seventh child that was due to be born the following month. Don Julian put off his annual spring trip to the Tulare Valley for matorral ash and lead ore. Every able-bodied man was needed to guard the hacienda and herd, which was shrinking. The loss of a heifer counted as four since she wouldn't be bearing calves in the coming years. It was estimated that over the previous five months, more than eighty head had died or been stolen, which was upward to a sixth of the herd. At that rate, the spring matanza wouldn't yield enough hides and tallow to provide the supplies needed for the summer and fall.

Guillermo didn't need to be told that he wouldn't be attending school in the fall. He didn't know who to blame for his predicament, Fremont or his father. Perhaps it was fate.

One unseasonably warm night in mid-February, the Foxens were awakened by shouts, gunfire, dogs barking, and the pounding of hooves outside the hacienda. Guillermo and Don Julian stumbled from their beds to grab their rifles, trying to orient themselves while shaking off the dregs of sleep.

Juanita shrieked, "They're BA-CK! They're BA-CK!" Martina could be heard trying to console her in the adjacent room.

As Don Julian unbolted the door, he ordered, "Mijo, stay inside and bolt the door! Open it only if you hear my voice!"

Guillermo did as he was told, though he was frustrated at having to remain inside. A flurry of shots were fired. He glanced down at his hand holding the rifle, which trembled uncontrollably. Would he be able to shoot accurately if someone stormed the house? He prayed he wouldn't have to find out.

Martina hustled the girls out of their bedchamber and had them crouch in the hallway. Guillermo ordered her to close their door as a precaution against a stray bullet entering the interior of the house.

Juanita cried, "Guillermo, are they going to kill Papá?"

Before he had a chance to reply, another round of gunfire was exchanged outside, causing everyone to duck. It sounded as if the shots were coming from the patio. Ay, caramba! That was way too close! Guillermo assumed that

223

Angel and Manuel, who were on guard duty, were reinforced by Sal and the others. He wished his father hadn't rushed outside, as there was no telling what he had walked into. If his father were killed, he'd be thrust into the role of head of the household overnight, and he was not prepared to take that role. "No, they're just trying to scare us."

Martina and Ramona knew he was downplaying the seriousness of the situation. Doña Eduarda lumbered around the corner, her braid hanging to her waist. The terrified Juanita threw her arms around her mother's side, sobbing, and Doña Eduarda staggered as she absorbed the jolt of her daughter's body. She soothed her youngest daughter by stroking her head, murmuring, "Hush, dear, it will be all right. They'll be gone soon."

Martina, Ramona, and Panchita stared up at Guillermo, searching his face for reassurance.

"Mamacita's right. They'll be gone soon," he said.

Petra joined Doña Eduarda and the children in the hallway. She tried to hold Alejandro in her arms, but he refused, kicking and squirming to get to his mother.

Doña Eduarda said, "No, no. It's all right, Petra." She scooped up the toddler and bounced him in her arms, closed her eyes, made the sign of the cross, and began to pray. "Hail Mary, full of grace, the Lord is with thee."

Petra and the three older girls knelt on the rug and joined her in prayer.

The attacks were taking their toll on his mother and sisters. By all rights his father should have evacuated them to the safety of his grandparents' new home in San Luis Obispo. Worry lines were etched in his mother's pale face, along with fatigue. Though normally a source of strength and comfort to others, she looked vulnerable, her flannel nightgown stretched over her swollen stomach. Loose strands of hair framed her pinched face. Alejandro laid his cherubic face against her cheek, gazing over her shoulder at his older brother and sucking his thumb.

A lump caught in Guillermo's throat. Usually his father was unavailable, too busy, or gone somewhere. He had a sudden urge to abandon his post so he could hold his mother protectively, but he had been ordered to guard the door against intruders, so he was duty bound to ignore the nudging of his heart.

The gunfire had become sporadic. Surely the attackers realized they were outnumbered and would flee, escaping into the night. What an outrageous state of affairs it was that his family should be huddled in the middle of the night quaking with fear, wrested from their sleep by marauders. He wondered how his father, the Gonzalezes, and Manuel were faring and prayed none of the horses in the corral would be hit in the crossfire. It was frustrating being holed up inside.

Guillermo heard excited shouting outside and strained to make out the words. Could it be "Fire!"? O Dios mio! Not again! The gunfire ceased, but now there was more yelling. His first impulse was to throw open the door, but he needed to be sure the attackers were gone. After a few moments, there was the thud of heavy footsteps on the veranda and pounding on the door.

"Guillermo, it's me! They're gone now! Open the door!"

Don Julian came inside and reassured Doña Eduarda and the others that it was safe to return to bed. Their anxious faces broke into smiles, and they hugged one another in relief. Guillermo joined his father outside to be debriefed. According to Angel, three riders had come down the trail and boldly entered the yard from the main entrance. It was Manuel's turn to keep awake, and he managed to get off two shots with Angel's rifle before Angel awoke and grabbed it from him. The riders seemed surprised that they met gunfire so soon. Guillermo could see Manuel and Juan in the corral calming the horses. He knew this would go a long way to help Manuel get over his sense of failure for falling asleep while on guard duty the previous year.

"I-If Manuel hadn't been so quick to respond to the dogs barking," said Angel, "w-we, w-woulda lost precious time. The rifle was loaded, and he fired at the rider in the lead as he passed the corral. He missed, but it caught them off guard. At that point, they knew we were waiting for them. The loft and its firing post have saved us twice now. Yowee! F-feels good to beat them at their own g-game!"

"Did you see who it was?" asked Don Julian.

"They had kerchiefs pulled up over their faces, but it sounded like Fuentes who yelled to the other rider to light the torch in the hornito."

Chico spoke up. "You're right. I recognized Fuentes' voice too. When he spotted me, he dismounted and hid around the corner of the house. He fired two shots in my direction. I fired back, but he ducked around the corner, saddled up again."

"What do you expect when you've been seeing his girl-friend?" said Guillermo.

Chico's head bolted back in surprise, and he sneered. "Why do you say that?"

"Cuz Alfredo told me last Easter."

Chico shrugged it off. "They're gone now, and that's all that matters."

"Having someone on guard at all times saved us," said Don Julian. "Angel, you and Manuel did a good job. With all the shots fired, we're lucky none of the animals were hit." He raked a hand through his wiry hair that stood on end and gazed out into the moonlit night. "After all these months, I was hoping the raids had ended. Looks like I was wrong."

"I agree. This is headed in a bad direction," said Sal. "They would have set the roof on fire if Angel hadn't grazed the one who was trying to light the torch in the hornito. I'm sure they were hoping to be gone by the time we were roused from a dead sleep. By then, the roof would have been engulfed in flames."

Chico slapped Angel on the back and said with a wolf-ish grin, "Well, what do you know, little brother! You're the first of us draw blood. Congratulations!"

Angel's eyes widened, and his chin trembled. "'Fore tonight, I-I wondered if I-I'd be able to h-hit someone when I-I needed to, b-but it all happened so fast I-I didn't have time t-to think about it. W-when someone's shooting at you, y-you, sh-shoot back."

Guillermo stared at him. "Are you all right?"

Before Angel had a chance to answer, Sal said, "It's just shock setting in. He'll be all right."

Angel's hand shook so violently that Chico said, "Here, hand me that thing before you hurt someone."

Angel handed over the rifle. "Did I do the r-right th-thing by aiming for him, el jefe, or should I have shot over his head to scare him off?"

Don Julian tucked his hands under his armpits to keep them warm. "You did the right thing, mijo. When someone's shooting at you, all bets are off." He motioned with a hand. "I had a bullet whiz past my head. I fired back but missed.

Make no doubt about it, I aimed to kill. It infuriates me how they're terrorizing the women and children, trying to force me to throw in my cards and abandon the rancho."

Guillermo and Sal exchanged glances, recalling their discussion some weeks back.

Sal said, "We can't go on this way. It's just a matter of time before someone's killed. I say we let Officer Janssens know about this latest attack. A couple of us could ride out to his rancho tomorrow. He can pay a visit to Corral de Cuati and La Laguna in an official capacity and see if anyone's nursing an injury, and maybe that will be proof enough for him to make an arrest."

Don Julian nodded. "It's worth a try. How about you and Felipe make the trip in the morning?"

"I'll go," said Chico.

"I know you're itching to cross paths with Fuentes," said Don Julian wearily, "but I don't want to take that chance. I need you to stick around here and help us guard the rancho. Comprende?"

Chico's shoulders slumped. He reluctantly said, "Sí, el jefe."

Guillermo wondered now if the upcoming confrontation between Janssens and Davila would escalate their troubles.

CHAPTER 40

al and Felipe returned by sundown the following day after informing Janssens of the previous night's attack. After some discussion, Janssens rode to the mission to confer with the padres about how to proceed.

Three days later, Janssens and Padre Jimeño were seated in the Foxens' sala, grimly sipping tea. They had met with Gustavo Davila hours before, and he claimed no knowledge of the recent attack but allowed his crew to be questioned. Not surprisingly, they denied any involvement. Rios had one arm in a sling, which he claimed was the result of being thrown from his horse.

Janssens noticed that some of the cattle grazing on Corral de Cuati bore the Foxens' anchor brand. "Why is that?" he asked.

Fuentes complained that Foxen allowed his cattle to wander. He and the other Corral de Cuati crew members repeatedly herded them back onto Tinaquaic land, but they kept returning. When Janssens and Padre Jimeño exchanged skeptical looks, Fuentes said, "How can you defend someone who was quick to accept Mexico's land but refused to defend it against invaders when it became inconvenient? He's responsible for us losing more than twenty of our best cow ponies to Fremont."

Padre Jimeño suggested that Doña Eduarda and the

children leave with him and stay at the mission for the time being. "I fear for your safety, señora. You're too isolated for anyone from the outside to protect you. If they've tried to burn your house down with family members in it, they'll stop at nothing to run you off your land."

Don Julian spoke up. "Why should she and the children be forced to leave their home because of outlaws? We all know Fuentes and Rios are lying, so why can't someone official examine Rios' injury? Arrest him if it's a gunshot wound. Besides, as you can see, it's too late for my wife to travel in her delicate condition."

Doña Eduarda blushed and studied her teacup as if looking for answers. "Thank you for your concern, Padre, but Julian is right. The baby is due in weeks. I promise we'll leave as soon as I'm able to travel after the birth. Until then, we have to trust our Heavenly Father to protect us."

Padre Jimeño and Janssens bid the Foxens farewell with heavy hearts. Padre Jimeño promised the family would be in his daily prayers, and Janssens left behind a pouch of gunpowder. "Here. At least you'll be able to defend yourselves if the need arises. I pray it doesn't but just in case."

"Thank you, Augustin. I appreciate everything you've done to help us," said Don Julian.

The visitors galloped down the trail and out of sight. Guillermo was overwhelmed by a desire to call out to them to wait. He yearned to gather up his family and ride out with them under armed escort. He prayed they would be able to hold out until his mother was able to travel.

A few weeks later on a blustery night in early March, Guillermo and Angel sat in Fernando's blacksmith shed, molding bullets for the rifles and two pistolas on the rancho. Nearly a hundred rounds were neatly stacked according to size. Every man carried a loaded weapon at all times.

Guillermo asked, "You think things have been quiet around here because of Rios' injury or because they were paid a visit by Janssens?"

"Probably both," said Angel.

Guillermo poured the molten lead into the round mold and squeezed the long handles shut. "It could go one of two ways. They could back off or become angrier."

"Are you kidding? Mark my words, this is the lull before the storm."

"Why do you always have to believe the worst?"

"Because sugarcoating things don't work," said Angel. "I'd rather face facts and not be disappointed. Saves a lot of grief."

"That's where we're different. I need to hold onto hope. Otherwise, what's the point? We may as well chuck it in and abandon all that we've worked so hard for."

"Sorry to be the one to break it to you, but you think things are going to improve after your mother and sisters leave for the mission?" Angel shook his head. "Nuh-uh. Don't you get it, prince? They want us gone! They burned your father's crops, they're killing off the livestock or stealing them, they set fire to the roof, and they terrified the womenfolk. Even on days when there are no attacks, we're all on edge, snapping at each other, waiting for the next one!"

"I can't believe you're saying this." Guillermo whispered, "It's because you shot Rios, right?"

The words struck a chord. As Angel filed the ridge off a bullet, a tear trickled down his cheek. He swiped it away and turned from Guillermo, his head lowered in despair. In a defeated voice, he said, "I feel like a dead man walking. I keep asking myself why it had to be my bullet that grazed him. It should have been Chico's. Sure, I was proud at the time, but then it sunk in that I'm their number one target now. I'm sure they're plotting revenge. I'm a marked man now. Even in my dreams I'm tormented. Every night it's the same. My gun jams, and I'm a sitting duck. I can hear Fuentes laughing as I'm waiting to be shot. When I wake up, it's hard to shake the sense of dread." His shoulders heaved, and the floodgate opened. Guillermo couldn't recall a time he'd seen Angel cry, not even when Chico dared him to jump out of the tree and he broke an ankle.

"I don't know what to say. I'm sorry. If I were you, I'd feel the same," said Guillermo. "Don't seem right that we got sucked into this mess. This is way beyond us. Just once I'd like to hear my father apologize for bringing all this trouble down on us."

Angel wiped his face with his poncho and sighed deeply. Still slumped, he turned around. "I don't hold it against your father. It's Fuentes and Rios with their black leather hearts that I blame." Angel had always believed that el jefe could do no wrong.

"Least we have enough ammunition to last us for a while. Want me to talk to my father about having you stick around the hacienda, not out on the open range?"

"No! Promise me you won't ask him. I don't want him to know I'm scared. Swear on Ausencio's grave you won't tell."

"Tell him what, Angel?"

They swiveled and spotted Old Fernando standing in the doorway, a cigarette dangling from his lips.

"What are you doing, Tio, sneaking up on us like that?" said Angel. "Good way to get yourself shot."

"You seem to forget you're in my workshop." Fernando eyed the piles of bullets. "Looks like you spent your time well tonight. What's the big secret?

232

Guillermo stared at Angel. "Go ahead. He won't tell."

Angel glared at Guillermo and sighed heavily. "I don't want el jefe to know I'm…worried about Fuentes and Rios coming after me for revenge, that's all." He shrugged.

"Of course you're on edge. We all are except for that crazy brother of yours. I would think that with all the chaos that night, they don't know for sure whose bullet hit Rios. I'm guessing we all have a target on our backs. We're all the enemy."

Angel nodded. "You're right. It was chaotic. Bullets flying everywhere. Maybe they don't know it was me, but still, it's not much better that we're all targets."

Fernando removed a chain from around his neck and handed it to Angel. "Here, take it. This Saint Christopher medal has protected me from rattlers, puma, even a she-bear with cubs that I came face to face with one time."

Angel fingered the medal and slipped the chain over his head. "Hope you don't regret giving this up."

"It's served me well. Time to pass it on."

"Where'd you get it anyway?" asked Angel.

"From an amigo years before you were born."

"Why did he give it to you?"

"He didn't exactly. He got gored by a bull and I took it."

"Doesn't sound like it protected him so well," said Guillermo.

"It protects against danger, not stupidity."

Concha passed by the door opening and leaned in. "You boys still up? It's late. Angel, you can finish that in the morning. You need your sleep." She wagged a finger at Guillermo. "By morning, you should have a baby sister or brother." Her round face broke into a broad smile, and her eyes twinkled.

"Really? Mamá's having the baby tonight?"

"Sí! I'm going home to change my clothes and then back

to spend the night and help Petra."

Angel left, and Guillermo poured the last of the molten lead into the bullet mold. "Well, this should last us for a while. Maybe until Mamá and the girls leave in another month or so."

"I remember how it was when you were born," said Fernando. "For weeks before, the night sky was lit up by a star with a long tail. Petra and the other Chumash were convinced the señora's baby would be born under a good sign. You were destined for something special. When I heard about what you did on the mountain, I said to myself, well, there you have it, Fernando, proof that sometimes there's more to Indian superstition than we think."

"Do you believe in destiny?"

"You've played enough hands of cards to know about odds. What do you think the odds were that you, a mere boy, would be placed on that mountain to lead an army down in a torrential rainstorm?"

"Hmm...slim, but it could just mean I'm unlucky."

"What's wrong with you, boy? Hasn't any of your mamá's faith rubbed off on you? Not just anyone could have done what you did. Now don't get me wrong, I suspect you had plenty of divine intervention working for you that day, but the point is you made yourself available to be used. I have no doubt men returned home to their families because you led them down the mountain safely. Remember that when you start bellyaching about things not being fair. Life isn't fair, but sometimes, despite our frailties, we can contribute to the common good by helping where we can. Simple as that."

Guillermo stared at Fernando in amazement. "I've never heard you talk like that."

"Yeah, well, just because I don't go saying every thought

that passes through my head don't mean I don't have deep ones from time to time."

Guillermo was touched by the old man's sentiments. Life certainly was mysterious. If he had been divinely ordained to lead an army down the San Marcos Trail in a deluge, why wouldn't God protect his family so they wouldn't have to abandon their beloved rancho? It didn't make sense. "Even though it's been quiet these past couple weeks, the air feels strange. I can't explain it. Do you feel it too?"

Fernando nodded. "What you're sensing is impending danger. We all feel it."

"I'm expecting at any moment to hear the crack of gunfire or someone yell, "Fire!" I'm on edge all the time. Every time the dogs bark, I think they're alerting us. I drive myself crazy constantly thinking I hear something, so I rein Benito in so I can strain to hear, and then it's just the wind. I can't relax, ever. In some ways, waiting is harder than the actual attack. Every night I dream we're under attack, but I'm never ready. I fumble with my rifle. I wake up in a sweat and try to shake the feeling, and I'm afraid to fall back to sleep for fear I'll slip back into the dream. Have you ever shot anyone?"

"Nope, only critters," said Fernando. "When your life is threatened, doesn't matter if it's human or animal. Your aim needs to be dead-on. No maiming. An injured animal is a dangerous one. Same goes for a man if he's out to get you."

Guillermo gave a mirthless chuckle. "Rios is probably gnashing his teeth wanting to repay us for grazing his arm. That's the problem. If you shoot and miss, you're in danger, and if you maim, you're in worse danger. If you manage to kill someone, then his friend is out to get you." He shrugged and spread his arms in exasperation. "There's no winning."

"There is if you survive," said Fernando.

CHAPTER 41

I n the wee hours of the morning, Maria Antonia de la Cruz arrived, the first of the Foxens to be born under the Stars and Stripes. Although Toñita, as she would be called, was not the brother Guillermo hoped for, she was healthy with lots of dark hair and strong lungs.

In the coming weeks, there were no night raids, but there were other kinds of harassment. Several times as the crew herded cattle, they were fired at by a sniper. On two of those occasions, a lone gunman was spotted under some oaks before he disappeared.

One afternoon when Concha was cooking in the ramada, a bullet hit the triangular gong hanging a few feet from her head. Startled, she looked up the hill behind the house, and a male figure on horseback saluted her. By the time Fernando shuffled from his shed to see what the matter was, the gunman had disappeared. Fernando spent the rest of the afternoon standing guard while Concha prepared supper.

On the Thursday before Easter, Guillermo and Sal rode in from the range with disturbing news. Before they had a chance to tell Don Julian, he asked, "What now? I can tell something's wrong." He leaned against the plow he had been sharpening and mopped his face with a kerchief. "Out with it."

Sal sighed heavily. "I'm sorry to have to tell you this,

jefe, but we came across El Mauro and his harem. They've all been shot dead. Thirteen heifers and their calves."

Don Julian groaned. "Oh no. Not El Mauro." He slumped onto a bale of hay and hung his head in his hands.

"I'm sorry, Papá," said Guillermo. There was no point in telling his father that from the looks of it, it had taken a fusillade of bullets to bring down the noble black beast. He had been Don Julian's prize bull—a gift from his godfather, Daniel Hill, when he began ranching. The bull killed the previous year had been El Mauro's son. Practically and symbolically, the vengeful act dealt a major blow to the rancho's ability to replenish its dwindling herd.

Don Julian picked up the scythe leaning against the bale of hay he was sitting on and hurled it across the storage room. It crashed into a bucket of oats, sending it rolling across the dirt floor and spilling its contents in an arc. Guillermo and Sal flinched at the outburst and braced for what was to come.

"They're determined to ruin me! They'll stop at nothing! I've had it! I'm going over there to have it out with Gustavo! If he can't control his crew, someone needs to."

Sal put up his hands. "No, no, no, jefe. You can't do that, not by yourself."

"Papá, please don't go! They'll shoot you!" said Guillermo.

"Mijo, sometimes a man has to take a stand. I've taken as much as I'm going to. This has gotta stop!" He grabbed his rifle and stomped out of the stable.

Sal tried blocking his way. "El jefe, I can't let you do this! It's too dangerous!"

Don Julian barreled past him. "Sorry, Sal. It's no use. This has gone far enough." He strode toward the corral, bellowing. "Juan, saddle up Joaquin!"

Juan appeared from the workshop, wide-eyed at seeing Sal and Guillermo trying to restrain Don Julian. Confused, he hesitated.

"Ahora!" yelled his beet-faced boss.

Juan sprang into action, "Sí, señor!"

Doña Eduarda rushed from the house with Toñita in her arms. "Julian! Julian! What's the matter?"

Don Julian stopped in his tracks, whirled, and pointed. "Eduarda! I need you to go back into the house. This doesn't concern you!"

Undeterred, she lifted her skirt with one hand to cover the distance more quickly. "Julian, por favor!

Flushed with anger, Don Julian ordered Guillermo, "I need you to get your mother back in the house!" He pointed toward Doña Eduarda and bellowed hoarsely, "Now! Do you understand?"

Guillermo turned to intercept his mother. He extended his arms and grabbed her by the shoulders, careful not to squeeze her bundle. "Mamá, por favor! Stop!"

She struggled to break loose. "What happened? Why is your father so upset?"

"El Mauro and his harem were shot."

"Oh no." She moaned. "He's going after the men who did it? You must stop him, mijo!"

Guillermo put his arms around her. "Mamá, por favor. Don't worry. He'll be stopped. Sal won't let him get far. Chico and Felipe will help stop him."

By this time, Juan had saddled Joaquin, and Don Julian was swinging into the saddle.

Sal ran alongside him. "El jefe, por favor! Don't do this! Stop!"

Don Julian yanked on the reins and galloped out of

the yard and down the south trail. Doña Eduarda buried her face into Guillermo's chest and sobbed. He rubbed her back and tried to console her, whispering in her ear, "Mamá, don't worry. He needs to blow off some steam. It'll be all right. I promise."

She peered up at him and caressed his face. "Promise me you'll stay here. Don't go after him. I couldn't bear it if anything happened to you. We need you, mijo." Strands of dark hair hung loose on each side of her tear-streaked face.

He had never seen her so distraught, not even after learning of her brother's fatal accident. "Don't worry, I'll stay. Now go inside. Angel, Fernando, and I will be right here."

"Gracias." She tenderly pulled away the blanket covering the tiny face of her newest child. Toñita squirmed and whimpered, and Doña Eduarda smiled down at her and cooed, "You poor little thing. Don't you worry, your Papá's coming back." She glanced back at Guillermo and caressed his unshaven cheek. "Where have the years gone? It seems like yesterday I was holding you in my arms, and look at you, all grown up, comforting me."

Petra and Concha each took an elbow and escorted Doña Eduarda past her bewildered daughters back into the house.

After Sal fired two warning shots, it didn't take long for Chico and Felipe to come galloping in from the range. Upon hearing where Don Julian had gone, they joined their father in racing to intercept him before he arrived at Davila's Corral de Cuati.

As promised, Guillermo stayed behind with Angel and Fernando, waiting by the campfire. Witnessing his parents' outbursts had left him shaken. If his father confronted Fuentes, there would be violence. *Dear God, please let him be stopped before he arrives. We need him.*

An hour and a half later, the group rode back into the yard, somberly dismounted, and handed the horses to Juan and Manuel. While Don Julian went into the casa to speak privately with his wife, Sal told Guillermo and Angel that they had caught up with Don Julian a league down the trail and persuaded him to stop and talk. By then, most of the bluster had gone out of him. Dejected, he acknowledged it would be foolhardy for him to confront Fuentes or Rios, as his family and crew depended on him. He turned around and headed home.

When Don Julian emerged from the casa, he explained that it was too dangerous for them to continue trying to ranch. He and Sal would make arrangements with the Tepusquet crew for the Gonzalezes to join them. The remainder of the Foxens' herd would be combined with theirs for the time being.

"Why can't Mamá and the children stay at her parents' until things blow over?" asked Guillermo.

"Because the harassment isn't going to let up until we're all gone. Your mother's right. It's just a matter of time before someone is killed. She pleaded with me to abandon the rancho for now, and I agreed. It's too far for her to travel to her parents with the little one, so we'll stay at the mission until she and the baby are strong enough to make the trip to San Luis Obispo. It won't be forever, maybe a year...or two. Eventually, the furor will die down, and it will be safe for us to return. We'll start over."

Angel stared into the fire, poking at it with a stick. "I don't understand why my family can't stay here and tend the herd. That way you won't have to worry about squatters."

"I wish you could too, but it's a matter of safety," said Don Julian. "There's your mother and sister to think of. During

240

the day, they'd be left unprotected. It would be safer for all of you to be at Tepusquet."

Sal said, "He's right, mijo. Your mother still hasn't recovered from the bullet whizzing past her head a few weeks ago. These outlaws will stop at nothing, even terrifying women. This will be temporary, and we'll be reunited."

Angel hung his head, continuing to poke disconsolately at the fire. A short time later, he tossed the stick in the fire and stomped off toward the corral.

As for Guillermo, what he had taken for granted a year earlier was now in jeopardy. Maybe he wouldn't inherit his portion of Rancho Tinaquaic—his birthright. He feared that once they abandoned their land, they'd never be able to reclaim it, and the course of his life would be forever changed for the worse.

CHAPTER 42

The three weeks leading up to the Foxens abandoning their rancho were marked by somber preparations. The remaining cattle were driven onto the northern part of Tinaquaic that bordered Rancho Tepusquet, and the dogs, flocks of sheep, and geese were relocated. The Gonzalezes, Juan, and Manuel would revert to being employees of Don Tomás, as they had been years before. The Foxens would take the barest of essentials, which all fit into the ox-pulled carreta, to set up housekeeping at the Santa Inés Mission.

On a chilly day in late April, six weeks after Toñita's birth, the family saddled up and bid farewell to the Gonzalezes and their faithful servants, Juan and Manuel. God willing, when the "loco fever" of their neighbors abated, they would return. Until then, it was "Vayan con Dios." Guillermo waved to Angel and said, "I hope to be back before long to help you herd cattle."

With heavy hearts, the Foxens rode off down the south trail, leaving behind their beloved home, rancho hands, hard work, and memories. Don Julian led the way on Joaquin, his rifle resting across the pommel of his saddle.

Guillermo followed woodenly in the rear. He felt hollow inside, strangely devoid of emotion. It was as if the very hills and trees had betrayed them. How could such a tranquil setting allow his family to be driven away? His family wasn't the first to abandon the land that had been an Indian cross-road. Long ago, a Chumash village had been abandoned, though the reason was lost to time. How many souls had called this place home down through the centuries? How long would it be before the land reclaimed all that his family had done to carve out a living in the hostile wilderness? Weeds would overtake the wheat and barley fields, the orchard, and his mother's garden within months. Better nature reclaim her land than Yankee squatters.

They traveled through the narrow canyon, still green from the winter rains but fading toward gold each day. As the caravan made its way through a grove of oaks, its resident magpies squawked at the passersby. The exiled family plodded onward, retracing its steps from eight years earlier. Back then, a lifetime ago, a smaller group eagerly made its first trip to claim its land grant. Guillermo recalled his boyhood sense of wonder at what lay beyond each bend. He had his first sighting of a puma slinking through the chaparral, its muscles rippling under its tawny coat. It had paused, stared with amber eyes, and moved on. A pair of condors had soared majestically overhead on splayed, white-tipped wings, seemingly curious about the travelers. Perhaps his family had been the first humans the giant birds had ever glimpsed. An hour later when they trotted across the Zaca Mesa, Guillermo glanced up at the mountain to his left, remembering the murder of the Palchaljet family by the same Tulares who raided the Foxen rancho when Don Julian went to Santa Barbara to sell hides. They too had lost their battle to survive in the hostile backcountry. At least his family was escaping with their lives and the few possessions they could carry with them.

To the southwest, they saw a distant plume of soft gray smoke coming from the Davilas' adobe, which was obscured in a cluster of trees. That evening, Gustavo and his family would enjoy the comforts of home in front of their cozy fire while their former friends sought refuge at the crumbling mission.

When they arrived at the mission in the late afternoon, Padre Jimeño showed the weary family to their quarters in the back of the courtyard. Two adjacent rooms had been swept in preparation for their arrival. Judging from the stench and the feathers that littered the dirt floor, chickens had been the most recent occupants. The two-story building that housed the dormitories and classrooms for the school students was a stone's throw away. Guillermo dreaded the inevitable encounter with Alfredo and Marco.

After the livestock were unloaded, fed, and corralled, Guillermo lingered on the bluff that overlooked the Santa Inés River. Rays from the setting sun sparkled off its gently flowing current as it made its way to the sea, some eight leagues to the west. The leeward side of the towering mountains in front of him were darkening, their shadows reaching to the river's edge. A red-tailed hawk wheeled overhead and then perched high in a sycamore across the way. Guillermo envied the bird's freedom. The creature was spared the indignity of having others observe its fall from grace, of feeling like an outcast with no home of its own.

How had it come to this? Exiled from the land he loved, his birthright abandoned.

Guillermo declined to join the family in their quarters though a bed had been prepared for him. Sleeping in it would have been an admission that he accepted his circumstances, which he did not. He was anxious to accompany his father when he returned home to collect more of their belongings.

When Don Julian saddled Joaquin the following morning, he insisted that Guillermo stay behind.

"Why? Mamá and the children couldn't be any safer," Guillermo said. "Please, Papá, I can't stand it here. I want to go back home even if it's only to help you gather our things."

"No, I need you to watch over the family and make sure the animals are cared for."

"Mamá has Petra and Martina to help her, and Ramona can look after the animals. Please. We both know it would be safer for you to have some help."

Don Julian's craggy face bore the strain of months of conflict. He barked irritably, "I'm in no mood for arguing! The matter's settled." He squeezed Joaquin's sides and galloped away with Sadie in toe.

Guillermo threw up his hands in exasperation. It made no sense. He burned with resentment at being treated like a child, not the co-protector he had been for the past year.

Later, his mother said, "Mijo, I know this is hard on you. You're used to herding cattle and guarding the hacienda. Think of this as a break from all that. Padre Jimeño said you're welcome to attend classes with the students. Maybe that would help you pass the time."

"I don't need a break from herding. Don't you understand that's all I want to do? I'm fifteen now, not a child. I don't understand why I'm here when I could be helping Papá or the Gonzalezes. This is a waste of time." He shook his head in despair. "I keep hoping I'm going to wake up, and it'll all just be a bad dream."

Doña Eduarda peered up at him. "Our family needs to be together until we figure out what we're going to do. We can talk at a later time about you joining the Gonzalezes. Please try to be patient, mijo I'm not ready for you to live away from us yet."

"The longer I'm away from the rancho, the more I fear we'll never return. What if squatters claim it?"

"It's too dangerous for any of us to be on the land for now. If it's God's will, He'll save it, however long it takes for us to return."

"If it isn't, then what? That was supposed to be my birthright. What am I supposed to do, be someone else's hired hand for the rest of my life?"

Doña Eduarda said, "You're putting too much value on the rancho. It's just land. You have a gift for working with horses. You can do that anywhere."

Frustrated, he wandered back to the pasture and checked on the horses. From that vantage point, he could see the back side of the seminary and wondered which classroom Alfredo and Marco were in. Had they heard he was staying at the mission? If so, would they seek him out? Probably so, but he wasn't ready to see them. He had never felt so lost. A pain had taken up residence in his chest. Rancho Tinaquaic had been his home, his world.

He took off his tio's hat and ran his fingers over its brim. "Tio, who am I if I can't be a vaquero on Rancho Tinaquaic?"

CHAPTER 43

Guillermo was grooming Benito in the corral when he heard, "Hola, amigo." He turned around, and there stood Marco and Alfredo.

Marco said, "Padre Jimeño said we'd find you here. What's going on?"

Guillermo sauntered over to the fence and shrugged. "We had to abandon our rancho. It was getting too dangerous."

"What's been happening since we last saw you?" asked Marco.

"You name it. Our cattle have been killed, crops burned, our roof was set on fire three times, we've been shot at, threats." He shrugged. "We're staying here being until my father decides where to go next."

"That's too bad. Who's been harassing you, Davila and his crew?" asked Alfredo.

Guillermo nodded. "For sure Fuentes and Rios. We think they recruited Tulares as well. We suspect Davila's also responsible in some way, though he's denied it."

"I'm sorry, Guillermo," said Marco, shaking his head. He scuffed the dirt with his boot. "I don't know what to say. Except…well, your father had to have known there'd be retribution for helping Fremont. He made that choice, and now your family is paying the price."

"Hey, how about we take a ride to Nojoqui Falls?" said

Alfredo. "Maybe a change in scenery will cheer you up."

Marco said, "I'll go back and ask our teacher, Padre Sanchez, if it's all right."

After promising Father Sanchez they would return before sundown, the three boys crossed the river and headed into the foothills. When they came to a creek, they followed it deep into a canyon. Steep slopes on either side were dotted with a profusion of spindly V-shaped oaks. Blocked by hills from the cooling winds of the Pacific, the canyon became sweltering, and the pungent smells of sage and mustard permeated the air. Finally, they found a cow path that led into the recesses of the canyon. It followed the creek and gnarled sycamores that provided welcome shade. The clomping of hooves echoed in the tunnel of trees. Scattered boulders told of torrential rains that had brought them tumbling down the mountain. The sound of rushing water came from farther down the trail.

The trio rounded a bend and came upon a shaded grotto. They sat on horseback, gazing up at a rushing waterfall that cascaded over a hundred feet of moss-covered cliff. Ferns grew out of the vertical rock, and a mist covered the pool, giving the scene an otherworldly look.

Alfredo raised his gloved hand. "What do you think?"

"It's amazing," said Guillermo. "I've heard about Nojoqui Falls but had no idea it was so high. It's so secluded, no one would know it's here." He swung off Benito to allow him to drink. Standing on the edge of the pool, he gazed up and asked, "Isn't there some Chumash legend about this?"

Marco took a deep breath. "Long before the mission was built, back when several Chumash villages occupied the area, a group got caught in a storm on the mountain and took refuge in a cave. A young maiden thought she heard someone calling for help outside, but her father and the others insisted it was just the wind howling. After all, who would be out on such a dark and fearsome night? As the story goes, the chief's daughter ventured out to investigate and discovered a young brave trapped under a fallen tree. Not strong enough to lift it herself, she made her way back to the cave. Others rescued the injured warrior and carried him back to the cave, and the following day, they took him to their village to recuperate. As fate would have it, the maiden and the brave fell in love, but her father had promised her in marriage to the son of an elder. Suspicion grew among the villagers that the stranger might persuade the girl to run away with him, so the couple was watched carefully. One moonless night, both went missing. A search party tracked them to the trail above." Marco pointed to the top of the waterfall. "As pursuers closed in, the couple found themselves perched on that rocky ledge up there. No one knows if they slipped and fell to their deaths or chose to leap together rather than be separated in life."

The boys stared up at the vertical cliff in awe. The roar of the rushing water nearly drowned out Guillermo's musing. "If the girl was drawn to his cry for help by some unseen force so he could be saved, why wouldn't it allow them to be together? Seems like a cruel twist of fate."

"Maybe it's just a tale." Alfredo shrugged. "Or maybe the young warrior wasn't supposed to be there. He could have disobeyed his elders and wandered onto another tribe's land. As Padre Sanchez says, when we sin, bad things happen."

"That doesn't seem fair for the girl," said Guillermo. "Why should some people have to pay for the sins of others?" He stared up through the mist, contemplated falling from such a high ledge, and shook his head. "Sometimes life doesn't make any sense."

After an awkward pause, Alfredo asked, "How long will you be staying at the mission? If you're still here in the fall, you could attend classes with us."

"Who knows?" Guillermo shrugged. The thought of staying that long sounded unbearable. "My mother's parents moved to San Luis Obispo. We'll probably go there."

When they returned to the mission, the sun was sinking over the hills. Guillermo was relieved to spot Joaquin and Sadie grazing in the pasture. As the boys uncinched the saddles, Guillermo said, "Thank you for showing me the falls. It was good to get away from here for a while."

Marco and Alfredo headed to their dormitory, and Guillermo went to his family's quarters. When he opened the door, Petra and his sisters were huddled on the makeshift bed, ashen faced.

"What's wrong? Did something happen?"

Martina stood, trembling. "Yes, but we don't know what exactly. Papá returned but went right to Padre Jimeño's office. Mamá went to be with him."

Petra rocked Toñita in her arms and whispered to Martina, "Best to talk outside so the baby doesn't wake."

Martina put on her shawl and stepped into the corridor. She led her brother around the corner where they could see a faint glow of candlelight coming from the padre's office. "Oh, Guillermo, I'm so scared. I could tell from the expression on Padre Jimeño's face when he came to get Mamá that something bad happened." Her lips trembled.

He glanced around self-consciously, unsure what to do next. He hugged her awkwardly, patting her on the back, trying to soothe her. "What happened?"

She straightened, wiped her face with her handkerchief, and blew her nose. "Half an hour ago," her voice quavered,

"Padre Jimeño"—sniff—"knocked on our door"—sniff—
"and asked Mamá to accompany"—sniff—"him to his
chamber." She inhaled deeply. "His expression was so grim.
When Mamá asked if he had heard anything about Papá,
he replied that he was waiting for her in his office. It was a
relief to know he was alive, but we could tell by the expression on his face that something bad had happened. Mamá
went out into the corridor. Through the door I heard her
ask if Papá was all right, and padre said 'Sí,' and something
about a shooting. Then they were gone. I think he had an
encounter with Fuentes and Rios."

"Tell you what. You go back inside to be with the girls.
I'll hang around here and wait for news. I'll let you know
as soon as I hear something."

Martina agreed and returned to their quarters.

Guillermo staggered on wobbly legs down the tiled corridor, leaned against the wall to collect himself, and took
deep breaths to calm the wild pounding in his chest. Looking out on the courtyard, he recalled a much different time.
The Easter fiesta a year ago had been marked with joyous
laughing and gaiety—that is, until Gustavo Davila barged
onto the scene, confronting his father in front of the revelers. After that, Maria had disappeared, presumably whisked
away by a member of the Ortega clan. He yearned to see
her again but only when this trouble was behind him. *Dear
God, what has happened? Has my father killed someone? Ay,
yi, yi…is he going to jail?*

He stared down the corridor at the light in Padre Jimeño's chamber. He knew better than to knock on the door,
so he did the only thing he could think of. He entered the
church sanctuary through the side door and kneeled in
one of the pews. Gazing up at the statue of Saint Inés, he

251

searched her serene face for assurance that whatever happened, his father would not be taken away. *Why is it that whenever I think things can't get any worse, another calamity befalls my family? Why is God allowing this to happen?*

He bowed his head and prayed more fervently than ever, pleading with God and the saints to intervene. He remembered the Easter message of sacrifice and offered up his most valuable possession, Benito.

Later, he heard the creaking of the door and footsteps echoing on the tile behind him. He raised his head and turned to see Padre Sanchez approaching. From the expression on the old friar's face, the news was not good.

CHAPTER 44

P adre Sanchez led Guillermo to the rectory and ushered him inside.

Padre Jimeño rose and gestured with his hand. "Please come in, Guillermo. You may take a seat next to your mother." He nodded solemnly at the other friar, who closed the door softly and retreated down the arched corridor.

Don Julian gave Guillermo a slight nod of acknowledgement. He was leaning forward in his chair, resting his forearms on his thighs and rotating his hat in his hands. His slumped shoulders and the tight line of his lips confirmed the news was grim. He had the look of a defeated man. Guillermo had never seen him like this before, not even the day El Mauro was found killed. Guillermo could deal with his father's anger, but this was unnerving. His faded eyes were etched in…what? Sadness? Regret? Wiry mutton chops couldn't conceal his clenched jaw.

Doña Eduarda reached over, took her son's hand in hers, and gave it a squeeze. In her other hand she clutched a handkerchief. The air was thick with tension.

Guillermo scanned the sparsely furnished room, taking in the carved crucifix on the wall behind the friar's desk and a bookcase filled with dusty volumes that stood against an adjacent wall. It was a room where matters of grave importance were discussed.

Padre Jimeño sat with his gnarled fingers entwined on top of his desk and regarded Guillermo solemnly. "Son, I'm afraid there's been an unfortunate incident. There was a confrontation between your father and Gustavo Davila that resulted in your father shooting him in self-defense. He'll leave shortly to turn himself in to the authorities in Santa Barbara. There will most likely be a trial."

At hearing "shooting" and "Davila," Guillermo's vision narrowed. He turned from Padre Jimeño to his father. "So he's…dead?"

"Yes." Don Julian nodded gravely. "When I arrived home, I discovered it had been ransacked and looted. Pictures and ollas were pulled off the wall, thrown on the floor and smashed. The furniture I had shipped around the Horn was gone, even the Oriental rug. As I was going from room to room, I heard hooves and voices. Since I'd left Joaquin and Sadie tied to a tree down in the creek, I figured whoever it was didn't know I was inside. When I peeked out the window, I saw Davila and two servants tying their horses and an ox-cart to the hitching post. I heard him boasting how they were going to burn the house after they finished taking what they wanted. I had left my rifle holstered with Joaquin, so I grabbed the old carbine off the wall. I stood in the doorway and called, 'You're not content to run off our land and ransack our home! Now you've come to strip it bare, then burn it? You're nothing but a vulture, Gustavo!'"

He continued. "Davila grabbed his rifle, aimed in my direction, and yelled back, 'You were a fool to return, Julian! You lost your right to this land when you helped Fremont! Leave now, or Eduarda will be a widow and your children fatherless!' I told him the peace treaty protected my own-ership, and I was only leaving temporarily to protect my family. I ordered him to leave or I'd shoot, but he scoffed and said, 'Careful that relic doesn't misfire!' He was right about that. It hadn't been fired in years, and I wasn't sure if it'd explode in my face. He laughed again and proceeded toward the veranda, so I took aim and warned him one last time. 'Don't come any closer, Gustavo, or I'll shoot.' He stopped and spread one arm wide and mocked me. 'You're going to risk your life for this?'"

"I can't explain what came over me. Something snapped. Next thing I knew, there was a loud explosion and a cry. When the smoke cleared, he was lying on the ground, bleeding from the chest. I knew he was mortally wounded. I ordered his servants to take him away, so they dragged him to the cart and loaded him into it. I gathered what I could and took off before Fuentes or Rios showed up."

Guillermo asked, "What about the Gonzalezes? Someone needs to warn them."

"They know to stay away for the time being. Promise me you won't go anywhere near there. It's too dangerous."

"But—"

"No buts. I'm ordering you to stay away, you hear? I need you to be here for your mother and the children. A messenger will send news of the trial, if there is one. Under the circumstances, I should be found not guilty. I'll return as soon as I can."

"Can't I at least escort you up the trail? Fuentes and Rios will be searching for you. Mamá and the children will be safe here at the mission, right, Padre?"

The friar shook his head. "Listen to your father. He knows what's best."

Don Julian said, "I need you to stay here. If I have to go to jail, you can pack things up and take the family to Daniel

Hill's. I know he'll let you stay with them until things are settled." Daniel Hill was Don Julian's godfather in Santa Barbara.

Before Don Julian departed, he stopped by the family quarters. Amid tears, he kissed and embraced each of the children. They knelt on the dirt floor and prayed for the repose of Gustavo Davila's soul, for his family, and for Don Julian's protection. He bid them goodbye, and Guillermo accompanied his mother and Martina to the corral to see him off.

Don Julian said, "Eduarda, I never wanted things to turn out this way."

She stood on her tiptoes and caressed his bristled cheek. "I know that, mi querido. You're a good man, and people know that."

"Well, let's hope so. Guillermo, Joaquin's been ridden hard today, so I need to take El Rey."

"Of course. I'll saddle him for you."

"Thank you."

Guillermo stood stiffly while his father hugged him and whispered in his ear, "You need to be brave for your mother and sisters. Don't go anywhere near home." He straightened his arms and stared intently into his son's eyes. "Promise me."

Guillermo reluctantly nodded as he peered into his father's eyes and thought, *How could you do this to us?*

"I'm sorry, mijo."

Guillermo gave a quick snort and stepped away.

His mother reached out to touch his arm, "Don't be like this, please. Not now. You don't know—"

He yanked his arm away from her. "This didn't need to happen. He could have let the Gonzalezes stay in our house to guard it, but no, he sent them away!"

Don Julian said, "I couldn't take the chance there'd be a confrontation between Chico and Fuentes with us gone. It's safer for them to be at Tepusquet. The house can be rebuilt if it comes to that."

Guillermo shook his head in disgust and stepped farther away. He thought of the new stable, vulnerable to a marauder's torch.

Martina reached out and touched him arm. "Please, Guillermo." He shrugged it away, but she tilted her head in anguish, looked back at her father, and said, "Oh, Papá…" Tears streamed down her face.

His mother admonished him. "Mijo, you mustn't be disrespectful to your father."

Don Julian held up his hand to placate them. "It's all right. Let him be. He's angry, and I can't blame him." He embraced the weeping Martina and kissed her on the head. "Now now, it'll be all right, don't cry. You're my big girl." He untied his neckerchief, wiped her face, and held her chin in his bear paw of a hand. "Now stop the tears, mija. I'll be fine. Before you know it, we'll all be together again."

Martina sniffed and put on a brave smile as her father swung into the saddle. She reached over and put an arm around her mother's narrow shoulder as Don Julian rode away into the dimming light of dusk.

Guillermo left them and headed to the pasture to check on the animals. The horses and Sadie nibbled on grass on the far side of the field. Benito trotted over and followed him around as he filled the trough with water, and the other animals moseyed over to investigate. When he was certain his mother and Martina had returned to their quarters, he dropped the bucket and collapsed to his knees, rocking and sobbing. How had things come to this? Just when he thought the worst calamity had happened, abandoning their rancho, his father kills Davila! Besides being branded a traitor, now his father was a killer! How many times over the years had his father chided him for not using his head, and what does he do? Shoot a former friend in a confrontation! If it had been Fuentes or Rios, it would have been easier to take, but Gustavo Davila was the father of five young children and a paisano. How could things have spiraled out of control so badly?

Benito nudged Guillermo on the shoulder, nickered, and pushed his hat onto the ground. Guillermo continued to rock, and Benito pawed at the ground to distract him, but to no avail. The moans were replaced by sniffling. Guillermo wiped his face with his poncho, slowly rose to his feet, and found himself in the middle of a circle, the five Foxen horses and Sadie watching him with sober eyes.

"It's okay, amigos. I'm all right." He reached down, swiped up his hat, and returned it to his head. Benito took a few steps and stretched his neck, his way of asking to be petted. Guillermo rubbed the horse's nose. "It's just the two of us now."

He lingered with the animals until nightfall and watched a quarter moon rise in the east before returning to his quarters. His mother came to check on him, but he refused her offer of beans and tortillas.

For hours, Guillermo lay in the darkness, thinking about the Davila household. As he recalled, the eldest child was a boy around nine years old. This was his first night of being fatherless and, like Guillermo, promoted to being the man of the family. Hopefully in his own case, it would be temporary. What an unnecessary tragedy. Now both families would be displaced, as it was doubtful Davila's widow would stay on the isolated rancho with five children.

Which father would the paisanos remember as the victim and which the aggressor? Guillermo suspected it would come down to the Anglos supporting his father and the former rebelistas siding with Davila. Where did that leave him? Probably further alienated from his mother's people, the people of his heart. Now what? He straddled both groups but would have to take a stand in defending his father. Only he and the Gonzalezes understood how the months of harassment had taken its toll on his father. If only he hadn't returned to the rancho by himself and had allowed the Gonzalezes to stay behind and guard it. If only Fremont had not camped on their land in the first place. His world as he knew it was forever changed. Would there ever be reason to smile again?

Three days later, Gustavo Davila's funeral was held at the Santa Inés Mission. Out of respect for the Davilas and to escape the prying eyes of their paisanos, the Foxens remained in seclusion in their quarters. Fuentes and Rios were expected to attend, and Guillermo had no intention of crossing paths with them. He worried about the horses in the pasture, so he corralled Benito and Joaquin in the stable with the padres' horses, out of sight.

When the last of the family members and attendees had departed, Padre Jimeño brought the Foxens some of the leftover food from the reception. This had been sent at the request of Señoras Janssens and Covarrubias. Several people had asked him to pass on their concern for Eduarda and the children. Some were probably expecting a funeral for Don Julian in the coming days.

CHAPTER 45

Doña Eduarda, the girls, and Petra spent much of the intervening days on their knees, praying. Guillermo's anger was directed toward his heavenly father as well as his earthly one, so rather than pray, he occupied himself doing chores for the friars and caring for the livestock.

The waiting was tortuous as the hours dragged by. His family's future hung in the balance. Would his father be freed or found guilty and imprisoned? Or worse yet, executed? Despite the anger and disappointment he felt toward his father, losing him was unfathomable. His mother had been right. He regretted how he behaved not long after his father left and could kick himself for his selfishness. His anger at God wavered, and he found himself pleading for a chance to undo his wrong.

It was as if time was suspended. The hours crept by with agonizing slowness.

The frustration of not being able to ride to Rancho Tepusquet and inform the Gonzalezes about what had occurred gnawed at him. For the past eight years, he had spent most every day in their company, riding the range. Now, in the hour of his greatest need, he was forbidden to see them.

Guillermo envied the companionship of the womenfolk. Killing time by himself was driving him loco. His was a prison without bars.

On day four, as Guillermo passed outside their quarters, he heard Alejandro fussing. He stopped and opened the door to see the toddler sitting on the floor, crying, and Martina flustered in trying to soothe him. He knelt beside his brother. "What's the matter, little man?"

"I want Papá!" the three-year-old wailed, slapping his pudgy hands on his knees.

"Nothing we do will distract him," Martina said, exasperated.

Guillermo bent down beside him. "Hey, little man, maybe fresh air will do you good. How about helping me with the horses? Would you like that?" He glanced at his mother, who was nursing Toñita. "Is it okay if I take him with me?"

His mother sighed with relief. "That would be good. Maybe the baby will take a nap if it's quiet." She pushed a strand of loose hair from her weary face. "Watch him carefully. He can get away from you quickly."

"Don't worry, he'll be fine. Maybe I'll take him for a ride."

"Can I go with you?" asked Ramona.

"Me too." Panchita chimed in.

"Tell you what. Come with me to keep an eye on him while I tend the animals, and then we'll go for a ride. How does that sound?"

"Really?" said Ramona. "That would be so nice!"

His mother and Martina exchanged surprised looks and smiled, and Guillermo picked up Alejandro. "Let's go." He waved his brother's arm for him and said, "Wave adios to everyone."

"A-di-os!" Alejandro giggled, his brown eyes shining. He wrapped an arm around his big brother's neck as he was carried outside.

Once they got to the stable, they let Alejandro play on bales of hay while Guillermo mucked out the stalls and spread fresh hay. The group went to the fenced pasture and checked on the horses and Sadie. Alejandro chased a lizard that had been sunning himself on a rock. He pointed and squealed with delight as he squatted to peer at the creature. "Look!"

"That's a lizard. Can you say lizard?" said Guillermo.

"Leez-erd." He picked up a stick and poked at it.

"No, no, don't hurt it." Guillermo bent and caught the little fellow in his hand as it tried to skitter away. "See, it has a blue belly. You can pet him if you're gentle. Like this."

Alejandro stared in wonder at the reptile. Guillermo took one of his baby fingers and stroked its back, and Alejandro giggled. "Leez-ard!"

Guillermo said, "Okay, now he wants to go home, so say adios, Señor Lizard."

"Home? He go home?"

"Sí, he lives in one of these holes. He wants to go back and see his family." Guillermo lowered his hand to the ground, and they watched as the lizard darted out of sight.

"No more leez-ard," said Alejandro, opening his hands. "Go home."

"Sí, he's going home."

"When we go home?"

The innocent words pierced Guillermo's heart like a knife. He shrugged. "I don't know, little fella. We're staying here for a while."

"Why?"

Guillermo and his sisters exchanged glances. "Well, it's better that we're here for now."

Perplexed, Alejandro scrunched up his face. "Why?"

Guillermo sighed. What would satisfy his curiosity? "Well, there were bad men who wanted to hurt us, so we had to come here for a while." He could tell by the confusion on the boy's face that more questions were coming, so he headed them off. "Hey, how about we go for a ride? Would you like that?"

"Sí! Ride!" Alejandro clapped.

Guillermo sent Ramona and Panchita back to their quarters to get the long piece of cloth, which Petra used to tie a baby to the front of her so she could move with her hands free. When they returned, he tied it around his waist and Alejandro's to make sure the boy didn't slide out of the saddle. They rode to the bluff where the Refugio Trail crossed the Santa Inés River. Guillermo took along his father's spyglass and used it to see if he could spot riders coming down the mountain. Perhaps he'd spy his father returning or a messenger coming with news. When he looked through it, the view was partially obscured. "Huh? What's wrong with this?" He shook it and heard something rattle inside, so he unscrewed the lens cap on the small end and peered inside.

"What in the world?" A rolled paper was inside. He tried getting hold of it, but his fingers were too big. Handing it off to Ramona, he asked, "See if you can stick your fingers in there and pull the paper out."

She deftly pulled out the rolled parchment. "What's this doing in here? It looks like the diseño to our rancho."

"What's a diseño?" asked Panchita.

"It's a map of and deed to our rancho," said Guillermo, looking it over. He recognized the Sisquoc River to the north and Alisos Creek to the south.

"It's very important," said Ramona. "I heard Papá tell

Mamá how we needed it to prove to the Americanos it's our land. Right, Guillermo?"

"Sí." Shaking his head in surprise, he said, "Well, I'll be. Papá must have put this in here for safekeeping. His sea chest was partially burned in one of the fires along with the script Fremont gave him so the Americano government would reimburse us for our livestock. I wonder why he didn't tell me though. That's strange."

"Maybe in all the confusion, he forgot. What are you going to do with it?" Ramona asked.

"Think I'll put it back in for now. This is as safe a place to store it as any." He rolled the yellowed parchment, slid it back into the tube of the tarnished spyglass, screwed the lens cap closed, and looped its rawhide thong around his saddle horn. "Híjole. I hate to think what would have happened if I'd accidentally misplaced it. It's good to know what's inside."

"When do you think we'll be able to go back home?" asked Ramona.

"I don't know. God willing it won't be too long."

"You're not mad at God anymore?"

"What makes you think I was?"

"Because you haven't joined us for evening prayers."

He pushed back his hat and sighed. "I admit I was angry at God for a while. Now I just want Papá returned to us. Don't worry about me. I've been doing my own praying at night."

"That's a relief. We're not supposed to be angry, especially at God," Ramona said soberly.

"Oh, I think He can handle it. I used to think I'd be struck down dead if I told God how I felt...but I'm here to tell you, it didn't happen. He even answered my prayer. This waiting's been driving me loco, but today passed much easier."

"That's because you're not off by yourself. Thank you for taking us on this ride. It feels good to be outside. I can tell he's happy too," Ramona said, reaching over to pat Alejandro's.

"Me too," said Panchita. "Can we do this tomorrow? Please?"

"Sure, why not? It'll help pass the time, and it's good for Alejandro to get used to the saddle. If we have to make the trip to Santa Barbara, he needs to learn to balance himself in it." Glancing down at Alejandro, he said, "You're getting the hang of it, aren't you, little fella?"

"Me ride Benito!"

That drew smiles from the three older siblings. They headed back to the mission at a gentle lope.

As it was springtime, the oak trees were alive with the sound of chirping birds. The magpies scolded them for getting too close to their nests. As they neared the mission, Ramona challenged Panchita to a race back to the corral. Guillermo watched as his sisters galloped away, their braids swinging behind them. It was good that they had gone for the ride. Soon it would be dinner time and, not long after that, bedtime. One more day down. Perhaps Papá would return tomorrow.

CHAPTER 46

Two days later on the afternoon of day six, a messenger arrived from Santa Barbara with a letter for Padre Jimeño regarding Guillermo's father. Doña Eduarda was summoned to his office so the friar could read it to her. Guillermo accompanied her, and his leg jiggled uncontrollably waiting for the letter to be read.

Padre Jimeño put on his spectacles and cleared his throat. "Dear Señora Foxen, I regret to inform you that your husband, Julian Benjamin Foxen, has been found guilty of manslaughter by a court of law. The punishment for this offense will be execution by firing squad. This will be held five days hence to provide time for your family to journey to Santa Barbara to say your final farewell. Signed, Judge Pedro Carrillo."

Doña Eduarda gasped. Guillermo sat frozen as the words sank in.

Padre Jimeño said, "I'm most sorry. This is as I feared. Judge Carrillo is a hard man, embittered over the Yankee takeover. We will pray for God's intervention. You mustn't lose hope."

Guillermo turned to see his mother's ashen face crumble. She buried it in her handkerchief and wept, her narrow shoulders heaving with grief. He was struck by how fragile she appeared. Since Toñita's birth, she seemed to diminish with each passing day. Fatigue and worry had taken their toll, leaving her cheeks sunken and dark shadows under her eyes.

Shaken, Guillermo escorted her back to their quarters. He left her to deliver the news to the others while he staggered out to the pasture. He hadn't gone far when Benito came to him and nuzzled the side of his head. He doubled over, fell to his knees, and sobbed. "Why, God? How could you let this happen? Now in addition to us being branded traitors, Papá's a convicted murderer and will be executed for defending what was left of our rancho! It's so unfair!"

Hatred for Fremont burned in his chest. Guillermo wished he could confront him with the tragic aftermath of his battalion's march across their land. He wondered what the mighty Fremont would say in response. However, he was contending with problems of his own. Word had reached the Foxens that Fremont had been court martialed by the Department of the Army for defying the orders of his commanding officer, General Kearney. After being stripped of his rank of colonel, Fremont resigned. Some hero he turned out to be.

He heard footsteps approaching and glanced behind him to see Padre Jimeño stepping through the grass in his sandals, trying to avoid horse dung. Wiping his face with his poncho, Guillermo struggled to compose himself. "You didn't need to come out here. I'll be all right," he croaked.

"Nonsense, my boy. You've had a terrible blow. This is not the time to be alone. Come, let's go sit under my favorite tree."

Guillermo preferred to be alone but dutifully followed the kindly friar. Padre Jimeño led the way to a gate that opened onto a path that took them to the edge of the bluff overlooking the river. Crude slabs of wood had been fashioned to form a bench under a pepper tree, whose graceful branches swayed in the breeze. Somewhere in its canopy, a meadowlark sang.

Padre Jimeño said, "I come here to think and meditate. I never tire of the beautiful view. The mountains never fail to humble me. They've been here for eons and have weathered countless storms and will continue to do so long after we're gone. They remind me our problems are temporary. Fleeting." He took a deep breath. "Guillermo, you've been through a lot these past two years and have stood alongside your father and the Gonzalezes to protect your family and rancho. It's prepared you for this next challenge. You're going to need to muster all the strength you can to be strong for your mother and sisters. They and your father are depending on you to get them to Santa Barbara by Tuesday. You can do it. Good Lord, if you can lead an army down a cow path in a blinding storm, you can lead your family over the Refugio Trail. By tomorrow at this time, you can be at the Ortegas', and the most difficult part of the journey will be over. The other padres and I will be praying for you."

Guillermo shook his head. "I don't know what's going to happen to us. Without our rancho and herd," he threw up his hands in defeat, "I can't support our family, even with the Gonzalezes' help. Mamá and the children will have to go live with my grandparents in San Luis Obispo. I could work as a vaquero on Rancho Tepusquet, but that means our family, what's left of it, will be broken up." His voice cracked, and he shook his head in despair. "I don't see any other way. We've lost everything—our rancho, our good name, our friends—and now Papá will be executed like a common criminal."

"Hold on. You're getting way ahead of yourself. Let's take stock of what you have going in your favor."

Guillermo squinted at Padre Jimeño with his head cocked. *Is he loco? Can't he see everything is stacked against us?*

"Number one, your father has influential friends. I'm sure they are doing all they can to get the American military commander to intervene."

"You think so?"

"Sí. Power has shifted in the gringos' favor. Anything can happen. Don't give up hope yet. Number two, your family is fortunate to have such a capable guide to escort them to Santa Barbara—you. Three, if the worst were to happen, you're a skilled horseman whose services will always be in demand. You mustn't take that for granted. It's your inheritance. You're not going out into the world empty handed. Your father's made sure that you're well prepared."

"But I don't have an education."

"True, not a formal one, but I've heard you can read and do sums. You're a hard worker and responsible, and those qualities will take you far. None of us escape trials and tribulations in this life. My mother died when I was younger than you, and three years later, my father died in a freak accident. We four children were split up and sent to live with relatives. I was sent by myself to live with an elderly great aunt. I too felt God had abandoned me, but it turned out my aunt helped the parish priest, and I ended up finding my calling. I remember Padre Ambrose telling me that God can turn earthly loss into heavenly gain. At the time, I didn't understand, but I've lived long enough to see it happen many times."

Padre Jimeño's matter-of-fact appraisal helped to quell Guillermo's fear.

The following day, he bid the padre farewell under a gray sky. With Alejandro sharing his saddle, he led his family and Petra on horseback up the Refugio Trail. The somber caravan slowly wended its way up the steep mountain. Each clomping step sounded to him like "A-di-os, a-di-os." They were leaving their former lives behind and riding into the unknown.

His father's spyglass hung from the saddle horn. From time to time, Guillermo slid his hand over it to reassure himself the diseño to Rancho Tinaquaic was safe. Hopefully someday it would be used to reclaim their land grant.

The remaining hours of his journey were running out, and it was imperative they arrive in Santa Barbara the following evening. Travelers were infrequent on the trail, but Guillermo was on constant alert for the sound of approaching hooves. His gun rested across the pommel, inches from Alejandro's clothbound tummy. The rhythm of Joaquin's steady gait rocked the toddler to sleep.

A few hours later, they reached the pine-studded summit and were greeted by a stiff breeze and the briny smell of ocean air. Guillermo paused to let Martina's horse catch up with him. He gazed back at the peaceful Santa Inés Valley below, catching sight of scattered haciendas tucked behind clusters of trees. At the northern edge of the valley was Rancho Corral de Cuati, its residents mourning the death of its don. Beyond that, out of sight, lay the sprawling hills of the Foxen rancho.

Farther north on Rancho Tepusquet, the Gonzalezes were herding what was left of the cattle bearing the anchor brand, possibly still unaware of the latest calamity to befall Guillermo's family. They had shared in the travails of the past year, and he sorely missed them. They had fought together, shoulder to shoulder, to hold on to the land they loved and called home, but in the end, they had been defeated by their embittered neighbors.

In the opposite direction lay the Santa Barbara channel, which on this day was a moody blue-green and topped by frothy whitecaps. He saw, through the mist, the brooding silhouettes of Santa Cruz and the Anacapa Islands on the horizon. Pale sunlight pierced charcoal clouds, giving Guillermo hope that the threatening sky would clear. With the most arduous part of the journey behind them, they would make faster progress on the seaward side of the mountain. Barring any delay, they should reach the Ortegas before sundown.

As head of the family now, the responsibility for its welfare weighed heavily on Guillermo. Traveling with a baby required that they stop every few hours for her to be fed and changed. During the midday break, he watered the horses and let them graze along the trail while Martina and Ramona sat on a blanket on the grass. They set out a meal of bean empañadas that had been prepared the day before along with wedges of cheese and olives. After the meal was over and the group was preparing to saddle up, the younger girls lingered in the shade of a sprawling oak, picking violets and hummingbird sage.

Guillermo called, "*Ándale!* We need to get going!"

"Un momento! We want to pick a bouquet for Señora Ortega," called Panchita.

"C'mon, you've had plenty of time to do that. Don't keep us waiting!" he barked. He bent over, the fingers of both hands entwined so Martina could step into them. He had boosted her into the saddle and handed her the reins when Benito neighed, shook his mane, took a couple steps back, and neighed again. His ears were pointed forward, at alert.

"What's the matter, boy?" No sooner had the words left Guillermo's mouth when he heard a rattle.

"Guillermo!" Juanita shrieked, pointing at the grass in front of her with terror in her eyes. "Rattlesnake!"

"Don't move, either of you!" he ordered.

Juanita stood frozen with her hand outstretched, holding the bouquet of wildflowers. Her pixie face was as pale as her apron. Panchita, several feet behind her, stared down at the coiled serpent with saucer-shaped eyes.

Guillermo drew his father's pistol from his hip holster and took three long strides toward the snake. Its tail had four rattles that were shaking amid the foot-high grass. *Bang!* Dirt sprayed where the bullet passed through the snake and into the ground. In an instant, the crisis was over.

"Bueno, bueno!" the girls exclaimed in relief. "You killed him!"

"Next time, do as I say and stay on the trail," snapped Guillermo as he holstered the smoking gun.

Doña Eduarda crossed herself. "Gracias a Dios. Come along girls!"

They rode on, passing hillsides covered in manzanita, toyon bushes, and yucca. Giant red paintbrushes, yellow buttercups, and delicate violets lined the curving trail. They had yet to encounter a fellow traveler on the lonely trail that afternoon, which was fine with Guillermo. He felt vulnerable without his father or the Gonzalezes and wouldn't relax until he delivered his family safely at Ortega Rancho. He had heard stories of riders being ambushed by highwaymen along lonely stretches of El Camino Real. Since the American takeover, the trickle of gringo settlers had increased many times over as emigrants poured into the territory to claim their 160 acres of free land. Most were law-abiding folks, but an unsavory element had drifted in as well. With every turn in the trail, Guillermo's eyes and ears strained for the approach of potential danger.

It was midafternoon when he came to a shaded creek that crossed the trail. Most of the year it was barely a trickle but rain a few nights before had brought it back to life, rising to Joaquin's tall knee. He sidestepped a pool that was several feet deep.

Alejandro awakened from his slumber and said groggily, "Agua, agua."

"Sí, agua, Alejandro." Although his brother was tied to him with the long piece of cloth, Guillermo steadied him with one of his hands as he led Joaquin across. He warned the others behind him. "Be careful! The rocks!"

When he got to the other side, he watched as each of his sisters forded the pool in succession, passing through it easily, and then it was his mother's turn. Aleta, the gentlest horse in the remuda, started across. Guillermo was chatting with Martina when he heard a splash and his mother scream, "Oh dear mother of God! Help!" When he glanced back, he saw to his horror that the shawl his infant sister had been swathed in was floating in the creek! He yanked hard on Joaquin's reins and charged back up the thirty feet of trail. By the time he reached the pool, his mother was scooping up the sodden bundle and rocking it to her breast, consoling the outraged Toñita. Petra, who was immediately behind her on the sure-footed Sadie, rushed to her mistress' side.

Doña Eduarda gasped, "Thanks be to God that Aleta didn't fall on her side and crush the poor thing!" She again crossed herself and soothed the squalling baby. "You're fine, you're fine." She reassured everyone that she and the baby were unharmed.

"It's all my fault," said Guillermo. "I shouldn't have been in such a hurry, should have stayed to help you across. I'm sorry, Mamá."

His mother waved off his apology. "Accidents happen, mijo. Aleta slipped. That's not your fault. You have done an excellent job of leading us."

Guillermo knew if his father were leading them, he'd have made sure nothing like this happened. After Doña Eduarda and Petra changed the shivering baby out of her wet clothes, a shaken Guillermo continued to lead the caravan down the curving mountain trail. As the sun sank lower in the sky, the shaded sections of the road became chilly. He worried about Toñita catching cold, despite being swaddled in dry clothes.

The sun had set into the Pacific by the time they arrived at the Ortegas' main house near the mouth of the canyon, overlooking a cove. Even though Guillermo knew traditional rules of hospitality would overrule political differences, he was still anxious about how his family would be received. His fears were for naught as Señora Ortega, his friend Estefana Maria's aunt, graciously welcomed them. When she heard about Toñita's tumble into the creek, she said, "Well, sounds like this little one's been baptized for the second time! She should be doubly blessed!" Her father-in-law, José Vicente, put aside his animosity for Don Julian and made sure his servants made the wayfarers comfortable.

When Guillermo was being led to their quarters, he passed under an imposing portrait of the former patriarch of the Ortega family, Don José Francisco. He was clad in his captain's uniform of the Spanish army. The rotund officer proudly held an engraved sword in front of his chest. Guillermo wondered what the distinguished hidalgo would think if he knew the son of a traitor was staying under his roof.

When the Foxens said their goodbyes the following morning, the courtly Don José said, "Of course you will be welcome to stay at Rafaela's." She was his eldest daughter and married to the former Yankee, Daniel Hill.

The caravan continued on the final five leagues to Santa Barbara under clear skies. The journey along the nearly deserted coast was an easy one after the previous day's arduous trek up and down the Refugio Trail. The slopes of the mountains facing the ocean were golden with mustard. Sleek, long-horned cattle grazed peacefully on the undulating plain. They passed through Rancho Dos Pueblos, named for the two Chumash villages located on opposite bluffs of the creek where it emptied into the ocean. Farther up on a gentle knoll, Guillermo marveled at Nicolas Den's hacienda. Besides building a handsome adobe for his wife, Rosa, who was the Hill's daughter and the Ortegas' granddaughter, the resourceful Irishman had numerous outbuildings, sheds, barns, and corrals.

The weary travelers arrived at the Hill's town home late afternoon and were greeted warmly by husband and wife. Daniel Hill took Doña Eduarda's hands in his own and said, "My deepest condolences for what you have gone through, my dear, but let me assure you that we have reason to believe Julian will be granted a new trial."

Doña Eduarda squeezed Guillermo's hand as she gasped. "Oh, Daniel! What a relief if that happens!"

"We all know he shot Gustavo in self-defense," said Hill. "A group of us—José de la Guerra, former commandante of the presidio, Ike Sparks, Lewis Burton, my son-in-law Nicolas, and me—petitioned Colonel Stevenson for help. He sent word to Governor Mason, requesting that an impartial judge retry the case. We Anglos are outraged at Pedro Carrillo's actions. He's demonstrated that he's too biased to render a fair verdict and sentence. Julian's cause has been taken up by some very determined men, and we have every hope that a new trial will bring a different verdict."

Guillermo could hardly believe his ears. Their eyes brimming with tears, he and his mother exchanged relieved looks. This was the best news they had heard in a long time.

Señora Hill escorted Doña Eduarda and the girls to two comfortably furnished rooms complete with wood floors and rugs. It was luxurious accommodations after their cramped quarters at the crumbling mission. A servant was assigned to attend to their personal needs.

Hill put a hand on Guillermo's shoulder. "For the time being, your family is welcome to stay here. How about we retire to the sala and I get you caught up on the developments here? Please follow me."

Guillermo followed Hill down a corridor into a sitting room. He took a seat on a red velvet settee and glanced around at the well-appointed room. On the wall above the fireplace hung a painting of a tall-masted Yankee clipper sailing through rough seas. The dark clouds hinted at a storm approaching, or was it clearing? He couldn't be sure. The golden glow of two oil lamps gave the room a coziness he hadn't experienced since his family fled their home two weeks before. A lifetime ago. They made small talk while Hill lit his pipe and a servant brought cups of tea.

Guillermo asked, "Señor Hill, how long has it been since you saw my father?"

"Please call me Daniel. Two days ago. Ike and I went for a brief visit. We wanted to update him about our latest meeting with Colonel Stevenson. He's convinced the governor will order a new trial. The first one was a travesty. We knew if Governor Mason heard about Judge Carrillo's actions, he'd order a new trial. As luck would have it, the *Songbird* was leaving port that day for Monterey, so we hurriedly arranged for a letter to be rowed out to the ship."

"My father's execution is scheduled for tomorrow. What if word doesn't come in time?"

"Colonel Stevenson intends to delay proceedings until it does."

"He has the authority to do that?" Guillermo asked.

Hill shrugged. "He seems to think so. Since it would be his soldiers who would carry out the execution by a firing squad, he can refuse to proceed until he's heard from the governor."

Guillermo's eyes went heavenward, and he crossed himself. "Oh, thank God! What a relief!" He slumped against the back of the settee, stared at the beamed ceiling for several moments, and then sat up abruptly. "What if Judge Carrillo goes ahead and makes some other arrangements? Will the colonel be ready to stop him?"

"Don't worry. That's already been discussed. Ike Spark's already made his own plans as a backup. He's a sharpshooter, and we trust that he'll protect your father."

Guillermo relaxed back into his seat. "Oh good. That makes me feel better." A knot had settled in his gut and he doubted any amount of reassurance would banish his worry. "What do you think the chances are that he'll be released after a new trial?"

"Given that Davila was trespassing and had ransacked your house and threatened your father in front of witnesses at the mission, a jury should find your father not guilty of murder. He could be charged with a lesser crime like manslaughter, but he wouldn't be sentenced to die. Jail time maybe, but not death. If he's imprisoned, your family is welcome to stay with us until he's released."

"That would be so unfair. He was only defending his property and himself."

"I know. It depends on the testimony of the witnesses, if any show up. If none do, they have only your father's word."

"Did anyone from Davila's family or crew show up for the first trial?"

"It all happened so fast that no one from Corral de Cuati was notified of what should have been a hearing. Carrillo convened court the day after your father arrived to turn himself in. It was clear from the start that Carrillo wasn't interested in hearing testimony. He wanted vengeance."

"Please tell me about it. What happened?"

Hill settled back in his high-back chair and took a draw on his pipe. "Well, let me tell you, it was dramatic the way it played out. There weren't many of us in the audience—four of us supporters. When the charges were read, your father stood in front of the judge with his hands and feet in chains and two guards at his side. Carrillo asked, 'Aren't you the traitorous Englishman who helped Fremont retake our pueblo?' When your father confirmed it, Carrillo pronounced him guilty of murder and sentenced him to be executed by a firing squad that afternoon. We all sat dumbfounded and looked at each other in disbelief. Ike rose and got 'but Your Honor' out of his mouth when Carrillo rapped his gavel, declared Ike was in contempt of court, and ordered a guard to escort him out. We were outraged, but we knew not to object, so we bit our tongues and watched helplessly. We'd never seen such a spectacle of obvious prejudice. It was a mockery. When Ike was escorted out of the courtroom, he went next door to notify Colonel Stevenson, the American commander. Your father was as stunned as we were but managed to keep his composure. I would have fainted on the spot. Anyway, your father requested that his execution be delayed until he had a chance to say a final goodbye to his family.

"Carrillo's face flushed scarlet, and his eyes nearly popped out of his head that your father had the audacity to make such a request. Looking back at it now, we think he expected your father to plead for mercy. Instead, he bravely accepted his fate. Next thing we knew, Carrillo bolted out of his chair and charged your father with his knife, gesturing that he was going to cut his throat. We all gasped. The two guards were holding your father's arms, and when he jerked away from Carrillo, his shirt popped open, revealing the tattoo of Jesus Christ on his chest, complete with a crown of thorns on his bloody head. Well, the sight of that made Carrillo's eyes big as saucers, and his face went ghostly white! He must have taken it as a sign from God that he'd been hasty in his judgment. He stumbled backward and announced that the execution would be delayed five days."

Guillermo put his hand to his forehead, reeling from the shocking story.

"Carrillo's blatant prejudice toward your father should help acquit him in the end or drastically reduce his sentence by causing a new panel of jurors to be convened. Hopefully this time around there'll be some Yankees on it. Before he was returned to his jail cell that day, we promised him we'd have Stevenson intervene, but he was mainly concerned about you and your family. I promised him you'd all be well cared for."

The past few weeks had been the darkest of Guillermo's fifteen years, but the support and encouragement of Daniel Hill and Ike Sparks gave him renewed hope his family would be reunited. It was a huge relief to know he wasn't alone in the responsibility for the care of his mother and siblings, but the grimness of what awaited his father kept his stomach clenched in fear.

CHAPTER 47

The following day, word arrived by steamship that Governor Mason had ordered a new trial. Pedro Carrillo would be replaced as judge by Alcalde Steven Ardisson, an ex-trader who had been formally educated in his native France.

Two days later, court reconvened in the former Aguirre mansion, which served as headquarters for Stevenson's Regiment of New York Volunteers. The sleepy pueblo had changed little since Guillermo's visit two years before except for the presence of young soldiers who casually patrolled the streets in pairs, flirting with the local señoritas.

Guillermo and Martina sat beside Daniel Hill and Ike Sparks. Their mother had stayed behind at the Hill home to care for six-week-old Toñita and pray. She was promised that when the jury met to deliberate, she would be notified so she could be present to hear her husband's fate. It was hoped that Padre Jimeño and Augustin Janssens would arrive in time to testify in support of Don Julian. So far, the only representatives in the courtroom for Davila were his foreman and an Indian servant. It was no surprise that neither Fuentes nor Rios were in attendance. They had good reason to fear arrest after the jury heard of their campaign of harassment.

Don Julian sat up front, his ankles and wrists shackled in iron chains. He managed to twist his body to catch a glimpse of his supporters and flash them an appreciative smile. His incarceration had left him thinner through the jowls and neck. He was grayer than Guillermo remembered and looked older than his fifty-two years.

At nine o'clock, Judge Ardisson called the court to order with a rap of his gavel. He was flanked by six Americanos on his left and six Californios on his right. After the charges were read, Don Julian stood and pled not guilty to the charge of murder.

The first witness called was Davila's majordomo. Arturo Guerrero testified that he was not present at the shooting but was at Corral de Cuati when two servants returned with Davila's body in an ox-cart. Nervously fingering his hat, the weathered vaquero verified there had been bad blood between his crew and those at Tinaquaic. It started eighteen months earlier when Fremont's army marched through the valley on its way to Santa Barbara. He and his crew had driven a dozen of their best-trained cow ponies into the backcountry to prevent them from being stolen by the Yankees. The horses were never found, and Guerrero believed Foxen took them for Fremont. Davila was angry and believed Foxen should be stripped of his Mexican land grant for his treasonous actions. The majordomo conceded he had been aware that two members of his crew had been harassing the Foxens for more than a year. Both Fuentes and Rios would disappear for hours at a time, and a couple times, he overheard them bragging to other crew members about how they had made a raid the previous night, burned the Foxens' crops, and lit their roof on fire. When he approached Davila about it, he was told to mind his own business. Guerrero finished by recounting how his boss made two trips to the Foxens' rancho in the days leading up to the shooting. One time, he took his Indian servants, and the other time, he took Fuentes and Rios. They returned with furniture, tools, and barrels of grain, brandy, and lead.

Guerrero's testimony was followed by one of the Indian servants who witnessed the shooting. As the servant walked forward to take a seat in front of Judge Ardisson, Guillermo heard the jingling of spurs coming through the door behind him. He turned to see Chico and Angel! Híjole! They had arrived! Chico winked as they took seats on the bench behind Guillermo, patting his shoulder in encouragement. It was great to see them after three long weeks. Martina turned and flashed them a grateful smile.

The shy Indian servant, José, admitted accompanying Davila to the Foxens' rancho to haul away what had been left behind when the family abandoned their adobe. On the final trip, they were surprised when Don Julian came out of the adobe with an old carbine pointed at them. Threats were exchanged, and there was a loud bang, and Davila fell to the ground with a wound to his chest. José and the other servant held up their arms in surrender. Don Julian ordered them to load Davila's body into the ox-cart and take him home. By the time they arrived at La Laguna for help, he was dead.

When it was Don Julian's turn to testify, he did so in a booming voice that echoed in the room. Guillermo observed the jurors' expressions and postures as they listened to his father recount the incident. Of the twelve jurors, nine sat up straight and listened intently. Three Californios slouched in their chairs, casting skeptical glares.

During the lunch break, Guillermo met the Gonzalezes in the courtyard. "Is everything all right with your father and Felipe?"

"They're fine," said Chico. "They wanted to come but stayed at Tepusquet to work. They said to tell you to keep your chin up. We didn't find out about the shooting until a few days ago when we went over to the hacienda to check on things and found a pool of dried blood on the ground and the house ransacked. We didn't know whose blood it was and were worried it was your father's. We raced over to La Laguna to see if they knew anything about it and found out about Davila being shot. They returned from his funeral a few days before and told us your father turned himself in to the authorities here in Santa Barbara. Wish someone would have notified us sooner."

"I begged Papá to let me ride over to tell you, but he made me promise not to go back there. He was worried about Fuentes and Rios seeking revenge. Have you heard anything about them?"

"Won't need to worry about Fuentes for a while," said Chico with a wolfish grin.

"What do you mean? Did something happen?"

Chico raised his hand. "Relax. It's not what you think. Heard from La Laguna's crew that he and Rios were returning from your house with an ox-cart loaded with barrels, your father's plow, and other equipment when a wheel got stuck in a rut. Fuentes got out of the cart and was whipping the ox to get it moving. He tripped and ended up getting his leg busted when he was stepped on. With your pa gone, there was no one around to set it. Guess he'll be a cripple for the rest of his life." He shrugged.

"Ay, caramba!" Guillermo pushed back his hat and stared at Chico and Angel in amazement. "I'd feel better if he broke his shooting arm. What about Rios?"

"Davila's widow is preparing to move to her parents' rancho near San Francisco, so he and Fuentes will be out of a job unless whoever buys the rancho decides to keep them on."

"Least Fuentes is out of the picture for the time being," said Guillermo. "I've been so worried they'd try to get revenge by killing one of you. It would be like the cowards to hide out and shoot you while you were herding cattle."

"I know. Don't think we haven't been looking over our shoulders a lot," said Angel. "I suspect they were more interested in ransacking your place than going after us. We stopped by the mission first, and Padre Sanchez filled us in about your father being found guilty and sentenced to die. We rode as fast as we could to get here in time. Passed Padre Jimeño and Janssens on the way, so they should be here soon. Their testimony should count in your father's favor since they witnessed Davila's threats against your father at the Easter fiesta."

Janssens and Padre Jimeño arrived shortly after court reconvened. They testified about witnessing Davila's angry confrontation at the mission the previous year and how they had been informed about the attacks on the Foxens' livestock, having their crops and roof set on fire, and the accusations that members of Davila's crew were waging war.

Janssens said, "We interviewed Davila and his crew, but they denied any involvement despite cattle bearing the Foxens' brand found grazing on Corral de Cuati. The crew claimed the cattle wandered onto their land, which was unlikely considering the league and a half separating the ranchos. During the visit, I couldn't help but notice Rios' arm was in a sling. Sal Gonzalez, Foxens' majordomo, informed me that one of the night marauders had been grazed by a bullet. Rios insisted he received his injury from a fall from his horse, but he refused to let us examine it."

Padre Jimeño testified that word reached him in February that Fuentes had been overheard to say someone would die if the Foxens didn't abandon their rancho soon. Fearing for the family's safety, he made a special trip to Rancho Tinaquaic to warn the Foxens. He pleaded with Don Julian to seek refuge at the mission immediately but learned that would have to be postponed until after the birth of the Foxens' seventh child. The family arrived at the mission on April 20. The confrontation occurred when Don Julian returned to retrieve some belongings they'd been forced to leave behind.

Octaviano Gutiérrez, the absentee owner of La Laguna, testified that he and his crew considered Don Julian a good neighbor. He found it difficult to believe that Foxen shot Davila in cold blood. Prominent citizens such as José de la Guerra, Daniel Hill, and Ike Sparks vouched for Don Julian's character as well.

The presentation of witnesses came to an end midafternoon. It was time for the jurors to decide his fate. Daniel Hill and Martina hurried the few blocks to Hill's home so they could escort Doña Eduarda back to the courtroom to hear the verdict.

Guillermo and his father's supporters milled about the courtyard, talking in hushed tones. The general consensus was that the verdict should be favorable, but Guillermo dared not allow himself to relax. His heart pounded wildly, and his throat constricted.

Doña Eduarda arrived shortly before the announcement was made that a verdict had been reached. Guillermo and Martina escorted her to a seat in the courtroom. She held herself erect and waved bravely when she caught Don Julian's eye. His stoic expression faltered as they exchanged looks and he caught sight of the swaddled bundle in Petra's arms. He gulped and ran a hand over his bristled jaw. He turned toward the judge and squared his broad shoulders, jutting out his chin as if defying the judge to pronounce him guilty.

Spectators filed into the courtroom and took their seats. After a few preliminary statements from Judge Ardisson, he was handed a piece of paper by the jury foreman, one of the Californios who had been slouching during his father's testimony. The courtroom held its collective breath as Ardisson unfolded the paper and began reading. When Guillermo heard "guilty of manslaughter," his heart stopped. Turning to his mother, he saw disbelief in her eyes and the color drain from her cheeks. Martina let out a small gasp.

The judge said, "Due to the unusual circumstances, the defendant will be released from jail and placed on probation for no less than four years. Jailer, please release Mr. Foxen from his shackles. Following that, you are free to leave, sir. However, if there are any violations of the law, you will be incarcerated immediately. Good day." He pounded his gavel. "Court is adjourned."

CHAPTER 48

Guillermo sat stunned and confused as his mother, Martina, and the Gonzalezes shook him in joy. The courtroom erupted in cheers, and he was swarmed by men slapping his back and pumping his hand vigorously. He rose to his feet in a daze, bewildered by the sudden turn of events. In a matter of seconds, he had gone from devastation to stunned relief, from dying to being reborn. His mother and sister wept in each other's arms as Hill and Padre Jimeño consoled them.

The next thing he knew, his father was pushing through the crowd to get to them. Guillermo was nearest the aisle and the first family member to congratulate him.

"By Jove, it's over, the nightmare is finally over! Thank God in heaven!" Don Julian exclaimed. After squeezing Guillermo in a bear hug, he wrapped an arm around Martina and his wife, who buried their faces in his barrel chest. Well-wishers crowded around him.

Guillermo felt his legs buckle. He moved out of the way and lowered himself onto a bench to collect himself. His hands trembled, and he broke out in a cold sweat.

"Mijo, are you all right?" asked his mother. "You look so pale."

"I-I'm fine…just a little sha-ky."

Angel plopped down next to him, and Guillermo heard

him say to Doña Eduarda, "Don't worry, I'll keep an eye on him."

Guillermo lowered his head between his knees. He felt pats on the back as voices said, "You'll be all right, lad," and "Just take a few deep breaths." It was mortifying to lose control of himself this way. As his breathing evened out, he heard Daniel Hill say, "Hear, hear! Everyone is welcome to join us for a celebration at my house!"

Guillermo struggled to regain his composure. On wobbly legs, he joined the crowd as it filed out of the courtroom into the open air corridor.

Colonel Stevenson stood in his office doorway and offered his congratulations as Don Julian passed. A jovial Hill invited the commander and his assistant to join them in celebrating the victory, of which he played a major role. The outpouring of goodwill filled Guillermo's heart with joy. After months of fending off attacks on the other side of the mountains, being supported by well-wishers was a welcome antidote to the isolation they had endured.

Passing through the former sala of the old Aguirre mansion that now served as Stevenson's headquarters, the revelers poured into the street.

Guillermo inhaled deeply and took in the beauty around him. The whitewashed adobes with red-tiled roofs that he had passed in the morning were now aglow in the late-afternoon sun. A balmy breeze blew in off the glittering water of the bay, fluttering the yellow acacias. Seagulls sailed overhead, seemingly joining in the celebration by squawking their delight that a man of the sea had regained his freedom. It was a glorious day—a homecoming of sorts, but not to Tinaquaic. This was the port where Don Julian had come ashore eighteen years earlier and fell under the spell of a shy, doe-eyed señorita named Eduarda. The ship captain readily gave up his life at sea and his Episcopalian faith to marry her. The couple had returned after an absence of nine years with a brood of seven children to begin anew. They were poor in possessions but full of gratitude for this second chance.

Destiny had intervened to rescue Don Julian from the retribution of a vindictive Californio judge. Guillermo recalled the day his father explained to him why he was helping the Americanos, and one reason was a fair and impartial justice system to replace the corrupt provincial courts. Now he understood its value.

It was a joyful reunion when the Foxen children who had remained behind spotted their father striding up the Hill's front steps. The girls spilled out of the house, their long braids swinging merrily behind them as they raced to embrace their father. Ramona, Panchita, and Juanita wrapped their arms around him, having feared they'd never see him again. Don Julian lifted each daughter and planted a kiss on her cheek. Alejandro toddled out with outstretched arms to get his hug. "Papá! Papá!" Don Julian tossed him into the air and swung him around as onlookers wiped away tears.

The men retreated to the patio while the womenfolk remained inside. Hill was a skilled craftsman who had designed and built their lovely home twenty-three years before. It was the first house in the pueblo to boast wood flooring. Magenta-colored bougainvillea vines trailed along the roofline, the pillars of the wide veranda, and on the low wall of the patio. Savory smoke from a side of beef barbecuing in a corner of the yard wafted in the air. Indian servants passed out glasses of homemade brandy to guests.

The guest of honor's godfather and host was the first to offer a toast. Raising his glass, Daniel Hill said, "To our good friend Benjamin! Thanks to Governor Mason, he got a fair trial this time around! It's a new day for justice in Santa Barbara! No longer are we Anglos treated like second-class citizens!"

"Hip, hip, hooray!" shouted the celebrants.

"May this be a new beginning for your family marked by peace and prosperity!" Sparks called out. "God bless the Foxens!"

"Salud!" shouted the others as they downed their drinks.

Guillermo stood alongside Chico and Angel with an arm stretched over their shoulders and a glass in one hand. "I can't tell you how good it is to have you here. This party would have been incomplete without your ugly faces."

"Look who's talking! You don't look so great yourself. You're so skinny you look like a scarecrow. Haven't you been eating?" asked Angel.

Patting his stomach, Guillermo said, "Haven't had much of an appetite since we left home. Guess I'm not too fond of anyone else's cooking but your mother's. She spoiled me. Looks like Papá's lost weight too."

"He's a mighty lucky man to have such loyal friends," said Angel. "Hate to think what would have happened if they hadn't pressed Colonel Stevenson to request a new trial. Feel sorry for the Davila children."

"I agree, but Toñita came close to never knowing her father. No one else besides you Gonzalezes know what we've been through these past months. When my grandfather sent your family to help my father learn to ranch, he knew what he was doing. We owe so much to your family."

"Well, it goes both ways. Your father's always looked out for us too," said Chico, smiling fondly as he watched Don Julian greet his well-wishers. "Probably no time more than when he sent us to Tepusquet instead of guarding the hacienda. He risked his possessions for the sake of our welfare. Having to leave the rancho was one of the hardest things I've ever done, but your father was right to do that…it spared us a lot of grief. I have no doubt if we'd stayed, there would have been more bloodshed."

"That's for sure," Angel said. "Someone would have been killed."

"You're right," said Guillermo. "I resented him for sending you away. Now I realize I was thinking only of myself and all the hard work that was put into the stable. I was blind to how it would have affected you. Like Mamá says, people come before things."

Don Julian ambled over and pounded Chico and Angel on the back. "Everyone, listen up!" he bellowed as if shouting orders in a gale. "I'd like to make a toast to the four Gonzalezes who stood alongside my son and me in fighting off the Tulares and Davila's crew. They're more than our crew, they're family. Thank you, Chico and Angel, for coming today. It means a lot to us." There were cheers and clapping. He moved over to Guillermo and draped his arm around him. "And to my son, who's grown from a boy to a man in the last year and a half."

Guillermo stared at the ground as his father spoke, aware of the eyes upon him. Heat rose in his cheeks, and his chest tightened as he held in a flood of emotions. His lower lip quivered, but he held himself taut, lest any movement start a chain reaction.

Don Julian continued, "He never shirked his duty and

assumed responsibility for our family when I was gone. Sitting in jail, I knew I could depend on him to do whatever had to be done." He squeezed Guillermo's shoulder and said, his voice quaking, "Thank you, mijo. Now I have one last request."

Guillermo glanced at him quizzically.

"That's exactly what I mean," Don Julian said, pointing to Guillermo's furrowed brow. "I want to see that crease between your eyes disappear and for you to flash those dimples your Mamá gave you. Hear me?" Good-natured laughter rang out. He gave Guillermo a misty-eyed wink and raised his glass. "Cheers!"

Guillermo ventured a self-conscious glance at the group before him and saw a gallery of smiling faces: Daniel Hill and his son-in-law, Nicolas Den, Ike Sparks, Padre Jimeño, Lewis Burton, Augustin Janssens, José de la Guerra, Octaviano Gutiérrez, and Colonel Stevenson and his aide. His father's arm was still around him, and the smoke from his pipe drifted into Guillermo's eyes, but it didn't matter. His father's words of approval struck a deep chord. He forgave him for the times he had been chastised for not using his head. They made this moment possible because they spurred him on to do better.

Guillermo was relieved when Ike started a story, shifting attention away from him. He turned to his father and whispered, "Thank you."

Don Julian chuckled and said, "I know I embarrassed you, but I wanted everyone to know how proud I am of you. C'mon, let's go over where we have some privacy." With his arm still draped around Guillermo's shoulder, he led him to a low, whitewashed adobe wall. It had a view of the shimmering blue harbor. No big ships were in the port, only a schooner that had dropped anchor a ways offshore. The sun was setting, and the sky was a brilliant splash of corals, pinks, and blues.

Guillermo said, "I've been wanting to tell you how sorry I am about the way I acted when you left." He ran his hand along the top of the wall and pounded it with his fist. "I felt guilty and worried that I wouldn't have a chance to apologize. I hated the thought of you sitting in jail, thinking I was angry with you. Thank God they let you go. I-I don't know what I would have done if you didn't come back to us." His voice caught, and he shook his head at the thought.

"Thank you, mijo. I know you well enough to know you regretted it not long after I left. I understood why you were upset, but what I never had a chance to tell you was that I returned to the rancho to get the diseño. There wasn't room in the ox-cart when we left for my sea chest, so I hastily grabbed some papers and stuffed them in my saddlebag. It wasn't until we got to the mission that I discovered the diseño wasn't among them. I realized it must have been under the scorched papers that Fremont gave me that I left behind. I didn't want to worry you or your mother, so I didn't explain why it was so important that I return when I did. When I went back, sure enough, it was at the bottom of the chest in perfect condition. Fremont's papers had protected it from the fire. Ironic, huh? I heard the ox-cart approaching, and I couldn't risk losing it, so I rolled it up, put it in my spyglass, and hung it around my neck by the leather thong. Please tell me it's safe and sound."

"Yes, it in my bedchamber here. Hiding it in the spyglass was a clever idea. I happened to discover it when I was waiting for a messenger to come with news about you."

"Aye, that's a relief. I figured you'd take care of it." A few moments passed. "I know I've been hard on you at times. After Ausencio died, I feared you'd be spoiled by your mother and sisters like he was. It would have been a disservice to you if I had allowed that. As it turned out, you possess his horsemanship and my work ethic—a great combination. You haven't had much reason to smile in the past couple years. I blame myself for your seriousness. I promise things will be different here on the coast."

"Now that the trial's over, where are we going to live?"

"Daniel Hill wants us to manage his La Goleta Rancho for him. They have a summer house there that we can live in."

Glancing back at Chico and Angel chatting with Sparks and Hill, Guillermo asked, "What about the Gonzalezes? Do you think Daniel would mind if they joined us?"

"They seem to be hitting it off well. Who knows? He could be talking about it with them as we speak."

"That would sure be great," said Guillermo wistfully.

His father eyed him curiously. "What? I can tell something's on your mind. Out with it."

Guillermo shifted his feet and took a deep breath. Meeting his father's faded-blue eyes, he said, "It's our herd or what's left of it. I worry about it wandering back on our land and falling prey to bears and coyotes. I wish we could drive at least some of the heifers over the mountain and bring them to graze on La Goleta for the time being. That way we could build our herd back up."

Don Julian rubbed his chin. "Hmm, not a bad idea. I'd have to talk to Daniel about that. I need to stay here for four years while I'm on probation. Afterward we can think about returning to Tinaquaic and starting over." He drew himself up and inhaled deeply. "In the meantime, I'm looking forward to enjoying the sea breeze and smell of brine. Heard there's a schooner that ran aground in the estuary at La Goleta. You could help me make it seaworthy again, and we could make extra money fishing in the channel. How does that sound?"

Guillermo's first thought was *Oh no, here we go again with another new project.* He surprised himself by saying, "Sure, and maybe you could teach me to sail."

"By Jove, that's been my dream since you were born!"

Nicolas Den and Padre Jimeño approached. Den extended his hand to Guillermo and pumped it vigorously. "Guillermo! So good to see you! You've grown. How old are you now, lad?"

"Fifteen, sir."

"My goodness, you're nearly as tall as your father but much better looking!" He arched his eyebrows and whispered out of the corner of his mouth, "You've made quite the impression on Rosa's sisters." Rosa was Nicolas' wife and Daniel's eldest daughter.

"Me? You're kidding?" It was a surprise to learn that the girls' whispers and giggling had to do with him. That was flattering. Truth be told, he found fourteen-year-old Adelaida Hill pretty with her rosy cheeks, pert nose, and green eyes.

"No, I'm not." Den said to Don Julian, "I understand from Daniel you'll be moving out to the summer house on La Goleta. It'll be grand to have you for neighbors. I wanted to let you know that your children are welcome to attend classes out at my place on Dos Pueblos with mine. I hired a tutor from Daniel's home state of Massachusetts who's come to live with us. Your children could ride over. It's not that far. How does that sound?"

Guillermo and his father exchanged surprised expressions. "Well, what do you know? Looks like you'll be able to get that education after all," Don Julian said with a twinkle in his eye.

"That would be wonderful! Thank you, Señor Den. That's very kind of you!" said Guillermo.

"Good! It's settled then." Glancing over at the barbecue, he said, "Looks like they're ready to start serving. I'm famished. Excuse me while I take my seat."

Guillermo shook his head in a daze. "Can you believe it? I get to attend school after all! My head is spinning. This is all too much to take in. A few days ago, I wondered if I'd ever smile again. Everything looked so bleak."

Both men chuckled, and Padre Jimeño said, "Let this be a lesson to you that no matter how bad things may look, we should never give up hope."

Guillermo was humbled by the realization these men had known his father longer than he had and had given him the benefit of the doubt. Without being witnesses to what had happened in the confrontation with Davila, they thought enough of Don Julian to ask the commander to write the governor and request a new trial. He said, "It pays to have loyal friends."

Padre Jimeño held up a finger to make a point. "It does, but it was earned."

Guillermo nodded. "Thank you, Padre, for coming today to testify and for all your help and encouragement."

"Yes," said Don Julian, "can't thank you enough for all you've done for us."

"Nonsense. This will give me an opportunity to discuss some important matters with Padre Rubio. Since the governor declared the sale of the missions to private citizens like Carrillo and Covarrubias illegal, we've been waiting for official word that our cattle will be returned to us. Perhaps he's heard some news."

"If that's the case, both Carrillo brothers will have even more reason to gnash their teeth over American rule." Don Julian chuckled and glanced at the people who were starting to eat. "Shall we join the others for dinner?"

Guillermo followed his father and the balding friar as they headed for the banquet table laden with platters of sliced beef, beans, rice, and tortillas. The celebrants were laughing and enjoying themselves. The Gonzalezes were still deep in conversation with Daniel and Ike. It was strange to see Chico and Angel in this setting, so far from the rancho. The celebration would not have been complete without them. Guillermo looked forward to the evening, sitting around the campfire, catching up on news.

Angel spotted him and called out, "C'mon over. We saved a place for you!" Chico and Ike, with mouths full of food, pointed to a chair across from them.

Guillermo waved a hand. "Be right there! Just need to check on the horses first."

CHAPTER 49

As he retreated to the stables behind the patio, Guillermo flashed back to his dread and loneliness on the trip over the Refugio Trail. Padre Jimeño's urging not to give up hope was laden with risk. In his dark mood, the virtue had masqueraded as a cruel ploy meant to delay yet another crushing disappointment. He couldn't have borne it. The matter had been settled after Toñita's frightening tumble into the creek. Still shaken from the near disaster, he'd happened to gaze up at the sky. Streams of light had peeked around the edges of indigo clouds that hung ominously out to sea. He had recalled the storm that rolled in on the San Marcos Trail a year ago Christmas. Surely God would spare his family from being caught in a storm when they were so vulnerable, wouldn't He? Gradually the rays had brightened until they shone brilliantly. Ramona had called attention to it. "Look! The clouds are breaking! It's like God is saying 'Hello, Foxen family. Welcome to this side of the mountains.'"

Leave it to Ramona, the most irrepressible of his sisters and most like their father with her fair skin and blue eyes, to have spoken the words that rekindled a glimmer of hope within his wounded spirit. She had been uncharacteristically quiet on the trip, reeling from the latest tragedy to befall the family. He had furtively wiped away a tear then, as he did now. There was no doubt in his mind that the dazzling rays on display that evening had been a confirmation of the answers to prayer awaiting them. Having his father returned and being reunited with Angel and Chico at this celebration—well, it overshadowed the temporary fate of Tinaquaic. He hoped that someday that too would be reclaimed, just as the missions were being restored to the church and their caretakers, the padres. For now, he was grateful to be on the coast with those he loved, including Benito and El Rey.

A smile spread across his face as he heard the horses whinny their greeting at his approach. "Hola, mis amigos! How are you liking your new quarters?"

Benito's ears perked forward, and he stretched his neck to nudge Guillermo as he entered the stall. El Rey leaned his white head over the rail of the adjacent stall to join the reunion. Both horses watched with interest as Guillermo dug through his pockets for a treat.

"Let's see if I have anything for you." He retrieved a chunk of amber-colored panoche and broke it in two, offering a piece to each. As the horses chewed, he stood between them, rubbing their necks. "I'm happy to report the trial turned out well! Papá is a free man, and our new home will be on La Goleta, a pleasant rancho not far from here."

Hoping to get more panoche, Benito nibbled at Guillermo's pants pocket.

"Sorry, that's all I have."

Benito responded by whinnying and playfully trying to nudge the hat off his head, but Guillermo jerked back. "Oh, no, you don't! Nuh, uh, uh…I'm not falling for that trick."

From behind, El Rey seized the opportunity to lift the hat off Guillermo's head by biting its brim. Guillermo pivoted. "What—?" He watched El Rey give it a couple of good shakes and then release it, sending it through the air where it landed on a bale of hay several feet away. Guillermo stood with his hands on his hips and stared in amazement. "What's gotten into you?" He chuckled. "Now Mr. Serious wants to join in the mischief?" Turning to Benito, he said, "See what you've done? Ay, yi, yi...looks like now I've got double trouble."

Benito neighed and shook his black mane, and Guillermo smiled as he retrieved his hat. Turning to El Rey, he patted the tall horse's neck. "You want to join in the fun, huh, buddy?" He ran his hand down the Appaloosa's muscular shoulder and over the scars on his front legs. "You've come a long way, amigo. I remember when you wouldn't let anyone near you, and people thought you were permanently soured." He chuckled. "Look at you now. If you can lighten up after everything you've been through, so can I." He stroked El Rey's neck and chest, admiring his rippling muscles. He was grateful that his skill with horses enabled him to befriend and rehabilitate El Rey. His horses were more than just mounts to him. Like the Gonzalezes, Sal, Angel, and Chico, the horses were his companions. His heart swelled with joy at the prospect of being reunited with all of them.

"I have a feeling this move to the coast will turn out to be good for us," he said.

He went on to tell them about Hill's daughters and Den's offer of receiving tutoring at his rancho. The horses' ears perked up at the news. Things were looking up indeed.

HISTORICAL NOTE

The Foxens remained on Daniel Hill's Rancho La Goleta for six years. During his time on the coast, Guillermo helped his father repair a schooner in the Goleta estuary. He also worked as a vaquero for Hill and Nicolas Den, likely helping to drive their cattle to the stockyards in San Juan Bautista and San Jose. During the raucous Gold Rush Days of 1848–50, the value of a cow skyrocketed from two dollars for its hide to fifty dollars for beef on the hoof to feed the hordes of gold seekers flooding into the Sierra foothills. Some enterprising rancheros like Nicolas Den became millionaires in a few short years.

Guillermo and Maria Estefana Ortega married in 1852. Two years later when his sister, Martina, became engaged to the Englishman Dr. Charles Freeman, her mother insisted the family return to Rancho Tinaquaic for the wedding. In preparation, Guillermo and his friend Alfredo José Gutierrez repaired the roof on the adobe and built a new ramada. The family returned to their beloved rancho in December 1854.

As an adult Guillermo became known as William "JJ" (Jose Juan) Foxen or simply Bill. In addition to being a stockman, he served as constable of nearby Los Alamos.

In subsequent years, the Foxens improved their bustling homestead by building a barn, a blacksmith shop, and corrals, planting orchards, and growing crops. The Foxen adobe became a stagecoach stop in the late 1800s. Benjamin Foxen and his sons bred draft horses which were sold to pull street cars in San Francisco. One particular stallion was sold to the industrialist and politician Leland Stanford for $3000, a princely sum in those days.

Ramona and her husband, Frederick Wickenden, led an effort with Rev. McNally of the Santa Ines Mission, to build a church to serve the spiritual needs of the sixty-five pioneer families in the area. Land was donated from Ramona's parcel on which to build San Ramon Chapel. It was completed in 1872 and remains open for Sunday services.

A handful of Foxen descendants continue to live and work on the remaining portion of the original land grant. Cattle and horses have grazed on its gently rolling hills for more than 180 years. Oil leases have also been granted. In recent decades acres of grazing land have been plowed under to plant vineyards along present day Foxen Canyon Road. Its fertile soil and Mediterranean microclimate have proven ideal for growing several varieties of wine grapes. Numerous vineyards and wineries have sprung up along the meandering road between the quaint hamlets of Los Olivos and Sisquoc. The Foxen Winery produces bottles labeled with Rancho Tinaquaic's distinctive anchor brand. Another enduring legacy of the pioneering family is an elementary school named for Benjamin Foxen in Sisquoc.

Made in the USA
Monee, IL
20 July 2023